THE GLORIOUS MYSTERY

British Library Cataloguing-in-Publication Data
A catalogue record for this book is available from the
British Library

Arthur Machen

Arthur Machen was born in Caerleon, Monmouthshire, Wales in 1863. At the age of eleven, he boarded at Hereford Cathedral School, where he received a comprehensive classical education. Family poverty ruled out going to university, and Machen was sent to London, where he sat entrance exams at medical school but failed to get in. In the capital, he lived in relative poverty, working in a variety of short-lived jobs and exploring the city during the evenings. However, he began to show literary promise; in 1881, at the age of just eighteen, he published a long poem, 'Eleusinia', and in 1884, he published his second work, the pastiche *The Anatomy of Tobacco*.

By 1890, Machen was publishing in literary magazines, and writing stories with Gothic and fantastic themes. His first major success came in 1894, with the novella *The Great God Pan*. Although widely denounced by the press as degenerate and horrific because of its decadent style and sexual content, it has since garnered a reputation as a classic of horror; indeed, author Stephen King has called it "maybe the best [horror story] in the English language." Machen next produced *The Three Impostors* (1895), a novel composed of a number of interwoven tales which are now regarded as some of his best works.

Between 1900 and 1910, Machen dabbled in acting,

and published what is generally seen as his *magnum opus, The Hill of Dreams* (1907). He accepted a full-time journalist's job at Alfred Harmsworth's *Evening News* in 1910, where he remained throughout the war, not leaving until 1921. Machen accepted this role mainly to pay his bills – fiction-writing was his true passion, and he carried on producing novels and short stories throughout the 1910s – but he came to be regarded as a great Fleet Street character by his contemporaries.

The early 1920s saw something of a Machen boom; his works became popular in America, and he brought out his two-volume autobiography. However, by 1929 he was struggling financially again, and left London with his family. It was only a literary appeal launched on the occasion of his eightieth birthday – which drew contributions from admirers such as T. S. Eliot and Bernard Shaw – that eventually ended Machen's money woes. He died some years later in Beaconsfield, Buckinghamshire, England, aged 84. His legacy remains formidable; his work has influenced countless other artists, and is seen as setting the stage for – amongst other things – the Cthulhu horrors of H. P. Lovecraft.

The Glorious Mystery

By
Arthur Machen

Edited by
Vincent Starrett

CONTENTS

FOREWORD

IN THIS final important volume drawn from my collection of the uncollected writings of Arthur Machen, for the first time are brought together in covers many of Mr. Machen's finest contributions to the periodical press. In each is expounded some part of the high doctrine that is so peculiarly and beautifully Machen's own, but which rapidly is becoming the possession of others in number as the sometime clandestine celebrity of Arthur Machen and his philosophy spreads through the world. In the history of religion, I believe no more arresting and challenging theological work has appeared than the present volume, in which a great mediaevalist, still living, sets forth his quest of the Graal, and finds a symbol of that sacred vessel in less holy cups; in which a High Church theologian of the first importance triumphantly asserts and perhaps proves his conviction that Protestantism is a revolt against Christianity and the industrial blight and a curse on civilization.

Most of the reviews and essays here collected were contributed years ago to London journals, and there appears in many of them names and references long since lost to memory with the passing of the men and of the issues; but for the most part the dogmas assailed and the doctrines celebrated are still fundamentally and vitally questions of the hour. Where it has seemed necessary to stress a date, for any reason, I have appended to the paper in question the date of the issue of the journal in which originally it appeared, although the arrangement of the essays is not necessarily chronological.

Supplementing the Graal symposium, with which the book opens, and the theological philippics, are a number of graceful essays in lighter vein, some short fictional studies, and a bit of literary criticism. The grim little tale called "The Iron

Maid" was originally a part of the volume known as "The Three Impostors," but when that engaging chronicle became a part of the larger collection called "The House of Souls" it was abridged by the omission of "The Iron Maid," which has not since been reprinted. It has seemed a good idea to include the story in the present collection to make it accessible to those readers who can not or do not care to possess "first editions." To all save ardent Machen collectors who have gone to the extreme of unearthing early magazine "appearances" of their idol, it is likely that the present collection from first to last will be quite new.

VINCENT STARRETT.

THE GLORIOUS MYSTERY

THE SANGRAAL

IT IS really rather refreshing. "Scare heads" are presumably inevitable; in the pleasing language of their inventors they seem to have "come to stay." Well; if we *must* have them it is much better to be confronted with:

MYSTERY OF A RELIC

FINDER BELIEVES IT TO BE THE HOLY GRAIL
TWO "VISIONS" DISCOVERED AT GLASTONBURY

than with an array of trumpet-toned capitals which tell us the King is going to meet the Kaiser at Marienbad. And the story told is quite a curious one. A saucer-shaped vessel, made of bluish-green glass into which silver leaf had been introduced, was found in a well at Glastonbury. The newspaper accounts leave its genuineness an open question; but we are informed that a British Museum expert who has seen the vessel pronounces in favour of its antiquity, and considers it to be of Phœnician workmanship. So goes the history of the matter; there is also a legend.

The legend is more difficult. It is an affair of spiritual voices, of visions declaring the vessel to be the cup used by our Lord at the Last Supper that He made, of seeresses who describe the object without seeing it, of dreams in which a woman appears holding the vessel in her hands, of a strange radiance which is diffused from this (possibly) Holy Relic.

But there are some curious points in the tale, apart from its super-normal ingredients. In the first place the newspaper reporters speak of the vessel as a cup. It is not a cup; it is a saucer; and therefore it is idle to speak of it as the chalice of the Last Supper. In the second place, the discoverers, who say it is the Holy Grail, once the great relic of Glastonbury Abbey, are apparently ignorant of the fact that Glastonbury never claimed the possession of any such object. William of Malmesbury, who wrote the Glastonbury Legend in the first half of the twelfth century, says that the body of Joseph of Arimathæa was buried somewhere in the abbey precinct, and that with his body there was a *phial* of the Precious Blood; the idea may have been suggested to Gul. Marisburiensis by the fact that a phial said to contain the Precious Blood had just been brought to Bruges. But so far as we are aware the monks of Glastonbury who "discovered" the body of King Arthur in the reign of Henry II. never "discovered" the body of St. Joseph or the phial.

Then, again, there is the consideration that, with one exception, the Romances insist on the final withdrawal of the Grail, either into a vague region of mystery, or as in the great Galahad Quest, first to Sarras and finally to heaven. The one exception is Wolfram's "Parzival," where the Grail is left at Montsalvatch guarded by the "Templesiens"; but Wolfram's continuators, pressed probably by the universal tradition, bore away the Grail at last to the realm of Prester John. Of course there is the question of what the word "grail" really means. Paulin Paris thought it came from "Grail Book" (Mass Book); as a matter of fact the Gradual was called the Grail in the middle ages, and according to Ducange a Grail Service meant a morning service or mass. But more modern scholarship derives the word from a conjectured form, *cratella,* a diminutive of *crater,* and the word seems to have implied to the twelfth-century mind a sort of shallow dessert-dish, standing on a stem or foot. Now there is neither foot nor stem to the vessel just "discovered" at Glastonbury; and yet it is odd enough that a sculptured stone at Nigg in Scotland depicts two Celtic priests bowing in adoration before something which resembles a saucer on a stem, over which hovers a dove bearing a Host in its beak. In this connection it must be remembered that the Grail was a vague object to the romance-writers; in the "High History, for example, the object assumes five different forms, the last of which is a chalice.

THE GLORIOUS MYSTERY

There is a very short and easy way of dealing with the legend. Somehow or other you get hold of a theory, make up your mind that it is true, and then manipulate the evidence. The simplest way is to select the particular romance which fits in best with the theory that you have acquired; and then you ignore all the other romances which may conflict with it more or less. The best instance of this method is Dr. Sebastian Evans's ingenious and attractive "In Quest of the Holy Graal." Dr. Evans, it must be said, is the accomplished and admirable, if somewhat archaistic translator of one of the Romances, to which he has given the title "The High History of the Holy Graal," and on this particular romance he has founded his theory. It is an attractive one, as I have said; but it is quite terrible!

There is a very odd and inexplicable incident in most versions of the legend. Logres, that is Britain, is supposed to be in the doleful condition of enchantment; physically and spiritually the land languishes, and the keeper of the Graal is sick of a mystic wound. All that is required is for the chosen knight of the adventure to come to the Graal Castle; and then the holy vessel is borne before him as he sits in the hall. He must then ask what the Graal is and whom it serves; whereupon the evil enchantments will be annulled, the sick keeper will be healed, and all that is broken will be made whole. For one reason or another the knight does not ask this question on his first visit; consequently the doleful state of Britain continues and the wounded keeper of the mysteries is unhealed. It should be mentioned that the keeper is sometimes called the King Fisherman, sometimes the Rich Fisher; and this title, be it noted, is not the smallest of the many difficulties in this extraordinary tale.

Well; Dr. Sebastian Evans knows what all this means. I should first mention that in the particular romance which he has selected Logres is not "enchanted" on the arrival of Percival at the Graal Castle; misfortunes fall upon the land afterwards, in consequence of Percival's unhappy failure to put the question to the keeper. Here again is another illustration of the difficulties which beset the Graal student—the romances disagree with one another on the most important points. But Dr. Evans's interpretation of the whole legend is, briefly, as follows. It is, he says, an allegory of the events which fell out in England in the reign of King John, when the realm was laid under an interdict by the Holy Father. Percival, the hero of the quest, is St. Dominic; King Fisherman is the Pope, the King of Castle Mortal (or Deadly Castle) is the Emperor, Sir Gawain is Fulke the Troubadour, Lancelot is the elder Simon de Montfort, and Galahad is St. Francis of Assisi. The silence of Percival means that St. Dominic omitted to ask the Holy Father a certain question, when he visited the Court of Innocent *c.* 1215. The circumstances were these: Dominic was conferring with the Pope on the Albigenses, with special reference to the question of interdict enjoyed by the Cistercian Order. But he never thought of discussing the question of interdict and Cistercian exemption in any other country besides Languedoc; and so when England was laid under interdict, the Cistercians were not allowed to say mass—and this was the dolorous enchantment of the Isle of Britain.

This is the crudest outline of Dr. Sebastian Evans's theory; and it must be said that it is worked out in his book with the greatest ingenuity and the nicest skill, and that some of the analogies between the history of the time and the "High History" are quite extraordinary. They are so extraordinary that I am almost tempted to believe that they were expressly contrived by the Great Enemy of Literary Students —a very malevolent devil he—that Dr. Evans might be led to adopt a theory which is, undoubtedly, quite preposterous.

It would be a tedious and lengthy task to demonstrate the vanity of the Evans theory; I hope its evident falsity will become apparent in the course of this note. But it may be said, by the way, that there is one fatal and manifest flaw which vitiates the whole argument, and that is that the Graal legend is the Legend of a Great Loss. The Graal in the "High History" is finally taken away into the unseen, in the

"Queste" it is removed to heaven; another romance ends with the statement that it was henceforth seen of none "so openly," and the tales which carry on the legend of Montsalvatch remove the sacred thing to the realms of Prester John. But, in actual history, the interdict was removed and mass was once more freely celebrated; the discrepancy is quite fatal. And from another point of view: is it credible that a Cistercian, writing *c.* 1220 in Norman French, would ever dream of "getting up" obscure Celtic legends and details of Welsh folk-lore with the idea of giving his ecclesiastico-political allegory a picturesque setting? Or yet again: I am "a man in the street," I am sorry to say, as to the precise dates of the manuscripts, but I believe the learned are tolerably well agreed that some of the Graal Romances at all events were written years before the English interdict was heard of.

I have gone so far with Dr. Sebastian Evans's theory because it is the most ingenious of all the "straightforward" explanations of the Graal story. There are many other writers who are quite as certain, and not nearly so interesting. There is the "pagan" school, which regards the whole story as a bit of pre-Christian Celtic folk-lore, into which "Christian fetichism" was crudely and pitiably introduced in the twelfth century; there is the frankly nonsensical "Sun Myth" theory, according to which Galahad and Merlin are "sun heroes." This latter explanation has now gone the way of all such rubbish; but I daresay it has been succeeded by the equally ridiculous "Covent Garden theory," and for all I know Galahad may now be explained in certain quarters as *Caulahad,* or Cabbage Hero. Then there is the notion that the Graal Romances are, somehow or other, a Templar manifesto, the veiled utterance of the "secret doctrine" of the poor fellow soldiers of Christ. Here again we may say: how account for the introduction of obscure Welsh names, for the mention of obscure Celtic customs in books which are supposed to represent the teachings of a cosmopolitan order of chivalry with its headquarters in the East? But the most decisive answer to this hypothesis is: that in the first place there is no earthly reason to suppose that the Templars had any secret doctrine, or, if we are to believe one or two very dubious charges made against them, their doctrine was distinctly anti-sacramental. And the doctrine of the Great Romances is, on the other hand, hyper-sacramental. It would be just as reasonable to declare that Ultra-montanism originated in the bosom of the Wee Kirk, but people *will* talk nonsense about the Templars. Then there is somebody who says that water was a symbol of purity, truth, wisdom, and salvation, and so the vessel which contained water became a symbol of these great things. It is fine; but as it happens the Graal did not contain water. There are other and still wilder theories, most of them devoid of the mere semblance of reason.

It seems likely that these attempts at explanation are so far from being satisfactory, because they attempt a task which is in the nature of things impossible. If you are asked to explain the Graal legend you are really being asked a dozen questions, not one single question; and the attempt to reply to all these interrogatories with a single answer is bound to end in failure. And again; it is always a mistake to say that X *is* A when you know in your heart that you should have remarked that: "There is a good deal to be said in favour of the statement that X is A" or even "There is a bare possibility that X is A." But it seems so weak to content oneself with such timid affirmations as these after a course of long and wearisome research; and so the bolder way is followed, and the truth is obscured. I want to say at the outset that I am content to be weak; what I *know* about the Graal is very little, but I have a vision of certain probabilities, some quite strong and some rather doubtful.

It is my opinion, then, that the Legend of the Graal, as it may be collected from the various Romances, is the glorified version of early Celtic Sacramental Legends, which legends had been married to certain elements of pre-Christian myth and folk-lore. I say legends, not legend, because it seems highly improbable that the numerous and important differences between the various romances could have arisen, if there had been one recognised legend, one *Textus Receptus* of the story. And the legend as we know it is a glorified version; it was the work of an age that knew how to transmute Norman architecture into the marvellous beauty of First Pointed, or Early English. I should think that this process in architecture, which we know did take place, offers a pretty fair analogy to the transmutation of scattered Celtic legends into the splendid and glorious history of Galahad and the Sangraal. Only, unfortunately, while we can point to tangible and mighty evidence in stone of the one process; we have only very fragmentary proofs of the other.

But I think we can say for certain that at least one X *is* A—that the origins of the Graal are certainly Celtic. Otherwise one would have to conceive the Anglo-Norman romance-writer as "mugging up" Celtic literature, learning Welsh, wandering over Glamorganshire and Caermarthenshire in search of obscure names on tombstones, which names he would presently carefully distort into a French form, making himself acquainted with the unending genealogies of the Welsh saints and heroes. He would, for instance, have discovered with some pains the name Avalloch in early Welsh pedigrees, and then have made it into Evelake, and have smiled at the result. He would have visited St. Dogmael's, inspected the Bilingual Ogham Stone with the inscription *Sagramni maqui Cunatemi,* and have gone on his way rejoicing, conscious that "Sir Sagramour" in his forthcoming romance would be both melodious and entirely correct. I do not think that this was the way in which romances were written in the twelfth century; though a twentieth-century story-teller might well use some such methods. In the same way the "High History" has the following passage:

> The history witnesseth us that in the land of King Arthur at this time there was not a single chalice. The Graal appeared at the sacring of the mass in five several manners that none ought not to tell, for the secret things of the sacrament ought none to tell openly but he to whom God hath given it.

THE GLORIOUS MYSTERY

The history goes on to say that the last of the forms assumed by the Graal was that of a chalice, and that from the pattern seen in the mystery King Arthur caused chalices to be made for the churches of Britain, a "brief" having been found under the corporal declaring that God's will was that in such a vessel should His Body be sacrificed. Now in the "Leabar Breac" (written *c.* 1097, but evidently following very ancient tradition) we hear that under the rule of Columcille or Columba there was a mass chalice in every church. It would be difficult to determine the exact force of these allusions to some very early Celtic peculiarity in the celebration of the Sacrifice; the point seems to me an extremely interesting one, and I venture to hope that some Celtic expert will enlighten me. But I cannot imagine anything more profoundly uninteresting than an attempt to show that there is no connection between the passage in the "High History" and the passage in the "Leabar Breac." Again, it is known, I suppose, even to those who know but very little of Celtic things, that every saint of Britain and Scotland and Ireland had his holy bell—many examples of these bells still remain in wonderful preservation, some of them still retaining the reputation of miraculous powers—and in the chapter of the "High History" which has been cited the holy bell is almost of as much importance as the Graal itself. It was one of those that had been cast by King Solomon, one for God, one for Our Lady, and one for the honour of the saints. King Arthur thought that he had heard this bell ringing all the way of his journey from Cardoil to the Graal Castle, and he commanded that bells should be made after the pattern of it. It is distinctly *not* conceivable that such details as these should be inserted to give an archaic and Celtic atmosphere to a twelfth-century tale; we are forced to conclude that the French or Anglo-French Romance writers were working on old Celtic materials; the people who say that the Normans made up the whole story out of their heads are clearly out of court.

So far good: but now comes the difficulty: what did

these Celtic materials amount to? Here knowledge ceases, and opinions, more or less probable, begin. But in the first place it would be well to be clear on one point: Percival was *not* the original Graal knight; though the first book (now existent) which utters the great word Graal is the Conte del Graal of Chrestien de Troyes, of which Percival is the hero. It seems certain that Percival was not the hero of the old Legend, because the "Peredur" of the Mabinogion, a late form of the Legend from which Chrestien doubtless derived his "Conte," has no mention of the Graal at all: and such is the case with the English metrical legends of Percival. Peredur (or Percival), is, as Mr. Nutt has pointed out, an Exile, Return, and Vengeance story, doubtless pre-Christian. Chrestien was engaged in turning the tale into French verse, hears some vague rumours of the Graal Legend, and mentions the Graal, so vaguely that it seems doubtful whether he knew what a Graal was. Wolfram von Eschenbach, who followed Chrestien, says, truly enough, that he had not got the right story; the appearance of the Graal is a mere dubious incident introduced without much reason into the tale of Percival. One can see, perhaps, what made Chrestien think of it; in the Mabinogion mention is made of a salver in which a man's head swims in blood—it was the head of Peredur's cousin slain by the sorceresses of Gloucester—it was the reminder to Peredur that he must execute vengeance on these sorceresses. But a dish full of blood might well remind Chrestien of another strange story that he had heard of a miraculous vessel; and so he, tentatively, introduces the Graal into his romance, into a tale of a quite distinct origin and meaning. Chrestien then, does not count: but he coupled the name of Percival with the Graal Legend, and so we find later writers, such as the authors of the "High History" and the "Parzival" adopting Percival as the Graal hero.

It is undoubtedly futile to make the story of the Sangraal a purely pagan legend, into which Christian Symbolism intruded at a late period. It is futile—to take one reason out of many—because the story of the Sangraal is essentially and chiefly a high, mystic, sacramental, and Christian legend —take away its Christianity and it is merely a queer bit of folk-lore. The Gargantua has, of course, folk-lore elements or traces, perhaps in the proportion of .0001 to the thousand, but the book does not owe its value or its interest to the old farmhouse tales about a giant. It is pretty much the same case with the Graal histories. There are, undoubtedly, pre-Christian elements in the mythos; the "feeding properties" of the Blessed Vessel are, perhaps, the most distinct of these, and carry one back to the Bardic Cauldrons, to the *mwys* of Gwyddno Garanhir, who, it may be noted, derived his revenue from a salmon-weir, and may have thus counted for something in the invention of the title "Rich Fisherman." These were miraculous feeding-vessels—illustrations of a conception which is perhaps worldwide, which is certainly not peculiar to Celtdom, since there is a mill which will give a perpetual supply of flour in the Kalevala. And one sees that these cauldrons of eternal refection could well be married to the instrument of the *dulcissimi convivii,* for there are numerous authorities which might be cited in favour of the belief that the Eucharist feeds not only the soul but the body. And on the other hand, the pagan cauldron was not wholly physical: it would not "cook the food of a coward." We can see, I think, without much difficulty that the Cauldron of Ceridwen might well be fused with the Chalice of the Eucharist; and we may allow that certain properties of the Sangraal were suggested by the basket of Gwyddno Garanhir, the horn of Bran Galed, the cauldron at Tyrnog, the pan and platter of Padarn Beisrudd and other such food-and-drink-multiplying rarities of the isle of Britain.

And there is another point in which pre-Christian legend may have had an influence; that is the "quest motive." Arthur ventured into the depths of the underworld in search of magic treasures, and here I think we have the origin of the search for the Graal, which I do not believe formed part of the sacramental legend in its earliest form. This was a legend of vanishing and of loss, not of finding; the two motives have been combined with wonderful skill in the "Queste," where Galahad achieves the Graal, discovers the holy and thaumaturgic object after many perils; and yet in the end Galahad dies and the Graal is borne up to heaven. And I really think that when we have admitted these "traces" we have given all the credit that can justly be given to the "pagan" elements in the story. And even in the matter of the "quest" idea, which is decidedly most important; I am not sure that we have a purely pre-Christian motive. The wanderings of the Celtic monks may count for a good deal; it is wonderful to think that the typical adventure of the mediæval knight-errant—the leaping into a boat without oars or sails, trusting utterly to the deep and the design of God, was, one might almost say, part of the ordinary routine of the average Celtic monk. Even as late as the reign of King Alfred such a boat, with three monks in it, drifted on to the coast of Cornwall from some "cell" on the shores of Ireland, and when the Northmen came to Iceland they found there a population of such adventurers. Celtic "monk-errantry" is a strange matter; one does not know how far these voyages were the expression of a wild missionary zeal, how far they were due to the desire for a greater solitude than might be had in the cell, for the "desart in ocean" that St. Columba's monk tried to discover, or how far they were really voyages to the semi-pagan, semi-Christian paradise, deep Avalon of the apple-blossoms far beyond the waves, the Glassy Isle where, some say, Merlin is hidden, having with him the Thirteen Rarities of Britain. In these voyages, undoubtedly, we have the origins of all that is most poetic and most romantic in the romances of chivalry; and the journeys of the Celtic monks may well have had some share in the Quests of the Knights of the Graal.

There is another possible element which must be examined and estimated for. Though Dr. Sebastian Evans is undoubtedly wrong in his main thesis, I should like to think that there is "something" in another theory of his. Dr.

Evans holds the view that Geoffrey of Monmouth's curious book was "written to order," written to further certain ambitions of the House of Anjou, which dreamed of a
British Empire and a British Church — the latter independent of the Ruman Curia. Geoffrey wrote of the
glories of the British kings, and these glories, according
to Dr. Evans, were to be "taken over" by the Normans, as
the legitimate successors of King Arthur. One wonders
whether this were so; if so it would explain certain things
which are at present hard to understand; it would explain,
for example, how men dared to set up Josephes, an imaginary
son of St. Joseph of Arimathæa, as a rival to St. Peter—
as infinitely superior to St. Peter. Christ himself, according
to one of the Romances, makes Josephes bishop, styling him
the Moses of the New Covenant. Was Josephes intended
to be the lengendary founder of a British Christianity, not
merely independent of, but infinitely more exalted than the
Christianity of St. Peter and his successors the Popes? This
is a question on which more light is needed; but if it were
established it would certainly do something to explain the
odd air of contemporary illusion which some of the Romances
certainly possess.

II.

THE evidence for the Celtic and Sacramental origins of
the Graal legend is to be found directly, in the lives of
the Welsh saints, especially in the life of St. David. Indi-
rectly; it may be gathered from many works which treat of
early British Christianity.

Now, before we begin to trace certain analogies between
our legend and the ecclesiastical histories, it will be as well
to say a word or two about Celtic Christianity. And in the
first place, there rises the question: was the Celtic Church
of the fifth, sixth and seventh centuries the continuous successor of the Christian Church which undoubtedly existed in
Britain during the Roman occupation? Or, again: did Chris-

tianity conquer the whole island during the Roman rule, or was it confined, with exceptions, to the garrison towns and to the country adjacent to such towns? There is no certain answer to either of the questions; not for the first time I call on the experts to come forward and be decisive, if they can. But the more probable opinion seems to be that the Christianity of St. David, St. Dyfrig, St. Teilo, St. Iltyd, and their successors was in the main a new, or a greatly modified form of Christianity, grafted perhaps on certain remnants which had survived the Roman exodus. There are reasons to be given for these (probable) conclusions. There are no early Welsh legends which profess to give the story of the first introduction of the religion into Britain, though all the legends take it for granted that the faith was established from early times. The hagiology of the British Church begins, for all practical purposes, with the post-Roman period, and tells how Pelagianism having overwhelmed the island, certain saints from Gaul came over, routed the heretics, and established orthodoxy. It has been suggested that for Pelagianism we should read Paganism, and that the two saints, Germanus and Lupus were, in reality, the evangelisers of Britain. No doubt there were Christians scattered about here and there; but the rather late monumental stone, with the inscription, *Homo Christianus fuit,* inclines one to believe that Christianity was the exception rather than the rule. Celtic scholars have wondered how an imaginative people could have been attracted by the heresy of Pelagius—which is more stupid and unenlightened than the common run of heresies—and the answer *may* be that the British never were attracted by this "New Theology" of the fifth century. Of course there is the story of Bran Vendigeid; but here we have an evident transmutation of a purely pagan demigod into a Christian saint. Gildas (a contemporary of King Arthur) knows nothing of this legend, nor indeed of any material whatsoever for the early history of British Christianity. We may take it then as a working hypothesis at all events that the early Celtic memory could go no farther back

[13]

than the period of the SS. Germanus and Lupus, and this period, therefore, would be, so far as our inquiry is concerned, the epoch of the Christianisation of Britain.

From which tentative but highly probable conclusion it follows that the Celtic legends which were available for the Anglo-French romance writers of the twelfth century were legends which referred to the saints of the fifth and sixth centuries, and not to the saints or missionaries of the first, second, and third centuries. These doubtless had existed; but for one reason or another they had not succeeded in dwelling in the Celtic memory. And so, when we read in a romance of Joseph of Arimathæa coming from Palestine to Britain in the first century, we may translate that sentence into: X came from Gaul to Britain in the fifth century. In other words, the British Church of the Romances is a glorification of the British Church from *c.* 420 to *c.* 666, about which time Cadwallader, the last king of Britain, died, the Relics of the Saints were removed or lost, and Celtdom and the Celtic Church began to suffer their long death-agony.

Now, the lives of St. David, St. Carannoc, and of other saints of the same period are accessible in histories which date from the end of the eleventh or the beginning of the twelfth century; but whatever may be said of the date of compilation, the material used is certainly antique. There is little or no trace of Norman or Roman influence, and the manner of the legends and of the incidents described is exactly similar to the manner of the seventh century life of St. Columba by St. Adamnan. As an example of the primitive and uncorrupted state of the Welsh hagiologies, I may mention that Arthur, whose name occurs a few times, is very far indeed from having attained the position which he occupies in Geoffrey of Monmouth; he does not even foreshadow the Arthur of the Romances. In one tale "a certain tyrant named Arthur" is punished by a saint for his impiety; in another Life he is represented as being in a district about twenty miles from Caerleon, the splendid capital of the later Arthurian legend, and Arthur does not know in the least where he is! Of course there may have been another set of early Welsh stories in which Arthur was already a mystic figure, indeed it is almost certain that this was the case; but the absence of all romantic treatment of him in the Lives of the Welsh Saints proves, I think, pretty conclusively that we may accept them as handing on faithfully traditions of the seventh and sixth centuries.

These traditions, then, are legends of the Christianising of Britain, and of the great men who carried out the work— and such done into high romantic dialect is the story of the coming of the Sangraal. To take the case of St. David first: his birth was foretold to his father by an angel in a dream. Sant (or Sandde) was to go out hunting, when he would find three things—a stag, a fish, and a honeycomb, prophetic of the son who should be born to him; and the adventure duly fell out as the angel had foretold. The honeycomb prophesied David's wisdom, "for as the honey is in the wax, so he will hold a spiritual sense in an historical instrument" —a sentence which I venture to think a very remarkable one. But "the fish denotes his aquatic life . . . therefore David will be surnamed David of Aquatic Life." Note here the analogy of the saint and the "Rich Fisherman" of the Graal Romances; and while this point is under considera- tion it may also be remarked that in South Wales there is a "Church of the Watermen"—they were rescued from the water and nourished by miraculous fishes—and that one of the saints—Ilar—is actually called Bysgottwr, or Fisherman. It is certain, that early Celtic Christianity was acquainted with the Ichthus symbolism, and it would appear that at a later period the significance of the fish had been forgotten. The phrase "denotes his aquatic life," the title "vir aquaticus" seems to show that the writer of the Life was ignorant of the fact that the fish is Christ, and more especially the Christ present in the Eucharist. It is not difficult, perhaps, to imagine that from this ignorance, this confusion, arose the figure of the Roi Pecheur, the Rich Fisherman, who keeps the Graal, the Holy Vessel which held "the Mighty, Unpolluted Fish," that is the Body and Blood of Christ: *panis ipse verus et aquae vivae Piscis.* In the earliest of the Romances the ancestor of the Graal keepers is made to catch a fish, which gives him his title; it is not difficult, I say, to suppose that such a story should be invented to account for a forgotten symbolism; and the associations which I have noted between certain of the Welsh saints and the Fish are at least worthy of attention.

There are many curious circumstances in this Life of St. David. At the Synod of Llandewibrefi it is said that David was acknowledged as "sovereign of the saints of the Isle of Britain . . . as God gave Mattheus in Judæa . . . Christ in Jerusalem, and Peter in Rome . . . so He has given St. David to be in the island of Britain." The passage is a curious one; there are already traces of the extravagant claims made for Josephes in the romances. Still more curious is another passage. The Patriarch of Jerusalem, who is represented as the consecrator of David, gave him: "a certain hallowed altar in which the Lord's Body had reposed, which abounded in innumerable virtues. Never was this altar seen after the death of the bishop [St. David] by any son of man; but it lies hidden, covered with skins. . . And hence the common people call it the Gift from Heaven." And in another passage this altar is called *anceps,* which may be interpreted by a passage from the life of St. Carannoc, to whom "Christ gave an honourable altar from on high, the colour of which no person could comprehend."

In these three quotations, it seems to me, one has already the germ of the Graal, and of the claims made by its keepers. For it should be noted that in the early romances the chalice idea is by no means a fixed and constant one. We have seen how in the "High History" the Graal assumed five forms, the last of which was the chalice, while in the metrical romance of Borron, and in the Grand Saint Graal, the Holy Vessel is taken as the antitype of the sepulchre in which Joseph of Arimathæa had laid the Lord, and Wolfram says the Graal is a stone called Lapsit Exillit—*lapis ex coelis?* It should be remarked also that the word graal (cratella) implies not so much a chalice as a shallow bowl on a stem; to the mediæval mind it must have given the idea of a vessel something like the dishes on which dessert is served. St. David's altar was, in the earlier legend, a gift from the Patriarch of Jerusalem, later it became a gift from heaven; and its "virtues," its thaumaturgic powers were due to the fact that in it, *dominicum jacebat corpus*. It is an altar, and yet there is already the suggestion of hollowness in its shape, and above all it is an altar in which the Lord's Body had been laid; it is not difficult to see how the name of Joseph of Arimathæa was suggested to later writers. And if the gifts which were called afterwards *e coelo venientia* were at first, in a more sober spirit, presents, though miraculous presents, from the patriarch of Jerusalem; then, it would be likely enough that St. David, at first consecrated by the Patriarch, should ultimately be consecrated by Christ from heaven. And the equations of St. David with St. Peter, with Christ Himself are undoubtedly in the same line of thought as the wild and extravagant claims made for Josephes in the Great Saint Graal. It is worth noting, too, how there is already something mysterious about the appearance of the Object; it is called *dubius, anceps;* the similar altar given from heaven to St. Carannoc is of a colour that no man can comprehend; St. David's altar was not seen openly after the saint's death, even as the Graal vanished in the romances. So, when William of Malmesbury was "writing up" Glastonbury Abbey (*c.* 1130, perhaps sixty years before the earliest of the romances was written) he speaks of St. David's altar, known as *Sapphirus,* as one of the treasures of the place; lost for a long time and then recovered. I do not think that it is temerarious to say that in the legends of these Welsh saints, hallowed in the east, endowed with miraculous altars of divine origin and of wondrous form, evangelisers of Britain, there is the probable ancestry of the great romances of the Graal.

So much for the direct analogies between the Celtic

legends and the Graal books; the indirect are perhaps as interesting. It is difficult, I think, to read the Lives of the Celtic Saints without recognising that a great deal of the "atmosphere" of the romances derives from the hagiologies. Take the following passage from the Life of St. Columba by St. Adamnan:

> For three days and three nights he allowed no one to approach him, and remained confined in a house which was filled with heavenly brightness. Yet out of that house, through the chinks of the doors and keyholes, rays of surpassing brilliancy were seen to issue during the night. Certain spiritual songs also, which had never been heard before, he was heard to sing. He came to see . . . many secrets, hidden from men since the foundation of the world, fully revealed.

One of St. Columba's monks saw him on another occasion enter the church; "and along with him at the same time a golden light that came down from the highest heavens"; this light was seen several times, and when the saint died the whole church was filled with heavenly brightness. It would be impossible to read of these appearances of celestial light without being reminded of the glorious brightness that accompanied the manifestations of the Graal. So when St. Cadoc (to whom the Church of Caerleon is dedicated) died: "a great brightness shone on the people devoutly engaged in performing his funeral rites, so that no one of them was able to sustain it." And again in the life of St. Fechin, a Scotch saint, we are told that when St. Fechin entered his church the multitudes saw light shining from the windows and the doors. Another topic of the romances is illustrated in the legend of St. Tathan, who found a little ship, without oars or sails, and entering boldly, was borne to Britain; and in the strange story of the Sacred Fire of St. Cadoc, we hear how this holy relic having been defiled by the profane, it vanished away, and hurts and doles were healed no more. St. Iltyd, again solitary in his cave by the shore, saw approaching a ship, on which was "an altar divinely supported." The oarsmen gave St. Iltyd "the perfumed body of a very holy man, whose name they told him, which he was never to utter." Taking these and other similar tales into consideration; we might almost pronounce that the heroes of the romances are Celtic monks in armour; there has been a certain fusion between the "monk errant" of the Celtic legends and the knights of Charlemagne, and from this admixture, which one may say was being realised at the time in the Templar Order, proceeded Galahad and the knights of the Graal.

Now, it is to be noted very carefully that when a Celtic biographer speaks of the "relics of the saints" he does *not* mean their bones. He means any holy vessels or objects which have belonged to them: such as the altars of which we have spoken; books, bells and croziers. This is of great importance in considering the passage in Geoffrey of Monmouth, who repeats the prophecy of the angel to Cadwallader, the last king of Britain. Cadwallader died in foreign lands—in Rome, according to the Normanised Welshman of the twelfth century, but almost certainly in the East, probably in Jerusalem, in the original legend. Prosperity shall return to Britain, says the angel, when Cadwallader's bones are restored to the island and when the relics of the other saints, which had been hidden on account of the fury of the pagans, should be revealed. Here, we see, there was an old legend which connected the vanishing of certain holy objects with the great loss and doom of Britain. In the romances the loss is a final one, so far as the relic—the Graal—is concerned; in the Celtic tradition there was to be a restoration of all things; Cadwallader was to return, Saxons were to be eradicated, and bards were to flourish, in the words of a poem in the (twelfth century) Red Book of Hergest, which, however, makes no mention of any relics. The romances contemplate a certain fashion of restoration—Arthur was to return and rule once more—but the Graal, it would appear, has gone forever. Does this mean that the House of Anjou still clung to the idea of a British Empire, but had given up the thought of an independent British Church? I do not venture to give even an opinion, much less a judgment; I scarcely dare suggest the possibility of the politics, ecclesiastical or civil, of the time having had any influence in the concoction of the Romances. Wolfram, it is true, following a Graal tradition which differs curiously from the tradition of the Anglo-French romances, refers to the Chronicles of the House of Anjou as one of the sources by which he corrected Chrestien's imperfect and erroneous story: this may be either an important clue or an empty compliment to a power-ful reigning house: I take refuge in confessed ignorance.

It is now time to examine a curious fact in Celtic tradition—that is the extraordinary veneration given to the relics of the saints, the remarkable powers ascribed to these relics, and the strange story of their hereditary keepers. We have already seen that in the Celtic Church practically every saint left relics behind him—bells, books, croziers, etc. So far as I know, the honour given to these objects, the miracles ascribed to them are quite unique in the history of Christianity; and I am strongly tempted to believe that the "relics" were, in reality, the sanctified successors of tribal palladia, of certain objects which, *mutatis mutandis,* had exercised the same powers, and commanded a like veneration in heathen times. The saint's relic, in Celtdom, could do almost anything: the prosperity of the tribe (afterwards, perhaps, of the race), was bound up with its safe preservation and reverent custody; and terrible penalties sanctioned the due observance of the relic ritual. Only those authorised by hereditary or acquired powers might so much as look on some of these objects; and in most cases they were enshrined in reliquaries, rich with all the splendour and mystic symbolism of Celtic art. The Book of St. Columba was borne in battle, and brought victory to the clan, if carried by one of pure heart— it is curious to note here the motive which perhaps developed into the conception of Galahad. Other relics gave oracles; there was a bell that refused to ring save in the hand of the saint for whom it was destined by God; another bell sailed through the air guiding its saint to an appointed place, other relics were angel-borne from heaven; one, being removed from its shrine and habitation cried aloud, day and night, till it was restored. Some healed diseases, others detected criminals or restored lost cattle. In a word, it would be very difficult to exaggerate the immense importance which these relics occupied in the Celtic mind; and at the present day the healing cup of Nant Eos is revered in Wales, not only for its potent cures, but also as "a Venerable Gift of the Almighty." So late as 1887 a harper, to whom the relic had been solemnly exhibited, felt profound remorse for having treated the holy thing lightly and irreverently. The man came again in a miserable condition of mind, and he was only pacified by a second exhibition of the relic, to which he paid devout reverence. In Scotland and in Ireland many of the relics also survive; and some, wonderful to say, still belong to the descendants of their original keepers. Indeed; the keeping of certain relics was in many cases incorporated into the feudal system; charters are extant granting land in return for the due custody of some holy bell or crozier, and in one or two instances the keeper was given a sort of popular title of nobility. Sad enough are the ends of some of these old songs; a battered iron bell, with faint traces of its former splendours still surviving, turned up by the plough, or found by boys playing in a cave by the seashore; a poor Irish schoolmaster of the eighteenth century, last of the keepers, bequeathing some wonderful piece of Celtic workmanship to the man who had befriended him—such are some of the last chapters of these strange histories. The keepers, it should be remarked, were in almost all cases the collateral descendants of the saints whose relics they had in custody; and there was more than a trace of the belief that something of the original virtue and sanctity of the saint descended to his successor in the guardianship of the relics. It was remarked that the Irish of the twelfth century were so ignorant that they believed the possessor of St. Patrick's relics to be *ipso facto* archbishop of Armagh. Such are the facts as to the hereditary relic keepers of Celtic Christendom: it is for the student

of the Graal romances to judge as to the probability of the
existence of these keepers having originated the wonderful
story of the hereditary guardians of the Holy Graal.

M. Paulin Paris had a most interesting theory as to
Galahad. We have seen that Cadwallader, the "last King of
Britain" was in Welsh legend expected to return once more,
restoring all things, and bringing with him the "relics of the
saints." Cadwallader, indeed, loomed a more heroic figure
than Arthur in the Welsh imagination; Celtdom canonised
him, and the churches bearing the name Llangadwaladr were
built in his honour. It is noteworthy that while all other
Welsh saints are styled *sant* (or sometimes, oddly enough,
agius), Cadwallader shares with the mystic Bran the title
of Blessed, or Vendigeid (*benedictus*). One does not know
what was the true history of the real man's life and death,
there are various stories; but it is certain that the date
assigned for his death coincided with the death sentence of
Celtdom, both in Church and State. The "yellow hag"—
some form of plague—swept away the Cymri by thousands,
the Saxons tightened their grip and extended it over the
whole island, and strangely enough, the "making" of Celtic
saints ceased. The Celtic monk-errants had swept all over
the continent of Europe; they had set up the rule of
St. Columbanus at Bobbio, by the Pope's door, and Columbanus had addressed the Holy Father as an equal, not without a hint that any case of error or heresy on the part of the
Chief Bishop of Christendom would meet with due correc-
tion from the Celtic monk. But the tide turned. Cadwallader died, the "relics of the saints" were lost, or taken
into concealment, and everywhere the Roman power prevailed, abolishing Celtic customs and rites, and doing its
work so thoroughly that no Celtic liturgy has survived.
A dreary enchantment (from the Celtic point of view) fell
upon the sanctuaries of the saints, and the abomination of
desolation, in the form of the Roman missal, succeeded the
High Offering of the Perpetual Choirs of the Isle of Britain.

Now M. Paulin Paris thinks that the name and the tale

of Galahad are derived from the name and the tale of Cadwallader. In the case of the name (which was sometimes spelt Catgualart and Catgualatyr) I think M. Paulin Paris is right; and for the tale—well, there is a good deal to be said for his point of view. As Galahad, the last possessor of the Graal in the *Queste,* went to Sarras, carrying the holy vessel with him, so Cadwallader went to Jerusalem (for "Rome" in Geoffrey of Monmouth is almost certainly a substitution, partly due to a confusion between the names of the Welsh hero and a Saxon king) carrying with him, presumably, the "relics" which are to return with him. It is to be noted, also, that as Galahad was of the lineages of Joseph of Arimathæa and of Our Lady so also was Cadwallader descended collaterally from the Blessed Virgin and St. David. But it would be rash, I think, to assert that the story of the British king was more than a rough sketch for that splendid and glowing figure of Galahad. The romance writer had heard an old legend perhaps, a wandering and uncertain and broken tale with the last glow of the Celtic fire still shining dimly from it; and from these poor fragments he built up the miracle of the *Queste.* It would be unsafe to say that the Celtic legend counted for much more than a hint in the execution of that wonderful romance.

III.

IT WILL be understood, I hope, that these papers do not pretend, in any sense whatever, to be so much as an outline of the great literary question of the Sangraal. They are merely notes and hints and suggestions on certain interesting points in the legend; and my hope is that they may stimulate more learned and more fortunate "questers" to a deeper research.

It is not altogether necessary, then, for me to apologise for omissions; since if I once began to do so, I should never have done; but there is one point which I should have mentioned in my first chapter, in treating of the "pagan" elements in the story. This is the very singular and significant appearance of "a Head so rich and beautiful that never mortal saw aught so glorious" in the wonderful description of the Graal worship at Sarras, in the Grand Saint Graal. This Head was borne by one of the angels in red vestments, who served ⁺he great Rite; it is impossible, I think, to deny its close relationship to the venerable Head of Bran, which would have made an eternal paradise for the heroes—if they had not disobeyed a certain prohibition. Meat and drink and entertainment, and the enchanted song of the Fairy Birds of Rhiannon were the portion of the followers of Bran—till they opened the door that looked towards Cornwall; and then all delights and pleasures vanished away. The "Rich Head" of the Graal Romance is undoubtedly the pre-Christian demigod or deity consecrated to the service of the Holy Vessel; it is interesting to find so positive a proof of the Celtic origin of the Legend. By the way, it may be remembered that there are many traces of this Head cultus in Celtdom; in Pembrokeshire, for instance, there is a well, sacred to St. Teilo, the water of which heals sickness, if administered by the Hereditary Keeper in the skull of the saint. In Scotland, again, there was a saint's skull which was washed, ritually, and the water of the washing was regarded as holy and salutary; and I should like to be instructed in the real meaning of such place names as Holyhead and Penzance. Do they mean "the Holy Headland," or do they imply that in these places there was a special cultus of the "Venerable Head"? It is interesting to note that Penzance bears as arms a head on a dish, supposed, of course, to be the Head of St. John the Baptist.

But, for our especial purpose this "Rich Head," strangely introduced into the Graal Ritual, is of very high interest. For one cannot help thinking of that other Head—the head of Peredur's slain cousin, exhibited to him in a dish full of blood. This latter was not a holy object; it was, apparently, an incitement to vengeance on the murderers. The dish full of blood, the spear ever dripping with blood, cried to Peredur for vengeance; we have here, I suppose, an instance of the traps and confusions and coincidences which lurk in the Romance Literature of the Sangraal.

To pass on to the more immediate purpose of this article: there are many reasons for supposing that the Romances celebrate and glorify the curious and ancient quarrel between Roman and Celtic Christianity. In some of the earliest versions of the Legend, we hear of a distinct rite called the "Graal Service." This ritual was performed at Terce (the mediæval hour for the principal mass of the day); it was called "going to Grace," and it would seem that the worshippers were rapt into an ecstasy. Again, in the "High History" we hear of "the priests and hermits of the Graal," who are removed by the Lord God into a sure place during the usurpation of the King of Castle Mortal; and in the Queste the "service of the Holy Graal" was performed divinely in the precious chapel where the Holy Graal used to appear. To me it seems difficult to avoid the conclusion that in such passages as these we have highly romantic allusions to the Celtic Church; the possessor of sacrosanct and Eucharistic Relics, *e coelo venientia,* and of a distinct Eucharistic Rite. How far we may take the Romance allusions is conjectural, and perhaps will always remain conjectural. It may be that the allusions of the "High History" and the Queste are fairly accurate accounts of events which really happened, it may be that they have the slenderest historical foundations; we do not know and probably we never shall know.

And now as to the peculiarities of the Celtic Church as distinct from the Roman. Here again we are in a region of few certainties and many possibilities and probabilities. One thing at least is certain: the anti-Celtic fervour of the Roman authorities was so thorough that there is no such thing as a Celtic Liturgy in existence; and perhaps the latest reference to such a thing dates back to the twelfth century, when the remnant of the Culdees are reported as celebrating "some kind of barbarous rite" in a corner of a Scotch church. There are few certainties beyond this; but there are probabilities.

I have already said that I accept as a working hypothesis the theory that the Celtic Church was really the work of the fifth century, and that it was organised by Gallican missionaries; and that being granted it follows necessarily that the churches of Britain and Ireland were of the type that is called Oriental. Of course all Christianity is, in origin, a Syrian mission; but for whatever reason or reasons, the local Roman Church became differentiated from all others at a very early period, and developed a Liturgy—the Latin Mass—which it is convenient to call Western. It would be tedious in the highest degree to examine minutely the variations between the Rite of Constantinople and the Rite of Rome; it will be sufficient to say that the most important of the many differences between the two services is the presence of the Epiclesis in the Eastern, and its absence from the Western Eucharist. The Epiclesis is the Invocation of the Holy Spirit on the Elements (in some Eastern Rites on the congregation also), and in the Divine Liturgy of St. James it runs as follows:—

Have mercy on us, O God, according to Thy great goodness, and send upon us, and upon these proposed gifts, Thy most Holy Ghost . . . who descended upon Thy holy Apostles in the likeness of fiery tongues in the upper room of the holy and glorious Sion, at the day of Pentecost: send down the same most HOLY GHOST, Lord, upon us, and upon these holy and proposed gifts, that coming upon them with His holy and good and glorious presence, He may hallow and make this bread the holy Body of THY CHRIST.
People. Amen.
Priest. And this cup the precious Blood of Thy CHRIST.
People. Amen.

It is by this formula, or by some equivalent prayer, that the present Orthodox Church of the East believes the mystery of the consecration to be effected; the West—the Roman and English churches—on the other hand, make the efficacy of the sacrament to depend upon the due recital of the Words of Institution. And yet I believe that the Eastern Church would hardly declare all the consecrations of the West to be void and of none effect.

This, then, is the Epiclesis, and it is almost certain that the British Liturgy possessed some such formula. It is not absolutely certain, because, as I have stated, there is no Celtic Liturgy in existence; but the probability is very high—indeed, since the derivation of the Celtic Church of the fifth century from the Church of Vienne and Lyons, is almost inevitable. It should be noted, by the way, that the early Gallican Church in question occupied a peculiar position with respect to the Epiclesis. The formula was not, as in the East, an integral and essential portion of every Mass; it occurred in the Eucharists on certain saints' days, and not on those of others, and such, we may presume, was its place in the ritual of Celtic Christendom—unless, indeed, the Celts followed the more primitive and allied Mozarabic Rite, in which, I think, the Invocation of the Holy Spirit is invariably used.

Now, in some of the Graal Romances there are curious references to certain "secret words" used in the Eucharist; a claim is made, if the expression may be allowed, for a "super-valid" consecration. Robert de Borron, for example, says that he dare not speak of the secrets revealed to Joseph, and if he would he could not, without the Great Book:—

> Ou les estoires sont escrites,
> Par les grans clercs feites et dites,
> La sont li grant secre escrit,
> Qu'on nomme le Graal.

Is this a reference to a Celtic Liturgy, or rather to a vague rumour of a Celtic Liturgy? Are the "grant secre" of the Graal Service the Prayer of Invocation? I think there is a remote possibility that this is so; I dare not say more. Wales conformed to the Roman Church between 750—809; and therefore we may conclude that the prescription of the Celtic Liturgy began towards the end of the eighth and the beginning of the ninth centuries. It is quite likely that the native ritual was not extinguished without a struggle; it is quite likely that it continued to be celebrated by patriot recluses, by "saints" who had oratories among the rocks and among the woods for a long period after the Roman Missal had become the only "legal" use; it is quite likely that the primitive Liturgy endured long enough for the rumour of it to have reached the ears of the Romance writers. The Graal Service was said divinely in the precious chapel where the Graal itself had once been wont to appear. This *may* mean that the Celtic Ritual was used, after long pretermission, in an oratory where once some venerated altar, reputed to be of heavenly origin, had been preserved—it would be temerarious to say more.

There is another probable argument in favour of this identification of the Graal Service with the British Rite. In the Grand Saint Graal, the first Mass is described—in connection with the alleged Apostolate and Primacy of Josephes, son of Joseph of Arimathæa. The passage is as follows:—

Laiens fist Josephe le premier sacrement qui onques fust fais a celui peule, mais il eut moult tost accompli, kar il ne dist que celes paroles seulement, qant Jhesu-Cris dist a ses dessiples a la chaine: "Venes, si mangies et chou est li miens cors qui pour vous et pour maintes autres gens sera livre a martire et a torment." Et autress; leur dist del vin: "Tenes et si beves tout Car chou est li sanc di ma nouviele loy, li miens meismes, ki pour vous sera espandus en remision des pechies."

Now the Roman Formula of Consecration is, for the bread:—

Hoc est enim Corpus meum,

and for the wine:—

Hic est enim Calix sanguinius mei, novi et æterni testamenti: mysterium fidei: qui pro vobis et pro multis effundetur in remissionem peccatorum.

The question is: where did the author of the Grand Saint Graal get his formulæ? Professor Warren, an authority on Celtic Christianity, thinks that there is "ground," but

[28]

not "proof" for *confrangetur,* as the word in use in the lost British Liturgy. It may be noted that there is proof of very early intercourse between the Egyptian and Celtic churches, and that the Coptic consecration formula is similar to that of the Romance in its use of the future tense. Again, it is not wise to do more than suggest a probability. It would be delightful if one could point to the words of the Grand Saint Graal as an undoubted fragment of the lost Ritual of our fathers: but to do this were to play the "Higher Critic" in his wildest moods. It may be that here we have a remnant of the Celtic Liturgy; we must not be more positive. The general position—that the "Graal Church" symbolises the Celtic Church—is, I think, probable in a very high degree; the particular conclusions must be left in doubt and in mist.

There is one very odd circumstance about the "Parzival" of Wolfram von Eschenbach. We have seen that he accused Chrestien of having told the wrong story; he himself professes that he corrected Chrestien by the Chronicles of the House of Anjou, and by the narrative of one Kyot, or Guiot, a Provencal. However that may be, the "Parzival" is in one most important respect entirely distinct from all the other romances. A graal, as we have seen, probably implied to the readers of the romance, a shallow bowl (or deep dish) on a stem and foot, and we have noted also the curious uncertainty which seems to have existed as to the exact shape of the Holy Vessel. In one romance it assumes five forms, the last of which is the chalice, in another it is an image of the sepulchre in which Christ's body was laid by Joseph; the paten being the stone slab placed on top of the grave. It is at once a chalice, and also the vessel in which Christ willed that His Body should be offered and sacrificed; there is a singular ambiguity. One story says that it was the vessel in which Christ washed the Apostles' feet; another that in it He "made His sacrament." And one cannot help thinking of St. David's Altar, *in quo dominicum jacebat corpus.*

In the "Parzival" the Graal is a stone called Lapsit

Exillit. It was hallowed, its virtue was ever renewed, by a Dove that brought on the Good Friday of each year a consecrated Host from heaven, laying It on the Graal. There is no reference whatever to the Precious Blood; and it seems impossible that the Graal of Wolfram's conception could have served any of the uses of a cup or chalice. It was a stone that had fallen from the crown of Lucifer when the great angel was driven from heaven; a precious stone presumably; and one is reminded of William of Malmesbury's reference to St. David's Altar lost, and restored (so he says) to Glastonbury, and called *Sapphirus*. I do not say that Wolfram's story proves that the Graal was originally an altar and not a chalice; I am content to affirm that it is evidence strongly in favour of that hypothesis. The sculptured stone (eighth or ninth century, I believe) at Nigg, in Scotland, would seem to illustrate an idea not remote from Wolfram's. In the centre of the stone there is figured a vessel like a very shallow champagne glass, or a saucer on a stem; above this hovers a dove, holding in its beak a round disc, resembling a wafer. On each side an ecclesiastic bows in adoration; and below two lions crouch to the ground.

Now, accepting as an hypothesis the altar theory, the question naturally arises: How did the altar become transformed into a chalice? This, I think, is not an insoluble enigma; and the answer may probably be obtained from William of Malmesbury's eulogy of Glastonbury Abbey, in which there are several notable points. Firstly it is said by William that the body of Joseph of Arimathæa was buried somewhere in the precincts of the abbey, and so far as I know there is no earlier mention of Joseph in connection with Glastonbury or with Britain. The story dates from *c.* 1130—40. Secondly, it states that with the body were buried two phials containing the Precious Blood of Christ; and here, it seems to me, we have the secret of the Graal of the Romance Writers. Nor is it difficult to trace this invention of the Legend to its origin. Somewhere in the thirties of the twelfth century, a crusading knight had remitted to the town of Brugs a phial said to contain the Blood of Christ, which the Church of Antioch had given him, in reward for great services rendered against the miscreants. The phial in question, which is still preserved at Bruges, and venerated by the faithful, is adorned with work of the seventh or eighth century; beyond that date, of course, history must give place to legend. But it is certain that in the beginning of the twelfth century the cultus of the Precious Blood received a great impetus; and the inventive William endowed Glastonbury with a Relic which would be certain to enhance the prestige of the convent. It does not seem hard to imagine that the Norman-French romance writers combined two distinct objects—the altar of St. David or of some other Welsh saint—with the supposed phials of Glastonbury, and that the union of the two instruments produced the Sangraal. An altar could not hold blood; a phial would not serve in the Eucharistic connection which attached to the altar, and so a compromise was effected, and the Holy Graal, at first a vague and ill-defined object, put on at last the form of the chalice, and yet was spoken of as the vessel in which God willed that His Body should be offered. There is no proof of all this: most likely there never will be; but it seems to be a very probable solution of a most difficult question.

Then, of course, there is the substitution of the name of Joseph of Arimathæa for our (hypothetical) Welsh saint; and here again the difficulties do not strike me as insuperable. So far as I know there is no reason to suppose that the Legend of Joseph as the Evangelist of Britain existed before the beginning of the twelfth century. But it was "fashionable," if we may use the term, for every Church in Christendom to claim an Apostolic or semi-apostolic origin; and it is easy to understand that such names as Dewi and Carannoc, Iltyd and Ilar, had no particular prestige or enchantment for Norman-French ears, or for readers of Paris town. The Precious Blood cultus had suggested the phials, the belief of the Glastonbury monks that the body of Joseph was buried in their abbey was, possibly, a convent tradition; it was simple to put things together to make Joseph the founder of British Christianity, and the possessor of a priceless relic. The apocryphal Gospel of Nicodemus supplied the tale of his imprisonment by the Jews; his voyage to Britain was probably suggested by the Legend of the Saintes Maries de la Mer, and, indeed, one of the names occurring in the Grand Saint Graal is taken bodily from the Provencal story; and so the romance grows, mingling Celtic legends, apocryphal gospels, missionary tales, a popular cultus, and sheer invention in books of the most wonderful and glorious inspiration. And this last is, after all, by far the greatest element. Matters of varying merit went into the crucible; it was the power of the mediæval artistry that was the red powder, glistering and glorious as the sun, which transformed, transmuted, re-created, glorified, changing copper into gold, wandering and broken legends into splendid romance. The change seems to me not improbable; for the thirteenth century was the age in which Salisbury Cathedral was built, and the time that could raise the rough ashlar to such power and glory and dominion and spiritual life, was doubtless able to form rough literary materials into the great temple of the Graal Romances.

Aug. 3, 1907.
Aug. 31, 1907.

THE HOLY GRAIL

A Reply to Arthur Machen

MR. ARTHUR MACHEN, if I mistake not, will not be disinclined to foregather for a while with a fellow quester, and to consider with him the paths he has tracked through the devious mazes of the Grail forest, and the clues that seem to him to lead to the unveiling of all the mysteries of the Grail. I have read with the greatest interest Mr. Machen's three articles; they are full of acute and sympathetic criticism; they illuminate and, in many ways, really advance our knowledge. I am grateful to Mr. Machen for them, and I can best, it seems to me, show my gratitude by giving them close and searching attention.

It may be well to premise, for the sake of readers less well-informed than Mr. Machen, that the complex of Grail romances resolves itself into two main elements, one definitely Christian in character and mainly (though whether entirely is a moot question) of Christian origin, another which, if Christian in origin (again a moot point), most certainly presents itself in the romances in most un-Christian guise. As regards this latter, I claim to have shown that it originated and largely developed in an un-Christian world of conception and fancy which finds its nearest parallel in the mythic and heroic literature of Celtdom. With the exception of a couple of scholars who, having once expressed a contrary opinion, think it concerns their honour to shut their eyes and deny the sun at midday, my demonstration has been practically accepted by all students, and is now practically accepted (though some expressions might lead the unknowing reader to doubt it) by Mr. Machen. For, if his various statements with regard to the pagan elements in the romances are carefully examined, they will be found to cover well-nigh all the claims I have ever made in vindication of the part played by Celtic pre-

Christian fancy in shaping the Grail cycle. One observation of his I would especially single out for its pregnant character, that which regards the relics of the Celtic saints as "in reality the sanctified successors of tribal palladia, of certain objects which, *mutatis mutandis,* had exercised the same powers, and commanded a like veneration in heathen times." If there is any force in my parallel between the talismans of the Grail castle—Grail and Lance and Sword—and the talismans of the Tuatha de Dannan (the Irish gods)—Cauldron and Spear and Sword—Mr. Machen's sentence might be taken as quintessencing my contentions. I am also much struck by his claim that the Head which figures in the Grand Saint Graal account of the Grail worship is related to the Venerable Head of Bran. The suggestion is a bolder one than at present I am prepared to accept, diffident as I am in drawing conclusions in favour of my views, however strong the evidence appears to be.

If we turn now to the Christian element, there are two main views respecting its nature. The one, dominant twenty years, regarded it as belonging wholly to the twelfth century, as derived from texts (canonical, apocryphal and legendary) known to us at first hand, and, as disconnected, save in a purely formal and unessential way, with Celtdom. I was never able to admit this view, and in so far as I considered the Christian element at all (my chief object being to display and illustrate the non-Christian element) urged that it took shape in Britain and was conditioned in its growth by British surroundings and events. This is also Mr. Machen's opinion; and he (laying stress upon the Christian as I laid stress upon the non-Christian element) has made the same claim for Celtic Christianity as I made for Celtic pre-Christianity. Both he and I had precursors in this respect; he has mentioned M. Paulin Paris; he might also have mentioned M. Th. H. de la Villemarque and M. Potvin, who wrote before the appearance of my *Studies;* whilst since then Mr. Wardle, in *Y Cymmrodor,* and Miss D. Kemp, in her introduction to the E.E.T.S. edition of the fifteen century version of the Grand St. Graal, have done valuable and suggestive work in this connection. But Mr. Machen has not only focussed the evidence with all the skill of an artist in letters: he has definitely elaborated the theory "that the Romances celebrate and glorify the curious and ancient quarrel between Roman and Celtic Christianity" in a way that carries it far beyond the point at which it was left by M. Potvin. In endeavoring to estimate the value of this theory, I am compelled to enter into some consideration of the way in which have been preserved the diverse elements which figure in the Grail Romance.

These latter are products of the twelfth and thirteenth centuries. Now, Celtic Christianity, as an organisation, had disappeared alike in Ireland and Wales by the year 800 A.D.; Welsh paganism, as an organisation, had almost certainly disappeared by the year 450 A.D., Irish paganism by the year 650 A.D. (this late date allowing for the possible reaction which some of the stories connected with Guaire and Senchan Torpeist seem to hint at). If, then, in the French twelfth-century romances we find specific Celtic traces, it would, at first sight, seem more reasonable to refer them to Celtic Christianity, which lived, as an organisation, into the ninth century, rather than to Celtic pre-Christianity, which had ceased to exist centuries before. And yet, paradoxical as it may seem, the contrary is the case. Of the specifically Celtic features it was the pre-Christian rather than the Christian which stood a chance of surviving into the twelfth century. Nor is the reason far to seek. The heathen myth, voided of its animating concept, lived on as a story, and might in that shape preserve its outline and framework substantially unaltered. Alike in Wales and in Ireland, stories continued to be told down to far beyond the twelfth century which are manifestly of pre-Christian mythic origin. The divine *dramatic personae* have been humanised or heroicised, incidents that conflicted too much with the new faith have been eliminated or modified, but substantially the story persisted, and yielded the twelfth-century minstrel a fixed sequence of incidents, which, as a rule, he respected alike because it was easier than not for him to do so, because the stories were first-rate examples of narrative, and the minstrel generally knew a good story when he saw it. The chief fault, indeed, of the twelfth-century French romances is not so much that they distort the original Celtic plot (though sometimes they do with disastrous results), as that they swamp it in an endless wash of repetition and irrelevant detail. Thus it happens that we can often parallel, in well-nigh the same sequence, incident for incident of the twelfth-century French romances and the centuries older Celtic tale, the differences between the two being external (manners, costumes, social life, etc.) rather than internal.

As regards the specifically Celto-Christian traits and features, we must make a distinction. Although Celtic Christianity ceased to exist as a separate organisation by the ninth century, the literature which it produced survived as a living, plastic thing. Mr. Machen has well pointed out that the Welsh Saints' Lives, which we possess in twelfth-century versions, betray a far earlier origin, both as regards context and form. There is thus no reason for doubting the possibility of a French romance writer even as late as the thirteenth century, coming in contact with a literature permeated and animated by the spirit of Celtic Christianity. Nay, more; it so happens that on Celtic soil the process had already begun of turning legend into romance. The *Navigatio Brendani* stands in a different category from the early lives of Patrick or Columba, or Brigit, or David, or Samson; it is not so much that it is fuller of miracle (that could hardly be), but in a way that is apparent at once to the attentive reader—whilst the one class of narrative aims at being a record of fact, the other is avowedly religious fiction. When, therefore, Miss Kemp traces many incidents in the Grand St. Graal to the Brendan literature, when Mr. Machen urges that "the journeys of the Celtic monks may well have had some share in the Quest of the Knights of the Graal," I am perfectly ready to agree. Indeed, it must now be regarded as past doubt that the Christian portion of the Grail complex is as permeated with the spirit of Celtic Christian legend as the non-Christian portion is with the spirit of Celtic pre-Christion saga.

But when Mr. Machen takes his further step, then doubt begins to assert itself in my mind. The Celtic hagiological legend and romance that survived into the twelfth century, though differing in tone and spirit from that of the remainder of the Catholic Church, yet displayed nothing antagonistic thereto. A very searching analysis of the early Saints' Lives does, it is true, reveal to the historical critic an ecclesiastical and social organisation profoundly differing from that of the Roman Church—at all events, in the twelfth century. But the differences are such as would be unintelligible—indifferent, anyhow—to the man of the twelfth century. Nothing in them would savour of heterodoxy to him. But Mr. Machen's hypothesis demands the survival into the twelfth century, not alone of mere traces, or even of unconnected and incoherent incidents, but of a definite sequence of incidents, forming a distinct plot and exhibiting and symbolising a vital difference between Celtdom and Rome; a plot, therefore, essentially heterodox in the eyes of the twelfth century. For, note, Mr. Machen's hypothesis requires not only that the assumed features of the lost Celtic liturgy had been worked up into a romantic form *before* the period of the French romances, but that this had been done as a kind of last protest on the part of Celtic Christianity. In other words, it must have been elaborated whilst there was still definite consciousness on the Celtic side of the reality and magnitude of the points at issue with Rome. I do not see how, if Mr. Machen follows up his own suggestions to their logical issue, he can avoid dating back the Galahad story, in some form, to the tenth or ninth century. Potvin and de la Villemarque were quite ready to do this. But I think Mr. Machen would hesitate, and I am sure the majority of Grail students would, on the present evidence, refuse assent.

Let me not be misunderstood. I have no *a priori* quarrel

with Mr. Machen's hypothesis as regards the formation of the legend. Grant his assumption of a Celtic Eucharistic rite kin to that of the Eastern Church, and I recognise in the inevitable ensuing conflict between this and the Roman rite sufficient ground for the elaboration and perpetuation (so long as the conflict lasted) of such a legend as he postulates. But how did it reach the twelfth-thirteenth-century writer of the *Queste* as an organic whole? How was it preserved among a people which, in this respect, had long since conformed to Roman orthodoxy? And if it did not reach the writer of the *Quests* as an organic whole, must we suppose that he, a Norman, knew enough about the ancient conflict (a wild surmise)—or (yet wilder surmise, if he perchance *did* know) sympathised sufficiently with the long dead Celtic Church, to give it the shape he did? The more definitely Mr. Machen traces in the Galahad story, as we have it, the faded lineaments of a conflict then four centuries old, the more improbable does the hypothesis seem. Its very logical perfectness impales it on one or other of the horns of the dilemma set forth above.

On the other hand, the hypothesis does undoubtedly account for that heterodox element in the Grail Romances which is not the least puzzling of the many enigmas they present. When I began the study of the legend twenty-five years ago, the dominant critical view took as little account of this heterodox Christian element as it did of the non-Christian mythic element; it treated both as meaningless freaks, due to the ignorance and ill-regulated fantasy of the romance writers. Such a view always seemed to me untenable. There must, I held, and hold, be a reasonable explanation for this feature of these romances. An hypothesis which offers such an explanation thus finds me biassed in its favour; and if I reject it, it is only because the objection I have stated seems to me fatal. If I am called to account, satisfactorily, for this perplexing element, I confess my inability. But I think Mr. Machen has been over-hasty in rejecting the Temple explanation. I quite agree that an infinity of nonsense has been talked about the Templars, as about all subjects which get into the hands of the occultists. But that is no reason for shutting one's eyes to facts. It *is* a fact that there is a Crusading, Eastern element in the Grail Romance complex, and that this element stands in some connection, ill-defined and obscure it may be, yet certain, with the Temple body. Moreover, although it is safe to treat the charges trumped up by King and Pope as malignantly exaggerated, still the evidence for an esoteric, heretical doctrine among the Templars is by no means so slight as Mr. Machen asserts. Nor do I understand what he means by styling this alleged heresy "distinctly anti-Sacramental." In the sense of Christian orthodoxy, it is undoubtedly, but not in a wider sense. Is it, then, quite impossible that a Sacramental doctrine, which, in the case of certain members of the body, had a definitely anti-Christian outcome, might, with others, result in a Christian hyper-Sacramental teaching? Mr. Machen apparently forgets that where the Grail Romances must have seemed most questionable to the "sound" ecclesiastic of the day is in their glorification of a priesthood constituted outside of, and without reference to, the official Church *cudres.* Is not this, *a priori,* what might be expected from an over-enthusiastic adherent of the Temple?

I am rather puzzled by Mr. Machen's statement that "we have had treatises to show that Adonis is somehow concerned in the story of the Sangraal." Indeed! I am aware that a paper by Miss Weston will shortly appear in *Folk Lore,* entitled "The Grail and the Rites of Adonis." Has Mr. Machen fore-knowledge of its contents and has it multiplied itself in his mind? I cannot, from Mr. Machen's point of view, account for his hostility to what he calls the Covent Garden theory—*i.e.,* the Mannhardt-Frazer view that the agricultural rites for the fostering of vegetable life, together with the conceptions on which those rites were based, have profoundly affected the mythological protoplasm out of which myth, romance and legend were to develop. For these animating conceptions these symbolic rites are distinctly Sacramental.

If Mr. Machen will recall his own words about the Christian relic exercising the *same* power and commanding the *same* veneration as its heathen prototype, he may perhaps admit that a Christian hyper-Sacramental legend, if resting at all upon a pre-Christian basis (and he fully recognises that it does so rest), is most likely to find such a basis in myths which themselves are, in their essence, Sacramental.

ALFRED NUTT.

THE SANGRAAL

A Reply to Alfred Nutt

MR. ALFRED NUTT is certainly quite right in thinking that I should welcome his most interesting and suggestive contribution on the question of the Sangraal. I read his letter with the keenest curiosity, and I am under the impression that he and I are very near agreement on this most puzzling and complicated problem. There are some minor points that I wish he would solve for me: for example, there is the introduction to the Grand Saint Graal. I want to know about that Hermit; what was the "sign" that he wore which enabled the knight to recognise him as having been a participator in some secret assembly? What assembly could this have been? Is it possible that this introduction is an adaptation of some very early document? The precision of date is curious.

I think, perhaps, that Mr. Nutt and myself would disagree as to the importance of remote origins. If I am asked to explain the meaning of the words *imbecile* and *idiot,* I do not think that I should be really explaining anything by referring to *baculus,* or to a Greek word signifying a private person. And if an intelligent little boy were to say, "What does 'virtuosity' mean?" I should not reply that it came from a Latin word meaning "a man," and that this Latin word was akin to *baro.* Excursions into Sanscrit I should regard as still more impertinent—hence my prophetic irritation at Miss Weston's Adonis paper, hence my dislike of the Spring Cabbage Doctrine. Mr. Nutt allows that I have done ample justice to the Pagan element in the Graal Legend; why not leave Adonis alone, with Buddha's Alms Dish and the Mill of Perpetual Flour in the Kalevala?

There are one or two details in Mr. Nutt's admirable letter which seem to me arguable. Mr. Nutt says:

THE GLORIOUS MYSTERY

Mr. Machen's hypothesis demands the survival into the twelfth century, not alone of mere traces, or even of unconnected and incoherent incidents, but a definite sequence of incidents, forming a distinct plot, and exhibiting and symbolising a vital difference between Celtdom and Rome: a plot, therefore, essentially heterodox in the eyes of the twelfth century.

But the plot of the early Graal Romances—the Percival of Chrestien excepted, but Percival does not count—*are* horribly unorthodox, not only according to twelfth century Roman standards, but according to any Christian standards. Practically the whole Apostolate disappears, to give place to Josephes, who occupies a position in the New Dispensation compared with which the most extravagant Roman doctrine as to the powers of St. Peter is mild and modest. So "unorthodoxy" is clearly no objection to any hypothesis in this Graal matter. I confess I do not understand how these Romances were tolerated; I can only suppose that they were treated as fairy tales without any doctrinal significance. I do not believe for a moment that the Romance writers were consciously heterodox; it seems probable that they merely inflated an ancient Celtic story, containing ancient Celtic claims against Rome, to the point of hyperbole and extravagance, without seeing what their Josephes legend really implied from an ecclesiastical point of view. I think I should believe that the Galahad story "in some form" was older than the ninth or tenth century; I should incline to place its origin early in the eighth century. But in what form? That I cannot tell. There was no Lancelot of the Romances, but there was probably illegitimate origin, since the parentage of many Welsh saints is of this character. I cannot agree with Mr. Nutt in thinking the survival of Celtic Church *versus* Roman Church stories as improbable. For in the first place, speaking generally, is there any assignable time limit to the survival of anything? I am continually being astonished by the vitality of things. The wandering tinkers, jabbering corrupt Gaelic to one another, the server in the Roman Mass lifting up the little, stiff chasuble of modern days, just as the server of the ninth century lifted up the heavy and voluminous vestment of his time, the children of Caerleon on Usk carrying round the gilded and fruit-bearing apple of Martial's *strenae*—the list of such amazing survivals is infinite. Then, particularly, we are dealing with Celts, with a people noted for their fierce attachment to their antique customs. Mr. Nutt asks how the legend was preserved "among a people which . . . had long conformed to Roman orthodoxy?" Frankly, I see no difficulty. Logically, no doubt, the Welsh had no business to be recollecting the legend; but, logically, that abbot whom Giraldus met had no business to be a married man, and those Irish whom St. Bernard mentions had no business to believe that the possessor of St. Patrick's staff was *ipso facto* Archbishop of Armagh. Logically, the orthodox French Romance writer should have cut off his right hand rather than dethrone St. Peter and the whole Apostolate; but he overturned the foundations of his Church gaily, without a scruple. There are tales in the Lives of the Welsh Saints about a Holy Bell, which refused to give any sound in the hands of the Holy Father; but uttered angelic notes when rung by St. Teilo or St. Iltyd—I write far from books. Here, in little, you have the whole anti-Roman claim, in spite of the fact that the Welsh Church had submitted, officially, by the beginning of the ninth century. One might speculate as to the probable continuance of a cryptic Celtic Church, in lonely hermitages, in little chapelries in wild, waste places, perhaps for centuries, perhaps into the eleventh century; but, this not improbable hypothesis apart, it seems to me that the persistence of a Celtic Church Legend is (almost) demonstrated. The references of the Chalice and the Saints' Bells in "The High History" are certainly not Norman-French inventions; what are they, then, if they are not the desiderated survival?

And now for the Templars. I am still unmoved on this point. I do not think that it is "a fact" that the "Crusading, Eastern Element" in the Graal Romances "stands in some connection, ill-defined and obscure it may be, yet certain, with the Temple body." I think it is an improbable hypothesis,

and that the only relation between the two things is that the
Templars were supposed to be conforming in real life to the
pattern of the Graal heroes—to the union of the saint and
knight—and that, in consequence of this conformity, the
Romance writers have, on occasion, put the Questers into
Templar costume, while Wolfram calls them Templesiens.
I have named the Templar Heresy (supposing it to have ever
existed) "distinctly anti-sacramental," because the only evidence which connects Templarism with the Holy Eucharist
is to the effect that one or two knights confessed that they
had secreted the Host and consumed an unconsecrated wafer.
The evidence is highly dubious, I suppose; but, granting its
truth, I should say that it is quite impossible that from any
doctrine indicated by this tale—whether it be taken to be a
doctrine of profanation, or a doctrine of mere contemptuous
negative—there should have sprung the Eucharistic ardours
and adorations of the Queste. The fruits of the interior
spiritual life assuredly never were borne by such wretched
thorns and thistles as these. And, if we suppose the Templars, or some of them, to have been partially infected by a
possibly surviving Gnosis in the East, then the hypothesis
is in no better condition. I am sorry, of course, to hurt my
friends the Occultists; but the cold truth is that a Gnostic
Redivivus would find himself most at home in the City
Temple of today. The resemblance between the fragment of
an Albigensian Liturgy of the thirteenth century and a
modern Dissenting service is really wonderful. Then, again,
Mr. Nutt seems to find some likeness between the "glorification of a priesthood constituted outside of and without
reference to" the official Church and the system of Templarism. Why? The Templars never claimed the *sacerdotium*. They were accused of doing so in one particular—of
exercising or claiming to exercise the power of absolution.
The truth was that the Master had the power of remitting
the punishment due to the breach of any articles of the Templar Rule; but even the most virulent foes of the Order never
charged the Knights with pretending to offer the Sacrifice

THE GLORIOUS MYSTERY

and to consecrate the elements. The "peculiar priesthood" of the Graal is, above all things, a Eucharistic priesthood that offers the sacrifice by the power of the Holy Spirit—Mr. Nutt will remember the beautiful comparison of Galahad's red armour with the Red Flame of Pentecost—and such a *sacerdotium* would proceed, oddly enough, from a body which certainly seems to have made the trampling under foot of the crucifix an initiatory ceremony. I do not say that this rite was evil in intention—probably it was not—but imagine Galahad performing it!   ARTHUR MACHEN.

THE GLORIOUS MYSTERY

THE GRAIL ROMANCES

A Reply to Arthur Machen

THERE are one or two definite points in Mr. Machen's last letter on which I should like to say a few words. The Introduction to the Grand St. Graal, as I pointed out twenty years ago, is certainly connected with the Brendan literature. On re-reading it now, after several years, I am inclined to say—is certainly *derived* from some Brendan romance. The same atmosphere, invention and exposition of incident are unmistakably those of Celtic hagiology in its romantic, fictional form. Note, too, the emphasis upon the doctrine of the Trinity; it is to remove the Hermit's doubts on this subject that the vision is vouchsafed and the quest imposed. This is quite *dans la gamme* of the Irish stories. It is by this reference to an Irish Brendan story that I would explain the date, 717 years after Christ, assigned to the vision. Most of the Irish romances of the *Imrama* type, whether in pre-Christian or Christian form, open with precise chronological indications; as a rule, it is true, involving purely Irish data. I think it quite probable that the date figured in the romance accepted by the writer of the Grand St. Graal. I don't quite understand what Mr. Machen means by saying that the knight who knew the hermit "recognised him as having been a participator in some secret assembly." The text merely says that the hermit is disquieted because "il (the knight) me connut a un saing ke jou avoie sour moi, et dist qu'il m'avoit autrefois veu, et dist en quel liu" (Hacher, II., p. 30). The incident, like the immediately preceding one, is told in an abrupt and elliptic fashion, clear evidence to my mind that the writer is abridging and adapting, not taking out of his own head.

Mr. Machen thinks I attach too much importance to origins. May I quote his own words: "Is there any assignable time-limit to the survival of anything?" Precisely. There really is not, and it is quite legitimate to trace back practice and rite and expression of fancy or emotion throughout their varying manifestations to their pristine source. Be it noted, too, that the word survival connotes two markedly different things; as a rule it indicates that the thing so described is a mere husk from out of which the quick element has disappeared—as, *e.g.*, the *Calenig* custom to which Mr. Machen refers. But it may also indicate a conception or practice out of joint with its surroundings, but nevertheless still informed by a vital spirit. The belief in the possibility of interchange between the mortal and the fairy world, which had so shocking an outcome at Clonmel only ten years ago, is much more than a survival in the sense ordinarily attached to the word. And it is precisely the rites and conceptions of the peasant religion, dismissed by Mr. Machen as "the Spring Cabbage doctrine," which do still not merely survive, but, in howsoever maimed a form, live. And they do so because they expressed a symbolised, a vital, a supreme preoccupation of mankind in a given stage of culture.

As regards the hererodoxy of the romances, the difficulty is intensified if, as Dr. Paul Hagan claims, the author of the lost French romance, adapted by Wolfram von Eschenbach, who was himself an ecclesiastic, died indeed Bishop of Durham; for the Parzival is in many respects the most essentially heterodox member of the whole cycle. This is a point which Mr. Waite should keep in view in his forthcoming work. Meanwhile, I would ask Mr. Machen to remember that whilst the emphasis in the *Quete* is undoubtedly upon the Eucharistic sacrificial aspect, it is quite otherwise in the Parzival—there the stress is upon a conception of militant, governing, but *not* ecclesiastic theocracy. And the Temple seems to me the only body which would have suggested such a conception.

ALFRED NUTT.

THE GLORIOUS MYSTERY

THE MATTER OF ROMANCE

SO MUCH has been written recently about the Arthurian Legend, that it would be wearisome to enter into a detailed discussion of the many interesting points raised by Professor Maynadier in the course of his study of the great romances of the Round Table.* It may be said, however, that for literary students—as distinct from specialists—who wish to gain a good general view of the rise and flourishing of the Legend the book will be most useful. The writer is evidently ignorant of the valuable assistance rendered by the Welsh Hagiology in estimating the various elements which went to the formation of the wonderful story of the Graal; he makes the mistake of quoting Professor Rhys's nonsense about "Sun Gods" with some appearance of respect; but with these deductions, the earlier pages of "The Arthur of the English Poets" gives, as we have said, an excellent account of the growth of the great romance cycle that has Arthur as its central figure. There is curious reading, too, in the latter portion of the book, which deals with the fate of the legend in the dark ages of the eighteenth century; and the chapter on Tennyson's treatment of Malory is interesting enough, though it is always melancholy to be reminded how a great poet missed a great opportunity. One sighs as one reads that mighty fragment, the "Morte d'Arthur," thinking of what an epic the Laureate Poet might have given us; one groans over some of the later Idylls, in which the Mystic King is rapidly being transmuted into a variant of John Halifax, Gentleman, in which Vivien appears as an adventuress from town, disturbing the repose of a country vicarage. The opportunity was lost, the poet was conformed to the world, and it is hardly surprising to find that Lord Ten-

---

* *The Arthur of the English Poets.* By Howard Maynadier.

nyson considered the Round Table as a symbol of "Liberal Institutions," which is as much as to say that the central flame of the Universe is in reality a symbol of "The Domestic" Gas Stove, hired, on liberal terms, from the Company. The pages, then, that treat of the Idylls are to be read in the way of warning; and so may increase the usefulness of an excellent book. One may pass over the phrases which demonstrate the selfish, unpractical nature of Galahad's character, his failure to rise to the heights of "Modern Christianity":

> Nor can Galahad (says Prof. Maynadier) . . . be called other than fanatical. As he rides round the world singing, "I yearn to breathe the airs of heaven that often meet me here," he is either not normal and healthy or not honest. . . . Galahad shows himself after all only a knightly brother of the revivalists who manifest their religion nowadays with so much noisy emotion and so little sanity.

This is painful and foolish enough, but it is clear that Professor Maynadier has not heard the command: "Let the dead bury their dead; rise and follow Me." It is idle to attempt to steer a magic bark in faery seas by the assistance of the quadrant, a chronometer adjusted to the meridian of Greenwich, and the mariner's compass.

One point raised by Professor Maynadier deserves some discussion. It is apart from the special matter of the Arthurian Legend, and concerns the whole question, so often debated, of the Celtic Spirit or Celtic Genius. Speaking of the tale of "Kilhwch and Olwen," the author remarks:

> It is not a tale to impress human imagination for centuries, like the legends of Lancelot, Perceval, and Tristram and Iseult, for it is after all best characterised by that adjective which Matthew Arnold applies to Celtic Art in general, "ineffectual." Celtic Art, he says, so long as it remained purely Celtic, has never profoundly impressed the world like Greek or Roman Art, or the best German, French, English, Spanish, and Italian Art. Now, it was because French Art was able to join reason and significance to the fantastic poetry of such Celtic tales as *Kilhwch and Olwen,* to give the old charming but "ineffectual" stories substantial meaning, that they have become effectual and permanent contributions to the literature of the world.

And here lies a matter of perennial interest to all lovers of literature. It is, perhaps, idle to insist on the term Celtic; for, as Mr. Yeats has confessed, the spirit that we often call Celtic is, in reality, the spirit that is common to many if not all primitive peoples. It would be difficult to express its qualities in a phrase; it is the spirit of enchantment, of ecstasy, of wonder, of adoration; it is the spirit which protests for ever against all modern materialistic theories; it is the eternal witness, as some of us think, to the existence of that Avalon from which we have been driven, for which we long during the days of our banishment, *exules filii Hevoe.* The existence of the Brook by the way may be deduced from the thirst of the wayfarer; and so Paradise may be inferred by our longing for it. It is this longing, and the expression of this longing, which distinguish, in the last resort, Art from Artifice; without it a book, or a picture, or a statue is nothing but a more or less ingenious contrivance, with the excellence, perhaps, of a beehive or an ant hill, but no true work of art.

And here is the tragedy to which Matthew Arnold made allusion in the adjective "ineffectual." Take the "Morte d'Arthur" of Malory even; there the material which came from Celtdom—or, let us say, from a primitive race—had been worked over by many hands, both French and English, for more than two hundred years. And yet: compare Malory's book with the average "clever" modern novel; not with the dregs and drivel of the publishers' stock, which is, surely, the most offensively pretentious stuff that ever found expression in writing or print or articulate speech, but with the well-made, well-dressed, decently written story of these "educated" days. Well, of course, the modern book is nought, and worse than nought when compared with Malory; it is as the ingenuities of an amiable bee, or of an observant butterfly beside the "Morte"; and yet, how vastly the latter is excelled, in mere artifice, by the former. The modern writer "jines his flats," he has a story to tell, and he tells it in more or less logical order; the old romancer, not content with the wanderings of his heroes, must wander too; breaking off, turning from the track, indulging in episodes without end, returning to the high road of his story, only to stroll away from it again in the course of a few chapters. In a word: the spirit is undoubtedly present in the romance, but the body which the writer has provided is often deplorably ill-jointed and shapen in strange sort, and sometimes in no sort at all. And, nevertheless, we know that the old romance is a part of the lost paradise; while the new novel is just very entertaining reading. One may call this a tragedy of litera-ture, that the perfect spirit—the one element which makes literature, which transmutes the lead of human things into the pure gold of art—has so often been manifested in very dim and imperfect vessels; while well-chased flagons hold but poor, thin liquor, small wines of a second growth, agree-able enough with one's dinner, but not apt to serve in the celebration of the Greater Dionysian Mysteries. Of course, there may be people who think the faults of the old tales are beauties, just as there may be persons who think that the bad drawing of early stained-glass and illuminated manu-scripts is an added charm; but these are not tenable opinions. A glowing and glorious saint in his dyed robes is the less, not the more beautiful by the obvious dislocation of his neck; and so the wonderful old tale loses, not gains, by its awkward and rambling construction.

Here, then, is a great task for the writer who has the requisite vision, who is willing to be brave in his recounting of it. Let him think of this as his life's work, to tell the great dream truthfully, and yet to tell it coherently. The vision, of course, is above all things necessary; the chosen one must above all see the real things, he must be able to gaze on Paradise; and even if the especial gift have been vouchsafed him, he will have much ado to keep his eyes clear, to dispel, to dispel continually, the mists that rise from the rotten fens and dunghills of modern civilisation. He must purge his mind of cant; especially and principally of that noxious form of cant that caused Professor Maynadier to pen these dolorous pages concerning the selfish, fanatical, and unhealthy nature of Sir Galahad, which made poor Tennyson see in the marvellous imagery of the Round Table simply a pretty way of putting one's respect for the House of Commons, the County Council, and the School Board. The man who is to clothe the shining spirit with the perfect body must forget all this rubbish, he must forget that it exists, or the vision will be taken from him, as it was taken from the eyes of Tennyson; and Avalon, the isle beyond the glassy floods, will, perhaps, turn into a picture of modern society, or (worse still!) of "modern Christianity." Nay; he who is to write our great romance must himself be a knight-errant; he, too, must turn his back on the city, on the places where people sit by the cosy fires of social and convenient morality, and do business, and do each other, and deduce obvious moral lessons from everything, and pass Acts of Parliament, and make Religion a sort of shabby Moyen de Parvenir; he must fare forth on the wild ways by the dark wood, by the bare mountain heights, through fires and storms, over the billows of the great deep. In other words, he must be firmly and utterly convinced that man is here, not that he may be good-natured and kindly (so far as kindness and good-nature are consistent with business principles), but that he may be worthy of the Vision of the Most Blessed Cup of the Sangraal.

Now, this is no easy task. Our corruption is so profound that we have well-nigh lost the measure of all things; we have quite lost the measure of the highest things. Professor Maynadier's view of Galahad as a selfish and fanatical revivalist is probably quite a representative opinion in these sorry and besotted days; or rather, let us say, it is the representative opinion of the natural, bestial man of all ages. Since man was man the Primæval Pig has dwelt in him, grunting out the Pig Gospel: that the end of all things is Wash, that the Pig whose trough is full is a good, pious, religious and perfect Pig, and that, since one must work for Wash, the Pig who is always "doing business" is highly to

THE GLORIOUS MYSTERY

be revered. These dogmas, as we have said, are a portion of the early curse, of the doom that was laid on man when he lapsed from Paradise, when, according to William Law, the fluid and glorious universe became a grim and solid and brutal mass and fell upon "Adam," so that he was crushed beneath its weight. In every age the Bestial Evangel has been preached; Labour, which in the great Mythos of the Garden is denounced as a curse and a punishment, is proclaimed as a blessing, a pious exercise, a reward, in itself a heaven; and though the Christ denounced this vile heresy in no uncertain terms, though He stigmatised the saving of money and business forethought as wicked and senseless follies, though He placed before men the example of the lilies, though St. Paul declares that all actions of practical benevolence even are but dust and ashes if the secret fire, the divine ardours of Love are not present; still, in the Bright Ages there were doubtless many people who thought that the men called monks, who did nothing but pray and worship God, were useless idlers, that building cathedrals was a dreadful waste of money, and that the price of the incense at the Sacrifice would have been much better expended on "the poor"—that is, on themselves, on the hard-headed, practical men who usually keep the bag. If this were so—and it doubtless was so—in the Golden Ages of true faith and true reason and true art, what is now the depth to which we have fallen? Well, it may be said that we have almost reached the limit of utter confusion, of profound denial of all that is true, of firm asseveration of all that is false. The other day a bishop of the Catholic Church had the great opportunity of addressing certain of his flock, of confirming them, one might conjecture, in some dogma of the Faith, of unveiling to them some secret treasure of the Great Mysteries, of instructing them in some of the transcendent morals of the Christian religion. One would have conjectured all awry; for Dr. Diggle talked about the Lusitania's "record," and hoped that the proud and swelling, though legitimate, feelings aroused by this great achievement would move the people of Liverpool to a more liberal support of the Seamen's Orphanage! And it would not be true to say that this virulent nonsense is peculiar to Anglicanism or Protestantism; it is not many months since Father Bernard Vaughan allowed himself to speculate as to the probable conduct of St. Paul if he had edited a daily paper, and as to the likelihood of his appointing St. Timothy as assistant-editor.

Well, it is of all this *cochonnerie* that the man who would write great romance must clear his mind; he must silence, and silence effectually, the gruntings and squealings of the foul creature who dwells within him; he must pay no heed to the voice of the body of death to which he is chained in the valley of this pilgrimage. Utterly must he dismiss from his soul the thought that "success" means anything, that a man who has made a great deal of money or earned a great deal of praise, is anything but a *prima facie* suspect; for the dogma of success is one of the chiefest articles in the great Creed of the Stye. It is to those who are able to cleanse themselves of these defilements that the Vision may be vouchsafed, in them the old dream of the Celts may be renewed, and with clearer eyes for the struggle that has been endured they may see the wonder of the world and the wonder of man—the "things that really are" of Plato.

"Darkness and the shadow of death" is a very familiar phrase to many people; and one wonders to how many of these people the slightest gleam of the true meaning of these words has been given. As a matter of fact, one conjectures that ninety-nine out of a hundred, asked to explain the phrase, would reply that a thief, a pickpocket, an adulterer, a murderer would be described as being in this condition. The reply would, very likely, be true—in a sense; in the sense in which scarlet fever might be defined as an appearance of spots, or a great statue as a block of limestone, or a great picture as a collection of coloured earths, combined with oil, and applied to wood or canvas. But, essentially, such a reply would be imbecile; it is highly probable that the people who have never broken a single commandment are in a deeper darkness, in a more profound shadow of mortality than the criminals whom they scorn, or hate, or pity. The shadow of death and darkness, in reality, describes well enough the utter error and confusion of all men, "good" and "bad" alike, their ignorance as to what they are, and why they are, and what their end should be. The baser sort reply that they are here to make money, the better sort that they are here to do good, or even to be good; who answers that he is here to enjoy happiness, that he may enjoy a more perfect happiness in the life of the world to come? The people whom "the good" and "the respectable" call wastrels, Bohemians, vagabonds, have a sort of dim vision of this truth; they realise that happiness is man's true end; their mistake is in a confusion as to the means. Still, with all their error, they are infinitely nearer to the truth than the Scribes and the Pharisees, than the "practical men," the apostles of "plain common-sense," the vermin who infest church and chapel and the very altar itself. And it was no doubt because of this clearer vision that the Christ loved those whom the world called disreputable, while He hated all the representatives of respectability.

The hero of the Great Romance must, therefore, set his face continually to Syon; his ardours must consume him ever; through the wild and waste lands he must still wander, seeking Corbenic and the Blessed Vision of the Sangraal. "Liberal institutions," "modern Christianity," "practical philanthropy"—all the Nine Hundred and Ninety-Nine Articles of the Great Pig Philosophy have forever vanished from his eyes. His are the delights that are almost unendurable, the wonders that are almost incredible—that are, indeed, quite incredible to the world; his the eternal joys that the deadly flesh cannot comprehend; his the secret that renews the earth, restoring Paradise, rolling the heavy stone of the material universe from the grave whence he arises.

Of such matters will the High History treat—that High Romance which is yet to be written.
Nov. 30, 1907.

THE GLORIOUS MYSTERY

"CONSOLATUS" AND "CHURCH-MEMBER"

A YEAR or two ago, when I was beginning to investigate
the literature of the Holy Graal, a friend suggested
that the legend might have connections with what he called
"the mystic sects of southern France." I was not much
impressed with the likelihood of this hypothesis, chiefly
because I do not believe in the existence of "mystic sects"—
the true mystic is never a sectarian—and, secondly, because
I was already convinced that the main origins, the parent
sources of the Graal literature, were Celtic. Still, though
prejudices are indispensable things, one must not allow one's
self to be too bitterly swayed by them, and I sought among
the Albigenses for a while, finding, of course, some odd coincidences that made me hesitate for a moment—not for more
than a moment. Mont Segur, in the Pyrenees, the last
retreat of these Manichees, where the noble lady, Esclair-
monde, perished in the flames with a great number of "the
Consoled," suggested Mont Salvatch, and the date was fairly
coincident with the publication of the legend; there were
one or two other details which, as I say, made one think that
there might be "something" to be said for the hypothesis.
There was, for example, the prominence of the Fish Symbol
in a certain Albigensian Liturgy of the thirteenth century;
one could not help thinking of the very strange Fish symbolism in the Graal stories.

But all these things counted for nothing when one
began to enquire into the Albigensian *ethos* and the Albigensian doctrine. Whatever the Graal may be it is the
expression of a High Sacramentalism, one might say, of a
hyper-Sacramentalism. While the doctors of the Western
Church were defining the dogma of transubstantiation,
expressing (perhaps too scientifically) the logical side of a
great mystery, the imaginative spirit was opening its eyes to

the hidden glories, the transfiguration of all things that were latent in the central rite of Christendom. The wonder of the Mass is the very heart of the legend of the Graal; Galahad, who achieves the Graal, is the type of the perfect Christian.

And then the vanity of seeking for the origins of all this amongst the Albigenses became apparent; one might as well seek for the source of the present Holy Father's decrees in the secret councils of the City Temple. The one prominent characteristic of Albigensianism was its utter contempt for all sacraments, its constant denial of Baptism and Eucharist. By a different way it led to the same end as Pelagianism; to the latter the Eucharist was a needless superfluity, to the former it was an abomination. Clearly, then, the Great Visions of the Graal could never have proceeded from a sect which denied all sacramental efficacy. Albigensianism was as vain a field for the quest as Templarism (*pace* Mr. Alfred Nutt).

But one wonders whether the heresy of Southern France were not really the seed-plot of a very different scheme of thought. Many of us can remember the tortuous and dreary novels which appeared long ago in certain tortuous and dreary magazines—the *Quiet Sunday,* the *Sabbath Companion,* and so forth. Very often these novels were concerned with the persecution of the Waldenses and Albigeois; and one still recalls with relish the way in which all virtue was placed in the heretic heart and all vice in the breast of the evil and persecuting papist. The theory was that the Albigenses were witnesses to Protestantism before Protestantism had come into being; the Light of the Gospel was supposed by the writers to have been handed on from the Apostles to these evangelical men, and from them to Luther and Calvin. Children liked it, and older people laughed and called it nonsense. But the question is, was it quite such nonsense as we supposed? I hope I shall not be misunderstood; not for a moment do I imagine that the Albigenses were the veritable depositaries of Christianity in an age of manifest Popery and veiled Paganism. I am perfectly aware, as any honest person who has read the New Testament must be aware, that Christianity was from the very beginning a highly ceremonial and ritual religion, sacramental in its very heart and core; but the novelist of the *Sabbath Companion* was right, I think, for all that in believing that Albigensianism was the real ancestor of Protestantism. Not by historical pedigree and succession perhaps; there is no reason to suppose that Luther or Calvin deliberately borrowed from the older error: rather a blasphemy which was manifested in the early ages of Christianity as Manicheeism, then as Paulicianism, then as Albigensianism, finally appeared, *per saltum,* as Protestantism. In other words, the crowds which assemble to listen to "Dr." Clifford and Mr. Campbell are in reality the legitimate successors of the early Gnostics. They are not by any means so entertaining as their spiritual forefathers; the massive jewellery worn by the City Temple ladies, though doubtless valuable commercially, will never be as interesting as the Gnostic gems, and the jargon they employ is not so picturesque as that of the *Pistis Sophia.* But the doctrine of the one is strikingly similar to the doctrine of the other, and in ways apart from doctrine there are striking resemblances.

Of course, the leading idea of the Manicheean Gnosis is that the visible universe is devil-made, and from this judgment all sorts of consequences follow, legitimately enough. On the one hand such crazes as teetotalism and vegetarianism, the opposition to all that is cheerful, the deep hatred of gaiety in all its forms, the disapproval, veiled, unveiled, or partly veiled, of all the sensible works of God. On the other hand, there is the dislike of ceremonial worship, of ritual of all sorts, of decency itself, both in the religious and in the social life. It is amusing to trace the various manifestations of this feeling; the Manichee apologised even when he ate a wheaten cake. "*I,*" he would say, "did not cut you down with the sickle; *I* did not send you to the mill to be ground by the cruel millstones; *I* did not knead you into dough, nor cause you to be roasted in the heat of the fierce oven." This said, our Manichee made his dinner, satisfied that he, at all events, was not guilty of massacring the grains of wheat. In the same way the modern Puritan accepts the good things of life with apologetic grumble which he calls "grace," conscious in a dim way that he has no real right to enjoy his roast beef, that muffins are fundamentally sinful. Always to this tribe the exhilaration produced by good wine has been hateful and abhorred; to the Manichee wine was formally forbidden; to the modern Puritan teetotalism becomes more and more a prime article of faith, so that persons who call themselves by the name Christian are not ashamed to "communicate" in "non-alcoholic wine." The Psalmist speaks of wine that maketh glad the heart of man as one of the high blessings from heaven; the Christ performed the miracle of Cana in Galilee, and instituted the Sacrament of the Altar, promising the gift of the Eternal Vine in the world to come—the Manichees of old and the Protestants of to-day are better instructed. Again, in the antique sect and the modern there is the diseased abhorrence of what one calls, clumsily enough, the "sexual side of life." To the "Consoled" marriage and giving in marriage were utterly prohibited, regarded as essentially irreligious; the modern Puritan (certain especially uncleanly sects excepted) would not say as much in distinct words. There is certainly the instance of the Roman Catholic young lady—it is only the very simple who think that Roman Catholicism has escaped the Protestant virus—who thought Holy Matrimony "a very wicked sacrament"; but our Puritans to-day are content to hold the Manichee faith in their hearts without uttering it with their lips. They have not hit upon the happy idea of dividing the sect into the "Hearers" and the "Consoled"; the former of whom could do whatever they pleased, while the latter were forced to apologise to cottage loaves and cabbages before taking the liberty of devouring them. Yet, on second thoughts, some such division does exist, since the "church member" of whom we have heard in our American novels is not very different from the "consolatus" of the twelfth century. I believe a "church member" is not allowed to "go to circus."

THE GLORIOUS MYSTERY

Of course, it would be otiose to insist on the popular Protestant attitude towards sexual morality. Though he marries, the average Protestant is curiously ashamed of the action; he indulges in all kinds of odd and elaborate pretences and hypocrisies in order to veil from his own and from other people's eyes the real meaning of the Sacrament he blasphemes; he is secretly horrified at the imagery of the Song of Solomon; he only succeeds in accepting the Apocalyptic symbol of the Church as "the Bride" by forgetting, or pretending to forget, what the word "Bride" really implies. A voice crying in the wilderness, the voice of Coventry Patmore, said long ago how much more deadly it was to call good evil than to call evil good; this was the great sin of the Manichees, as it is now the great sin of our Protestants, who, be it said again, live in Canterbury and Rome as well as in Geneva and in Little Bethel. It was an English ecclesiastic who had the impudence to declare that "erotic" imagery in religion does not appeal to the Englishman, implying, of course, that the Englishman's opinion mattered. He might have said, just as wisely and as fitly, that swine do not much care for pearls. No; to the old Manichee and the new both the Marriage Feast and the Vessels of Wine are unclean things; and there is a sect apart which gives no obedience to the command, kill and eat.

It is, of course, not surprising to find a standard of "morality" which is, nominally, quite savage in its severity, accompanied in practice by morals of the very worst kind. The "morals" of Provence during the Albigensian *regime* were famous or infamous, and there is much the same tale to be told of the Protestant countries now. The illegitimacy statistics of Scotland have long been notorious; they form a pleasing contrast to the very different tale told by Popish Ireland. Gallant little Wales boasts constantly, perhaps too constantly, of its hatred of the Catholic Faith, of its fervent attachment to Calvinistic Methodism; it proclaimed its piety to the world by demanding and obtaining a special Sunday Closing Act. And it has been celebrating the passing of the

Act by getting drunk ever since! Of the sixteen counties with the most drunkenness in 1904, no fewer than eight were Welsh. Then, again, consider the United States of America, famous equally for the most rigid protestations of purity, for the most violent campaigns against everything that is beautiful—and also for the most horrible, revolting, systematised, organised vice that the world has ever seen. One dare not speak of the legs of the piano—and one draws revenue from the Hotel Nymphia!

There are many other points of resemblance between the old heresy and the new. The Albigensian "Liturgy," already mentioned, brings to one's nostrils in the most curious fashion the odour of the meeting house. The "Liturgy" is, frankly, "jaw," it cites texts in the approved Protestant style *ad nauseam;* it anticipates in its oily piety all the horrors of the conventicle. It is so destitute of beauty, of decency (in the true sense of the word) that one realises, more strongly than ever, that all the splendours of the Middle Ages were the gifts of the Church, flowers of the secret and hidden virtues which are to be found alone in the True Fold. One can divine from this "Liturgy" that if the Albigensians had prevailed there would have been no Salisbury Cathedral; barbarism would have made an earlier entry on the scene. At the present day Protestantism (of the "Literal" sort, I imagine) has its chief strongholds in Southern France, and accordingly one is not surprised by the hideous appearance of meeting-houses in those wonderful old cities—duplicates of the barbarous monstrosities with which we are so sadly familiar in our dim Northern streets.

It has been a certain satisfaction to me to trace the resemblances between the error of to-day and the error of the twelfth and thirteenth centuries. One sees, I think, that the "Reformation" was not altogether a new thing; it was but the repetition of an old cry, the resurgence of an old enemy that had laid the vineyards waste in very early times. *Dec. 21, 1907.*

THE GLORIOUS MYSTERY

A SECRET LANGUAGE

I SUPPOSE that there are certain scraps of wisdom, practical and theoretical, that very few of us have escaped.

There is the case of the mustard, for example. I was comparing notes on this matter with two of my friends the other day, and I found as I had expected to find that all three of us had been instructed in the fabled utterance of Mr. Colman: "Mr. Colman said that he hadn't made his fortune by the mustard which people put on their beef, but by the mustard which they left on their plates."

This instance, it is seen, is purely moral and practical in its nature; it cautions one against the wasteful use of an agreeable condiment. But there are two other anecdotes which all the young have received, I think, in their day, that are more to our purpose. One tells how Stephenson watched the kettle boil, the lid thereof vehemently rising and falling, and so was invented the steam-engine. The other shows the illustrious Newton, idling or meditating in the orchard. An apple drops to the ground; and the theory of gravitation is the result.

Few, I say, can have escaped these instructive stories; but I hardly think that the true moral has generally been drawn from them. So far as I am aware, they are usually employed to show that a mere trivial accident issues in a great discovery. Indeed, I am half inclined to believe that this moral belongs to the chapter called "The Malice of the Undistinguished." The Undistinguished do not compose music; so they make up a tale to the effect that Handel, walking through Edgeware, heard the church bells ringing and the blacksmith's hammer clinking; and thus wrote "The Harmonious Blacksmith." I regret to say that the actual process was still simpler; for Handel "cribbed" the tune in question from an old French composer. But I have always believed that the Undistinguished would fain say: "If I had been walking that day in Edgeware and had heard those bells and that hammer; then I should have written 'The Harmonious Blacksmith.'" And so, I fancy, the Undistinguished would insinuate that they would have thought out gravitation and invented the steam-engine easily enough, if they had been in that orchard and that kitchen. The Undistinguished hate genius, for it is a mystery, and mystery is anathema to them.

But this apart, I do not think that the real moral has been drawn from the instances of the apple and the kettle. The real moral is *not* that great things spring from trivial incidents. It is rather this: that great things can be and are before the eyes of men for countless ages, and yet are not perceived. For how many aeons had fruit fallen to the ground before the eyes of men? That is a question for the geologists and palæontologists; it may be answered briefly: so long as there have been men on the earth. I do not know the judged antiquity of hot water. I presume it must be nearly coeval with the age of fire; at any rate the steam must have lifted the lid of the pot for many rolling centuries before the day of Stephenson. Homer's heroes saw this marvel by the shores of the wine-dark sea; and yet they saw it not. They did not discern it.

Now, of course, it may be objected that the true state of the case is this: that both Newton and Stephenson had the prepared mind, the soil made ready for the seed; in one case the scientific mind, in the other the mechanical mind; and that in the case of the engine-inventor there had been for fifty or sixty years a great progress in mechanical work, which had made the way ready for him. And it might be alleged that the minds of the Homeric heroes—let us say—were so wholly alien and remote from physical theories of the universe and mechanical improvements that the phenomenon in question could not possibly make any impression on them. There is something in this. I confess that if I pass along the London streets and see in a bookseller's window a pamphlet with the title "The Lentil, the Secret of Everlasting Life," I go on without considering the matter, knowing that it is no sort of concern of mine. So, it may be urged, science and mechanics had to progress and be extended for many years before the apple and the kettle could become in any way significant.

This is very well; but how about the case of Logic? Here is a matter which has nothing to do with any applied science, with any long course of subsidiary inventions. It exists without any reference to the exterior state of man, to war or peace, riches or poverty, learning or ignorance. The matter of logic is of the matter of man himself: the man without it is no longer a man. It is inherent in every use of the word "because"; there cannot fail to be a syllogism in every action we perform. It is not, indeed, true to say that the reasoning process is the exclusive prerogative of man, for I believe it is pretty clear that many of the brutes reason; but it is true that a man who does not reason is inconceivable. It is not merely that without the reasoning process he could not write the "Ode on a Grecian Urn"; without it he could never catch his train to the city; without it the palæolithic man could never have overcome the mastodon.

Here, then, is a faculty which is absolutely necessary to man, infinitely more necessary to him than his arms or his legs: and yet it was not till the days of Aristotle that this faculty was, as it were, perceived, analysed, displayed as an intelligible thing, with its certain and fixed laws. Yet, centuries before the days of Aristotle, there had been mighty, prosperous, and peaceful civilizations. I remember reading that the Italian explorers finding the plumbing and the bathrooms of the Cretan—which flourished about 2500 B. C.—threw up their hands and said, "Absolutely English!" And I suppose perfect plumbing is an undeniable proof of a high civilization. Then there was Babylon; then there was Egypt; there were nations, that is, which had their leisured, thoughtful, philosophic classes: and yet this process of reasoning which they used every day and every hour of their lives was hidden from them. It was seen; and yet it was not seen. You see, we can no longer say as we said of the kettle and the apple: "But people weren't so curious about these things; their minds didn't run that way." In a certain sense, anybody's mind must run in the way of logic, if it is to run at all; and specifically, the leisured and cultured class that exists in every civilization cannot help turning its thoughts toward the reasoning process. Yet, I repeat, the analysis of ratiocination was not performed till the late age of Aristotle.

Now for an instance which I think is even more curious. Washington Irving, the American writer, was a man of very wide literature, of a very delicate and delightful perceptiveness; he was a man, I would say, alert in the discovery of beautiful things, and quaint things. He almost succeeded in enchanting the State of New York with his legend of it; and this seems to me an amazing achievement. Above all he was a lover of the old, gracious, kindly life of England and all its dear, merry observances; never was a man fonder of an ancient thing, just because it was ancient. Yet, this Washington Irving, writing in the twenties of the last century, speaks with a kindly contempt of the Gothic, of Westminster Abbey, as "barbarous ornament." He likes it, certainly, but merely because it is old; in his heart he despises himself for liking it; he knows that it is all savagery, that he has no business to like it.

Now this seems to me a most extraordinary case. Here is a man of very much more than average artistic sympathy absolutely blind to the wonder and beauty and splendour of Gothic. It is before him, great and visible; but he can't see it, and doesn't see it. A cloud, one would say, comes down and is heavy before his eyes so that all alike is hidden; both the spiritual aspiration, the divine poetry, of the whole building, and the marvel of the detailed ornament, which is as the marvel of the earth breaking into leaf and flower and greenness, in the season of spring. Washington Irving sees Westminster Abbey; but he sees it not.

And, of course, it had been so for two centuries or more.

THE GLORIOUS MYSTERY

From 1620 to 1820, one may say, nobody had seen Gothic at all. It is interesting to look at Eighteenth century prints of cathedrals; for it is at once quite evident that the artists did not really see what they drew. If you look at these engravings from a little distance, you might almost say that the artist had been gazing not at Peterboro or Lincoln Cathedral, but at a clever model made by a boy with wooden bricks and bits of wire. Draw closer and examine the detail, and it is all almost incredibly false; the tracery, the cusps, the mouldings are not a bit like the objects that were before the artist's eyes; everything is parodied, degraded, cheapened. It is difficult to believe that the man who drew the picture had really seen the cathedral at all; that he was not working from rough jottings supplied by a Chinaman or a Choctaw. But it is interesting to note that these bald cusps, these cheap-looking pillars, these cast iron piers and arches (in the View of the Interior) have very much the effect that is produced by many of the pieces of the Gothic revival. There is actually a church in Derby of which the window tracery is in cast iron: the effect is very similar to the effect of the eighteenth century print. And so here you have the artist, the man of the trained eye, whose business it is to see and represent, utterly unable to see what was before him. His case is more remarkable than that of the mere lay dreamer, such as Smollett, who speaks with actual horror of York Minster as a barbarous and altogether ghastly structure that should speedily be supplanted by a "neat Grecian room." Yet Smollett was an acute man, and a travelled man. But he saw York Minster; and it affected him as a coal cellar might affect us.

To take yet another instance. Dr. Johnson in the first place was an entirely honest man. He was utterly incapable of professing admiration if he did not sincerely feel admiration. He would never have praised that which he did not approve, merely because it was fashionable to praise. His great maxim was "clear your mind of cant:" think honestly, without regard to fashions or conventions of any kind. One is quite certain, then, that his literary judgments were absolutely honest judgments. And, again, he was a man of very wide reading. He loved his age, but he was very well read in the literature of all ages; he was well furnished, that is, with examples and standards of comparison. Yet Johnson firmly held that Pope's work was not merely poetry; it was the touchstone of poetry—"If Pope did not write poetry, what is poetry?" And he was not able to disguise his opinion that if Milton's Lycidas was not rubbish, it was something perilously near it.

Now we may almost say of Lycidas that which Johnson said of Pope's work: it is almost the touchstone of poetry. And Pope, with all his brilliance, his polish, and his wit, scarcely wrote poetry at all. So here is another instance of the honest and skilled and trained eye seeing and not seeing. Nay, though Lycidas is written with affectionate remembrance of the classic models in literature which Johnson loved, yet he could not see its shining beauty; he found it drivel or almost drivel.

And it will not do by any means to say that the late seventeenth century and the whole of the eighteenth century were "inartistic." They were nothing of the kind. St. Paul's Cathedral is not Gothic, but it is a mighty architectural masterpiece of its sort, both in its main design and in its detail. How great it is you may judge by comparing it with a modern attempt in the same order of architecture; that miserable joss-house in the Brompton Road called the Oratory. And if there be a pure art, it is music; and the late seventeenth century and the eighteenth century produced such masters as Purcell, Handel, Mozart, Pergolesi, and the arch-master of all musicians, John Sebastian Bach. And you had deep theology in Butler, and in Law, the followers of Bohme; and on the whole, one may say, you had what should have been the best jury in the world, an assemblage of men of learning, acuteness, wide reading, and much leisure who wrote and appreciated without either the desire or the necessity of pleasing the populace. Indeed, so far as they were concerned, there was no populace; the well-informed wrote for the well-informed.

Yet they could not see the beauty of Gothic—though Horace Walpole and a few others pretended that they saw it—they could not see the beauty of Lycidas. To these men an illuminated Book of Hours of the thirteenth century, which is one of the principal beauties of man's spirit and hands, would seem a mere grotesque. It would appeal to them as an oddity, much as some queer idol from the South Seas appeals to us, an affair of ugly, elaborate incongruity.

And now for the last instance of all, and the strangest, of this blindness of man to things that are evidently before his eyes. Whatever we see or do not see, we can not help seeing the visible world that is before our eyes, from the star above to the flower at our feet. And yet we may say that it was not till 1796 or thereabouts that men so much as approximated to the significance of the great sacrament of the world. It is true that there had been hints written in Hebrew and Greek and Latin, but they were but hints; it was left to the age of Coleridge and Wordsworth to discern that in the spectacle of external nature there is something much more than mere pleasantness or sensuous beauty— Horace found both these elements in his *"fons Bandusiae splendidior vitro"*—that in fact, there is a revelation of things hidden in things which are open to all. It is clear then, that in a sense Coleridge and his fellows discovered the significance of the invisible world; there was given to them a revelation of that which had been hidden from the beginning.

So it will seem pretty clear, I think, considering all the instances which I have quoted in physical science, in mental science, in architecture, in literature, in the contemplation of trees and clouds and streams and flowers, that things which are most clear may yet be most closely hidden, and hidden for long ages, and hidden not only from the gross and sensual man, but from the fine and cultured man. And that being evident, does not the consequence follow that we, who have certainly not attained to perfection of any kind, may be, nay, almost certainly are, as blind as those who have gone before us; that we, too, gaze at great wonders, both of the body and the spirit, without discerning the marvels that are all around us? And again, it would appear that we may be groping after the perception of things which we apprehend in a dim and broken and imperfect manner. I have alluded to Walpole and his sham Gothic, and I suppose that Walpole was beset by a sort of vague idea that there was something in this architecture of a past age which was somehow or other curious and admirable. So Walpole tried to attain to it; and it is quite clear from his imitations that he was far indeed from the truth of the matter.

Now one would not for a moment class the school of Coleridge in its appreciation of nature with the school of Walpole in its appreciation of the Gothic. But may it not be that Coleridge and his fellows were but the forerunners of a new doctrine which was not fully revealed to them? It was the misfortune, I think, of Coleridge that after his first rush and flood of inspiration he went after the strange metaphysical gods of Germany, clouding his soul with a more deadly drug than the opium which he applied to his body. He thought that he was drinking a strong spiritual wine; he was in reality swallowing the winds of the North Sea, which are but sour emptiness. The light within him became dim; he talked of his "system" in place of seeing visions. He forgot that he had already found truth; he thought he was going to find it by some wretched abracadabra charm of "object" and "subject," by some mumbo-jumbo incantation of the distinction between the reason and the understanding. I would not say at all that he despised his poetry; but he thought himself embarked in a far higher quest of something that he called the Truth; whereas the fact is that his poetry at its finest was the truth and the vital truth.

Let me say here: that in the Catholic Faith, the highest and final and uttermost mystery is not contained in the Symbol of St. Athanasius, but in the simplest rite in the world, in the matter of natural, familiar, physical things which all men know and taste and see, that is, in bread and in wine. That is the manner in which the Christian religion protests against all the horrible heresies which under various disguises have taught that the world and all that therein is, are the work, not of God but of the Devil; thus it signifies to us that the way to the spiritual things is by the gate of the sensible things. This is the secret language, open to all men but disregarded by all, or almost all. This is the witness against those who would maintain that lectures and "jawings" in general, and moralizings and philosophies, are higher matters than the scent and colour of a rose, rightly apprehended, than the flame of torches, than the odour of incense, than golden vestments, than High Mass: that is, than Bread and Wine.

Now I have said that all manner of things may be under the eyes of men through long ages, and yet be unperceived, undiscerned by them. This is true, and yet these things are none the less there. The stone-age man, hunting for his dinner and avoiding monstrous beasts, was arguing in Barbara and Celarent all the while, though he knew it not. And be sure, that he who tried to argue in Barbara and Celarent soon ceased to argue at all, for he died of hunger or was crushed by dinosaurs. And so, in spite of eighteenth century blindness, the splendour of Lincoln and Durham were not in any way veiled. They shone in glory, though dim eyes could only see barbarous confusion. And so this secret language of the visible universe, though it may not have been openly spoken, was everywhere whispered. It is the sure mark of a fool or an ignoramus or both to declare— for instance—that the Song of Solomon is just a beautiful Oriental love-song and nothing more. I believe that the Oriental scholar who is nothing more than an Oriental scholar can smash this falsity; he will be able to prove that the symbolism of the Song of Songs is in an age-old language of the East, which has persisted to this day; that the sacred books of the Sikhs speak in this tongue, that the Babis of

Persia are familiar with it. But, apart from all scholarship, those who have eyes and ears, the common senses of humanity, can perceive not only that the apples and wine and love and banqueting of the "Song" refer to divine and eternal mysteries; the Christian Church has always seen that, the Jewish Church always knew that the thirst of the heart for the waterbrooks really showed the longing of the soul for God. That is one side of the question, and an important side: but there is another. And that is, the correlative truth that all these things—apples, waterbrooks, wine, feasting, human love, owe all their significance, all their value, all their light, all their beauty to the fact that they are both images and sacraments of eternal joys and wonders and delights; to the fact that they are words, as it were, in the secret language of God; that they are communications, in varying degrees, of the divine mysteries. An old prayer says: "Let us so pass through things temporal, that we lose not the things eternal." Our blessed but idiotic reformers, in translating this prayer, inserted the word *finally*: "Let us so pass through things temporal, that we *finally* lose not the things eternal." This would mean: "Do let us be careful not to eat too many apples or drink too much wine or look at sunsets too long (when we might be writing business letters) or we shan't go to heaven." In fact, the great sentence would be turned into a choice piece of that twopenny morality which is so dear to the English heart, which leads, if not to the City of God, at all events to the City of London, which we call "the City."

But the true meaning of the ancient sentence is, of course: Let us apprehend the eternal savours of the things of time. Through all the beauties and delights of this earth, let us see, veiled, the beauties and delights of the everlasting. A cup of cold water will win paradise; but a cup of cold water is already a part of paradise. Wine maketh glad the heart of man; that is because its parent grape was grown in the vineyards of the Kingdom. An earthly feast is a goodly thing; because there is a heavenly feast. Dawn and sunset are wonders to look upon, being pale reflections of eternal splendours. And as to the feast: I was once talking to a Scottish philosopher, a Hegelian, who could not stomach Plato. "Why Plato maintains," said he, "that there is actually a table set in the heavens." Of course, Plato was perfectly right: if there were no table in the heavens, there would certainly be no table on earth. Two legged beasts would no doubt eat and drink to satisfy their hunger and their thirst after the fashion of other beasts; but there would be no table, and these beasts, though they might be cunning, would not be men; that is, sons of God.

The *adoro to devote Latens Deitas* of St. Thomas Aquinas has its special and sacred application to the Mystery of the Altar; but, like all universal truths as distinct from various pieces of information about things—which is the best definition of physical science—the doctrine implied "goes through" even to the uttermost parts of the earth. That which is on high is as that which is below; and the "latent deity" is latent in all things.

In all things, that is, that have not been clouded and defiled and deprived of their divinity by the ill will of man. I remember that there was an instruction given to me on joining a certain secret society, that one should so see and so think as to behold and know nothing but God. I considered this point, and when I next met my instructor I was frank with him. I said: "While I was reading that matter of finding nothing at all but God, I was sitting in my arm-chair in Gray's Inn and looking at the tiles about my hearth. They are horrible things though shiny, horrible both in colouring and in design. I must resolutely refuse to see anything of Divinity in them." And my teacher confessed that the matter was difficult. I cannot remember that he found me any solution.

But a few months ago, when I was writing a chapter in my reminiscences, this incident occurred to me, and my memory went back many long years, and I wrote somewhat as follows:

THE GLORIOUS MYSTERY

"Everything to me was wonderful, everything visible was the veil of an invisible secret. Before an oddly shaped or coloured stone I was ready to fall into a sort of reverie or meditation, as if it had been a fragment of paradise or fairyland. There was a certain herb of the fields that grew plentifully in Gwent that even now I cannot regard without a kind of reverence; it is a spire of small yellow blossoms, and its leaves when crushed give out a very pungent and aromatic odour. This odour was to me a separate revelation or mystery, as if no one in the world had smelt it but myself; and so the whole earth, down to the very pebbles, was but the veil of a quickening and adorable secret. I look back to the time when the mountain and the tiny shining stone, the flower and the brook, were all alike signs and evidences. I see myself all alone in the valley under hanging woods of a still summer evening, entranced, wondering what the secret was that here was almost told."

And that, or something like that, I suppose, must have been in the mind of the hierarch, whoever he may have been, who told those about to be initiated that they must find God in all things.

And so, I go on and say that you cannot write of anything or make the image of anything without writing of God or making the image of veiled divinity—heeding always, the example of the tiles in my sitting room in Gray's Inn. Man is almost omnipotent; he can quite destroy for himself and the fools who trust in him the great work of God. It is within the power of the sculptor—look about London—to say "Let us make man in the image of sheer stupidity and chaos and nonsense, or rather in the image of the fashion plates of this or that year, very badly carried out in bronze." It is in the power of the writer to be enormously clever, to shew the vastest knowledge of the common thoughts of people at large, and to write long, highly successful books which nearly everybody says are "like life" or "slices of life." Indeed these things are like life; as Madame Tussaud's wax work is like life, or as a beefsteak is, most undeniably, a slice of life.   But these things are not life, because the *latens deitas* which makes life is not discerned in them.   I will not take any English examples, though these be many and flagrant, but I would say that the short stories of Guy de Maupassant illustrate my meaning perfectly.   They are exquisite studies indeed; but in entomology, not in humanity.

But, as I say, corruption or blindness apart, it is impossible to write of anything without writing of God; and this is true of the simple homely things as well as of the splendid, glowing, and illustrious things.   The secret language is spoken everywhere and by all creatures.   The foolish and the folklorists read, for very different reasons, their Arabian Nights in Burton's version.   I always knew by instinct that Burton was all wrong from any point of view save that of the collector of oriental manners and customs; and when I had struggled through a page or two—I never could manage more—of his detestable English, I knew by experience that he was all wrong.   The wise read the Arabian Nights not for manners and customs, but for splendours and for wonders, for the story of hidden doors that are suddenly disclosed in ways of daily passage, for the vision of jewels which glow like the sun and moon and all the assemblage of the stars, for the magic carpet, for the tent which can shelter a host and yet be folded in the hand, for the magic, for the divinity, that is, which every uncorrupted mind perceives to be latent in life.   And I would go a step farther and say that I believe that the uncorrupted mind perceives by instinct that all these marvels are real.   Not actual, perhaps; I would not dare to say that that tent which can shelter an army and then be reduced to the compass of the palm of the hand will ever be a part of ordnance; but still it is real, real in the power of human imagination and transcendence.   Law, you know, following Bohme, as I suppose, taught that before the Fall the universe was "fluid"—this must refer to the period before the electrons became atoms—that is, obedient to the will of man.   After the Fall, it "hardened," but not altogether. Aladdin's Palace still rises in a single night.

THE GLORIOUS MYSTERY

I suppose then, it is no great task to see in such a book as the Arabian Nights a veiled picture of the wonders and the splendours of the world; that is of the glory of God in the world; but there are obscurer ways of the secret language, which speaks in the simplest things as well as in the most splendid things. Indeed, we have already seen that the Psalmist found a thirsty stag a good enough image of the great desire of the soul for God; and again in the twenty-third Psalm such homely symbols as wine, oil, and a table are sufficient in his view to convey a meaning which is deep and high enough. It is then, I think, to be considered whether bread and cheese and beer and a safe hearth and a roaring fire and a secure rooftree on a bitter and stormy night may not have their significance. These are vulgar things, I know, but oil is quite a vulgar thing to an oriental. To me an olive tree is a sacred tree; the first sight of it was a revelation, the silvery green of the olive orchards was a veritable magic-carpet journey in time rather than in space. But well do I remember how the old Provençal lady shook her sides when I confessed that I gazed with reverence on the olives about her farm.

I am sorry to refer you so often to the Holy Scriptures. I know it is an oriental book, but it has been so long translated into the tongues of the West that I am afraid that it has become almost as vulgar as bread and cheese and a warm fire on a cold night. Still, the Psalm *Benedicite omnia opera* —to put a good Latin face on it— is much to my purpose, and I would ask you to think over these measured appeals to showers and dew, winds and fire, winter and summer, frost and cold, ice and snow to "bless the Lord, praise Him and magnify Him forever." All these, you see, are the commonest of common things; yet they are addressed by the Children with Angels and Saints, as if they were creatures in the Eternal Chorus. And so addressed, as I believe, because they too, according to their degree, utter the eternal Word, and though of earth speak to the instructed ever of unearthly wonders. And thus I think it is that if you know how to describe a lonely man stumbling on his way up a long and winding lane on a winter's night, buffeted with mountain winds, drenched with driving rains, overwhelmed with darkness, and yet attaining at length to homely shelter, to a seat on the settle by a roaring fire, to a place whence he can listen to the storm without: well, incidentally, you have made literature, but essentially you have described the passage into paradise. And that, by the way, is no doubt the true definition of literature—of the secret language, well-expressed—it must deal with the passage to paradise; and if you are to apprehend this secret language you have got to understand that the villa at Dulwich where Mr. Pickwick rested from his pilgrimage is in fact paradise. I am sorry that Dulwich is just a suburb of London, with three stations, attainable from Victoria, Ludgate Hill, Holborn Viaduct, or London Bridge. I am aware that it ought to be called Oomtigala or Ispadan or something queer. Still, there it is; and I am afraid I must say that anybody who has difficulty in finding Dulwich a fit symbol of paradise had better abandon the study of the secret language forever. But such persons will have Blake against them. They will have Plato, a greater name, against them, with his Table in the Heavens. They will have Solomon the King with his wine and apples against them. They will have the Psalmist with his wine and oil against them. They will have every good man against them; they will be in the company of the accursed Manichees and in the company of all the fools who have maintained that the earth is not the Lord's but the Devil's. It is written that he who cannot love his visible brother can in no wise love the invisible Deity. That is, evidently, the same doctrine in another phrase. I would also say that he who cannot see the eternal gifts in bread and cheese and beer and homely friendship and kindly mirth may gabble occult abracadabras all his days; but he shall never taste of the eternal refections of paradise, or sing the new song of the redeemed. The stubborn child who will not learn the alphabet, it is clear, shall neither read nor write immortal verse; though the alphabet, to be sure, is a horrid, elemental thing with all sorts of silly and tedious associations about it.

It is curious how this secret language has informed all fine literature from all time. It has had many modes of expression; but there is one in particular that I would remark. When the great legend of the Holy Grail, and especially the Percival branch of that legend, came up before the Folklorists, they said, and said very justly, that the story of Percival was an example of the Exile and Return and Vengeance Formula. That is, your hero is, at the beginning of the tale, described as exiled from all, deprived of all, driven forth from pleasant and prosperous places into the wilderness. He sets forth from the wilderness on some kind of pilgrimage; he meets with all sorts of adventures, enemies, hardships, enigmas, terrors; and at last at the end of the story, he is restored to all that he has lost, and to far more than all. His wicked enemies have been trodden under his feet, all tears have been wiped from his eyes, all goods have been given back to him, nay given back tenfold; his Beloved is his; and, in the beautiful old ending, "he lives happily ever after."

That is the Exile, Return, and Vengeance Formula, which makes, according to the Folklorists, one of the age-old stories of the world. There the Folklorists stop; but we, I think, may be bold to say that, under these figures, is told the story of man, who comes from Paradise and at last returns to Paradise, having conquered all his adversaries and trampled down all the terrors that beset him. For my part, I very willingly receive this tale as a part of the primitive instinct of man, or if you will, a part of the primitive revelation made to man; and I hold, too, that if this be not accepted, then it follows that all literature and all art are but forms of mania, ravings about rests and palaces and refreshments that have no real existence in the universe. I should be sorry to accept this doctrine; and so I hold that Nicholas Nickleby is one of the great witnesses to the truth. It is true that in Nicholas Nickleby the word for Paradise is Dawlish, which is a small town in Devonshire on the Great Western line; but again I must maintain that Dawlish, as Dulwich, is no unfit symbol of the place of rest and refreshment and joys that are perdurable. For, you will remark that in the real books you feel that the hero and his friends are come to the place of the undying, to the paths of the immortals. Their sorrows are all over in the earlier chapters of the book; Squeers is sent overseas, Ralph is dead, Nicholas, with Madelaine, is returned to the old garden, and there he lives to this day, young and happy for evermore. They lived happy ever after.

I have only indicated possibilities. I have shewn that things most manifest have been before all eyes for long ages, and yet have remained concealed, even from the wise. I have spoken of a hot fire on a cold night, of bread and cheese and beer, and the tales of an early Victorian novelist; all these things being everywhere apparent to all. I leave you to judge of what else is known to all, and yet hidden from all, among the signs of the Kingdom.

THE GLORIOUS MYSTERY

EDGAR ALLAN POE
THE SUPREME REALIST

SOME time ago, I was endeavouring to intimate to a friend of mine, in the most ungentle terms of which I am master, that I did not want to hear any of his Bacon-Shakespeare nonsense. He said: "That's all very well, but I don't believe that the author of the 'Sonnets' would sue his neighbour for malt supplied." I don't understand the mechanism of this logical process, but I deny the proposition all the same. And here is an extract from a letter written by an American gentleman to his mother-in-law somewhere about April 7th, 1844:

> Last night, for supper, we had the nicest tea you ever drank, strong and hot—wheat bread and rye bread—cheese—tea-cakes (elegant), a great dish (two dishes) of elegant ham, and two of cold veal, piled up like a mountain.

This gentleman had just arrived at Morrison's boarding-house, New York—"it has brown stone steps with a porch with brown pillars." He is also responsible for the following lines:

> And all my days are trances,
> And all my nightly dreams
> Are where thy dark eye glances
> And where thy footstep gleams—
> In what ethereal dances,
> By what eternal streams.

His name was Edgar Allan Poe. Hence we learn that the vision of eternal beauty is not incompatible with a relish for a comfortable meal. After all, what did Dr. Johnson say: "I look upon it, that he who does not mind his belly will hardly mind anything else." And—the case of Lycidas excepted—Dr. Johnson was usually right.

THE GLORIOUS MYSTERY

This Edgar Allan Poe, who liked good ham and hot tea, and saw the dignity of brown stone (see Oliver Wendell Holmes on this matter), and was, in addition, a unique artist, was a child of a singular ancestry. One of the numerous "elegant" female friends who admired him seems to have manufactured a pedigree to match the pseudo-mediæval element in some of his tales: she babbles of De la Poers, of the Rhine, and so forth. And a bland male idiot, an American critic of some note, states, with ineffable imbecility that the name of Poe "antedates the river"! As a matter of fact, the greatest of all Americans came of a stock of tenant-farmers in County Cavan, Ireland. I learn from a curious and valuable little treatise, privately printed for Sir Edward Thomas Bewley (Dublin, 1906), that David Poe, of Dring, County Cavan, had a son named John. This John emigrated to America about 1750, having married Jane McBride. The son of these was David, wheelwright and D.A.Q.G. in the American Revolutionary Army. He married Elizabeth, daughter of ———— Cairnes, of Pennsylvania; their son was David, who married the young widow Hopkins; and of this couple was born Edgar Poe on January 19th, 1809. So much is absolutely certain; it is almost certain, according to Sir Thomas Bewley, that David Poe of Dring was descended from one of two brothers, David and Jonathan Powell, who invaded Ireland, under Cromwell, in the middle of the seventeenth century. And it would appear that the whole family were grim and rigid Puritans up to the father of the poet; and from this race of small farmers, of Puritans, of Welshmen, of Scots, highland and lowland, with probable dashes of Irish blood, was produced the man whom Mr. Arthur Ransome hails in his recent and admirable "Edgar Allan Poe: A Critical Study" as the supreme authority in literary æsthetics. Poe was this; he had penetrated deeply into the inmost secrets of Beauty in Literature; he was also a supreme creative artist; and that ancestry, from David of Dring at any rate, is an unassailable fact. And it seems to me that all this complicates the already complicated science of eugenics. It must have been a keen eye that could have detected "Ulalume" latent in David of Dring, the Presbyterian tenant-farmer.

I need only pass over in the briefest detail the well-known incidents of Poe's life. His mother and father, the strolling players, died when he was two years old; he was adopted by Allan, of Richmond, Virginia, the rich merchant, who lived in a wooden house that tried to look like a Greek temple. The Allans took Edgar to England, left him at school in the leafy village of Stoke Newington for some years, brought him back to Virginia. He was petted and scolded, went to a University, enlisted as a private in the U. S. army, tried West Point, accumulated extravagant habits and gambling debts, and was finally thrown on the world by Mr. Allan. He married his cousin, a little girl named Virginia, and attempted to make a living in the America of 1830-1849 by writing masterpieces of pure literary beauty. From this task he was mercifully released on October 7th of the latter year. As Mr. Ransome notes very sagely, it is hardly likely that Poe was the only literary man in America during this period who occasionally took too much to drink. But his bouts of intoxication (a single glass of wine, said N. P. Willis, was enough to madden him), are perhaps the only features in Poe's history and work that his fellow-countrymen have thoroughly understood. They have thus, naturally enough, been tempted to dwell overmuch on these lapses from the creed of the Brick Lane Branch of the United Grand Junction Ebenezer Temperance Association. A contemporary of Poe's tries in a friendly spirit to summon him to "the moral province of society"; a phrase which in its vague piety irresistibly recalls Mr. Pecksniff; and a writer of a much later day deplores the violence of his attack on Thomas Dunn English. Thomas Dunn English pretended to be a man of letters, and could scarcely string three words together grammatically—and Poe said as much. This was the violence in question. One wonders how the struggle lasted until 1849.

THE GLORIOUS MYSTERY

A man who knew Edgar Allan Poe told Messrs. Stedman and Woodberry that the poet's walk "was always slow and not graceful, and a little uncertain, as if his mind was on something else than walking." It is difficult from such reminiscences to gather a very definite idea of Poe's bodily presence, and the difficulty is not lessened by the inspection of the numerous portraits that adorn the Stedman-Woodberry edition of his works. One likeness is benign and tame and whiskered; the face suggests a mid-Victorian archdeacon of strictly moderate views. The second portrait has something of the filibuster about it; a third recalls Henry Clay as he appears on the cigar-boxes; yet a fourth, purporting to show Poe as he was at the age of thirty-five, looks as if it ought to be subscribed "Blank Fairchild" or "Blank Goodchild, Esquire, of Mildmay Park." Most of these reproduced daguerreotypes give him a straight mouth and normal brows; but one or two suggest strange twists or distortions of both features. Mr. Ransome has some interesting things about Poe's various "masks," speaking in metaphor, of the different aspects of his work; and it would seem that the phrase might be used almost literally. He was, we know, a man of many aspects, and there is one picture that might very well represent the descendant of a long line of Ulster Puritans: its sourness is terrific and its growth of whisker vicious in the extreme. But, comparing these portraits with the verbal likenesses that have been handed down, we have on the whole the image of a dark man with brilliant eyes; with brilliant eyes that appear to pierce beneath the surface of things, and lips that are by no means genial. There was no merriment in Poe; probably he was born of a melancholy disposition, his miseries and martyrdoms of the artist made him more melancholy, and the material wretchedness of his existence filled up the tale. And he had but the feeblest sense of humour; and it was this lack of humour, as it seems to me, which is responsible for the occasional lapses in his work, for such "trickery" as "The Bells," for that tendency to pile up the horror so heavily that (now and then) we smile—or would smile if we did not remember the man's greatness—instead of shuddering. There is a point, it must be remembered, where tragedy becomes melodrama, and Poe, it cannot be denied, sometimes overstepped the point in question, both in his prose and in his verse.

But this deduction being made, due weight being also given to his rare verbal infelicities—due, these latter, no doubt, as Mr. Ransome suggests, to infection from the speech of the barbarians with whom he was compelled to associate—we must place steadfastly before us the fact that Edgar Allan Poe is one of the very few writers who have understood human nature. The claim is a large one, and I am to justify it: Poe was a supremely natural writer.

In the first place it is necessary to define our terms. Many people, no doubt, think of the natural man as the man whom they meet at the street corner, in the 'bus, in the underground railway, at business, or at dinner-parties. The natural man is conceived of—is it not strange—as the man whom we see and read about in the papers. He is a person who is always hungry and thirsty, arid of pleasures, of sensible enjoyments, observant of conventions, of the opinions of his neighbours, desirous of reforming them—sometimes: a thoroughly social animal, conditioned at all points and on every side by his relations to other social animals. This is the natural man of the novelists; of this two-legged rational being, of his plots and interplots, they make their amiable and harmless tale. But if we think of it, this man is not in the least natural; he is wholly artificial and conventional when he is not purely animal. Or, to put it in another form, the creature of the so-called psychological novelists is man regarded not essentially, but accidentally, superficially, and not in his deep and secret and vital being. Becky in "Vanity Fair" looking for £5,000 a year is a delightful and amusing spectacle; but the procedure of Becky is not radically and essentially differentiated from that of a dog who has set his heart on a juicy bone and is determined to have it *per fas aut per nefas*—that is to say, Becky, as described by Thackeray, is not essentially natural. We have had novelists since the days of Thackeray who have drawn finer and more subtle (but never surer) lines; but from the standpoint which I am taking, the result is the same. The lines may be finer, but it is still the surface which is delineated. Now, place beside Becky at her brightest and best, in her most poignant moments of failure or success, the lines that I have already quoted:

> . . . where thy footstep gleams—
> In what ethereal dances,
> By what eternal streams.

Nay; let me copy out once more that oft-quoted and perfect lyric, "To Helen: ———

> Helen, thy beauty is to me
> Like those Nicæan barks of yore,
> That gently, o'er a perfumed sea,
> The weary, way-worn wanderer bore
> To his own native shore.
>
> On desperate seas long wont to roam
> Thy hyacinth hair, thy classic face,
> Thy Naiad airs, have brought me home
> To the glory that was Greece,
> And the grandeur that was Rome.
>
> Lo! in yon brilliant window-niche,
> How statue-like I see thee stand,
> The agate lamp within thy hand!
> Ah, Psyche, from the regions which
> Are Holy Land!

Yes, the careers of Jos and the return of Rawdon and the humours of old Sir Pitt and the Ribbons: all these things are capital; but it is Poe who is the true realist, the true depicter of essential humanity, the true interpreter of man to man. Such a poem as this, such a tale as "The Fall of the House of Usher," is truly natural; they mirror in forms beautiful and terrible the secret and innermost core of man's being.

THE GLORIOUS MYSTERY

Mr. Ransome points out in the course of his fascinating study that Poe never reduced his æsthetic theory to a perfect and consistent logical form. As the critic truly observes, Poe was an explorer, a discoverer, a Columbus of the spirit. He had to hew his way through trackless forests, to sail over uncharted and perilous seas; it is no wonder that now and then he wandered from the true course. For instance, in distinguishing between the offices of prose and poetry he says the business of the first is with truth, of the second with beauty. Here he falters; the business of both prose and poetry is with truth and beauty, the distinction being, as Poe himself recognises in another place, that poetry is rhythmical or measured, while prose is unrhythmical and not subject to metrical laws. Poe, no doubt, forgot for a moment the great distinction between essential and eternal truth and mere information; and with information, *qua* information, fine literature has no concern of any kind. A scientific text-book is in prose, but it is not prose, for Science, which is (or should be) accurate information, deals with surfaces and accidents, whereas literature has to do with essential and substantial realities. Again, Poe strays from the path when he makes melancholy the most fit subject for poetry. Beauty, as he rightly observes, is apt to fill the eyes with tears; but from this quite true premise he deduces, quite illegitimately, the conclusion that beauty is chiefly occupied with tears and human sorrows. Tears are a symptom common to both emotions, to the perception of great beauty, and to the perception of a great sorrow; and, again, Poe, reconsidering the matter, saw it in its true light. These are casual failures in his critical doctrine; they are better by far than the successes of the men who derided him as the "tinkling triangle" in the great orchestra of literary art. In the main he saw with piercing and exquisite clearness that the supreme quest of man is the quest of beauty, that the perception of beauty—which is truth, which is God—is the supreme differentia of man, and that, therefore, the creation of beauty is the supreme object of art, and, indeed, the sole and sufficient definition of art. And he lived amongst people, and he worked amongst people, and he was reviled by people who thought that the object of art was to make Jacky a good boy. Poor man!

I have noted Poe's error in making art the daughter of sadness. I suspect that here, where he reasoned amiss, he was in reality led astray by his own feelings. Poe, partly through his disposition, partly through the loss of that Helen who befriended him in his youth, was subject to what I must call the obsession of Death, in particular to the awful fear that death may not be the sudden stroke of a moment, but rather a slow and lingering process, in which, even after the flesh has been given over to corruption, a consciousness of being still survives. In this domain he has achieved wonders; but decay and dissolution are far from being the supreme subject for the artist, and hence we must often admire his prose tales more for their sub-conscious than for their conscious effects. As he said himself, anticipating Pater, "it is in music that the soul most nearly attains the supernal end for which it struggles," and it is a music both supreme and supernal that haunts us all through his wonderful work, that makes us, as it were, forget the literal tale—the plot—for the strange beauty of its phrases, for the murmured incantation of the melody to which he sets his story. It was thus that he strove to attain and did attain the final object of the human quest; it is thus that he deserves to be called the supreme realist, the truly natural writer. For others, the body, the superficies, the clothes conceal the man. But in the achievement of Edgar Allan Poe there is the quickening spirit, the sense of eternal reality and truth and beauty.

THE GLORIOUS MYSTERY

THE IRON MAID

I THINK the most extraordinary event which I can recall took place about five years ago. I was then still feeling my way; I had declared for business, and attended regularly at my office, but I had not succeeded in establishing a really profitable connection, and consequently I had a good deal of leisure time on my hands. I have never thought fit to trouble you with the details of my private life; they would be entirely devoid of interest. I must briefly say, however, that I had a numerous circle of acquaintance, and was never at a loss as to how to spend my evenings. I was so fortunate as to have friends in most of the ranks of the social order; there is nothing so unfortunate, to my mind, as a specialized circle, wherein a certain round of ideas is continually traversed and retraversed. I have always tried to find out new types and persons whose brains contained something fresh to me; one may chance to gain information even from the conversation of city men on an omnibus.

Amongst my acquaintance I knew a young doctor who lived in a far outlying suburb, and I used often to brave the intolerably slow railway journey, to have the pleasure of listening to his talk. One night we conversed so eagerly together over our pipes and whiskey that the clock passed unnoticed, and when I glanced up I realized with a shock that I had just five minutes in which to catch the last train. I made a dash for my hat and stick, and jumped out of the house and down the steps, and tore at full speed up the street. It was no good, however; there was a shriek of the engine whistle, and I stood there at the station door and saw far on the long dark line of the embankment a red light shine and vanish, and a porter came down and shut the door with a bang.

"How far to London?" I asked him.

THE GLORIOUS MYSTERY

"A good nine miles to Waterloo Bridge"; and with that he went off.

Before me was the long suburban street, its dreary distance marked by rows of twinkling lamps, and the air was poisoned by the faint sickly smell of burning bricks; it was not a cheerful prospect by any means, and I had to walk through nine miles of such streets, deserted as those of Pompeii. I knew pretty well what direction to take; so I set out wearily, looking at the stretch of lamps vanishing in perspective; and as I walked, street after street branched off to right and left—some far reaching to distances that seemed endless, communicating with other systems of thoroughfare; and some mere protoplasmic streets, beginning in orderly fashion with serried two-storied houses, and ending suddenly in waste, and pits, and rubbish heaps, and fields whence the magic had departed. I have spoken of systems of thoroughfare, and I assure you that, walking alone through these silent places, I felt phantasy growing on me, and some glamour of the infinite. There was here, I felt, an immensity as in the outer void of the universe. I passed from unknown to unknown, my way marked by lamps like stars, and on either hand was an unknown world where myriads of men dwelt and slept, street leading into street, as it seemed to world's end.

At first the road by which I was travelling was lined with houses of unutterable monotony—a wall of grey brick pierced by two stories of windows, drawn close to the very pavement. But by degrees I noticed an improvement: there were gardens, and these grew larger. The suburban builder began to allow himself a wider scope; and for a certain distance each flight of steps was guarded by twin lions of plaster, and scents of flowers prevailed over the fume of heated bricks. The road began to climb a hill, and, looking up a side street, I saw the half moon rise over plane-trees, and there on the other side was as if a white cloud had fallen, and the air around it was sweetened as with incense; it was a may-tree in full bloom. I pressed on stubbornly, listening

[90]

for the wheels and the clatter of some belated hansom; but into that land of men who go to the city in the morning and return in the evening, the hansom rarely enters, and I had resigned myself once more to the walk, when I suddenly became aware that some one was advancing to meet me along the sidewalk. The man was strolling rather aimlessly; and though the time and place would have allowed an unconventional style of dress, he was vested in the ordinary frock coat, black tie, and silk hat of civilization. We met each other under the lamp, and, as often happens in this great town, two casual passengers brought face to face found each in the other an acquaintance.

"Mr. Mathias, I think?" I said.

"Quite so. And you are Frank Burton. You know you are a man with a Christian name, so I won't apologize for my familiarity. But may I ask where you are going?"

I explained the situation to him, saying I have traversed a region as unknown to me as the darkest recesses of Africa. "I think I have only about five miles farther," I concluded.

"Nonsense; you must come home with me. My house is close by; in fact, I was just taking my evening walk when we met. Come along; I dare say you will find a makeshift bed easier than a five-mile walk."

I let him take my arm and lead me along, though I was a good deal surprised at so much geniality from a man who was, after all, a mere casual club acquaintance. I suppose I had not spoken to Mr. Mathias half a dozen times; he was a man who would sit silent in an armchair for hours, neither reading nor smoking, but now and again moistening his lips with his tongue and smiling queerly to himself. I confess he had never attracted me, and on the whole I should have preferred to continue my walk. But he took my arm and led me up a side street, and stopped at a door in a high wall. We passed through the still moonlit garden, beneath the black shadow of an old cedar, and into an old red brick house with many gables.

I was tired enough, and I sighed with relief as I let

myself fall into a great leather armchair. You know the infernal grit with which they strew the sidewalk in those suburban districts; it makes walking a penance, and I felt my four-mile tramp had made me more weary than ten miles on an honest country road. I looked about the room with some curiosity. There was a shaded lamp which threw a circle of brilliant light on a heap of papers lying on an old brass-bound secretaire of the last century; but the room was all vague and shadowy, and I could only see that it was long and low, and that it was filled with indistinct objects which might be furniture. Mr. Mathias sat down in a second arm-chair, and looked about him with that odd smile of his. He was a queer-looking man, clean-shaven, and white to the lips. I should think his age was something between fifty and sixty.

"Now I have got you here," he began, "I must inflict my hobby on you. You knew I was a collector? Oh, yes, I have devoted many years to collecting curiosities, which I think are really curious. But we must have a better light."

He advanced into the middle of the room, and lit a lamp which hung from the ceiling; and as the bright light flashed round the wick, from every corner and space there seemed to start a horror. Great wooden frames with complicated apparatus of ropes and pulleys stood against the wall; a wheel of strange shape had a place beside a thing that looked like a gigantic gridiron. Little tables glittered with bright steel instruments carelessly put down as if ready for use; a screw and vice loomed out, casting ugly shadows; and in another nook was a saw with cruel jagged teeth.

"Yes," said Mr. Mathias; "they are, as you suggest, instruments of torture—of torture and death. Some—many, I may say—have been used; a few are reproductions after ancient examples. Those knives were used for flaying; that frame is a rack, and a very fine specimen. Look at this; it comes from Venice. You see that sort of collar, something like a big horse-shoe? Well, the patient, let us call him, sat down quite comfortably, and the horse-shoe was neatly fitted round his neck. Then the two ends were joined with a silken band, and the executioner began to turn a handle connected with the band. The horse-shoe contracted very gradually as the band tightened, and the turning continued till the man was strangled. It all took place quietly, in one of those queer garrets under the Leads. But these things are all European; the Orientals are, of course, much more ingenious. These are the Chinese contrivances. You have heard of the 'heavy death'? It is my hobby, this sort of thing. Do you know, I often sit here, hour after hour, and meditate over the collection. I fancy I see the faces of the men who have suffered—faces lean with agony and wet with sweats of death—growing distinct out of the gloom, and I hear the echoes of their cries for mercy. But I must show you my latest acquisition. Come into the next room."

I followed Mr. Mathias out. The weariness of the walk, the late hour, and the strangeness of it all, made me feel like a man in a dream; nothing would have surprised me very much. The second room was as the first, crowded with ghastly instruments; but beneath the lamp was a wooden platform, and a figure stood on it. It was a large statue of a naked woman, fashioned in green bronze; the arms were stretched out, and there was a smile on the lips; it might well have been intended for a Venus, and yet there was about the thing an evil and a deadly look.

Mr. Mathias looked at it complacently. "Quite a work of art, isn't it?" he said. "It's made of bronze, as you see, but it has long had the name of the Iron Maid. I got it from Germany, and it was only unpacked this afternoon; indeed, I have not yet had time to open the letter of advice. You see that very small knob between the breasts? Well, the victim was bound to the Maid, the knob was pressed, and the arms slowly tightened round the neck. You can imagine the result."

As Mr. Mathias talked, he patted the figure affectionately. I had turned away, for I sickened at the sight of the man and his loathsome treasure. There was a slight click, of which I took no notice—it was not much louder than the tick of a clock; and then I heard a sudden whir, the noise of machinery in motion, and I faced round. I have never forgotten the hideous agony on Mathias's face as those relentless arms tightened about his neck; there was a wild struggle as of a beast in the toils, and then a shriek that ended in a choking groan. The whirring noise had suddenly changed into a heavy droning. I tore with all my might at the bronze arms, and strove to wrench them apart, but I could do nothing. The head had slowly bent down, and the green lips were on the lips of Mathias.

Of course I had to attend the inquest. The letter which had accompanied the figure was found unopened on the study table. The German firm of dealers cautioned their client to be most careful in touching the Iron Maid, as the machinery had been put in thorough working order.

THE ROSE GARDEN

AND afterwards she went very softly, and opened the window and looked out. Behind her the room was in a mystical semi-darkness; chairs and tables were hovering, ill-defined shapes, there was but the faintest illusory glitter from the talc moons in the rich Indian curtain which she had drawn across the door. The yellow silk draperies of the bed were but suggestions of colour, and the pillow and the white sheets glimmered as a white cloud in a far sky at twilight.

She turned from the dusky room, and with dewy tender eyes gazed out across the garden towards the lake. She could not rest nor lay herself down to sleep; though it was late, and half the night had passed, she could not rest. A sickle moon was slowly drawing upwards through certain filmy clouds that stretched in a long band from east to west, and a pallid light began to flow from the dark water, as if there also some vague planet were rising. She looked with eyes insatiable for wonder; and she found a strange eastern effect in the bordering of reeds, in their spear-like shapes, in the liquid ebony that they shadowed, in the fine inlay of pearl and silver as the moon shone free; a bright symbol in the steadfast calm of the sky.

There were faint stirring sounds heard from the fringe of reeds, and now and then the drowsy broken cry of water-fowl, for they knew that the dawn was not far off. In the centre of the lake was a carved white pedestal, and on it shone a white boy holding the double flute to his lips.

Beyond the lake the park began, and sloped gently to the verge of the wood, now but a dark cloud beneath the sickle moon. And then beyond, and farther still, undiscovered hills, grey bands of cloud, and the steep pale height of the heaven.

She gazed on with her tender eyes, bathing herself as it were in the deep rest of the night, veiling her soul with the

[95]

half-light and the half-shadow, stretching out her delicate
hands into the coolness of the misty silvered air, wondering
at her hands.

And then she turned from the window, and made herself
a divan of cushions on the Persian carpet, and half-sat, half-
lay there, as motionless, as ecstatic as a poet dreaming under
roses, far in Ispanhan. She had gazed out, after all, to assure
herself that sight and the eyes showed nothing but a glimmer-
ing veil, a gauze of curious lights and figures, that in it there
was no reality nor substance. He had always told her that
there was only one existence, one science, one religion, that
the external world was but a variegated shadow, which might
either conceal or reveal the truth; and now she believed.

He had shown her that bodily rapture might be the
ritual and expression of the ineffable mysteries, of the world
beyond sense, that must be entered by the way of sense; and
now she believed. She had never much doubted any of his
words, from the moment of their meeting a month before.
She had looked up as she sat in the arbour, and her father
was walking down between the avenue of roses bringing to
her the stranger, thin and dark with a pointed beard and
melancholy eyes. He murmured something to himself as they
shook hands; she could hear the rich unknown words that
sounded as the echo of far music. Afterwards he had told her
what the lines were:

How say ye that I was lost? I wandered among roses.
Can he go astray who enters the rose garden?
The lover in the house of his Darling is not forlorn.
I wandered among roses. How say ye that I was lost?

His voice, murmuring the strange words, had persuaded
her, and now she had the rapture of the perfect knowledge.
She had looked out into the silvery uncertain night in order
that she might experience the sense that for her these things
no longer existed. She was not any more a part of the garden,
or of the lake, or of the wood, or of the life that she had led
hitherto. Another line that he had quoted came to her:

THE GLORIOUS MYSTERY

The kingdom of I and We forsake, and your home in
annihilation make.

It had seemed at first almost nonsense, if it had been
possible for him to talk nonsense; but now she was thrilled
and filled with the meaning of it. Herself was annihilated;
at his bidding she had destroyed all her old feelings and
emotions, her likes and dislikes, all the inherited loves and
hates that her father and mother had given her; the old life
had been thrown utterly away.

It grew light, and when the dawn burned she fell asleep,
murmuring:

"How say ye that I was lost?"

THE GLORIOUS MYSTERY

FRAGMENTS OF PAPER

MR. DALE, who had quiet rooms in a western part of London, was very busily occupied one day with a pencil and little scraps of paper. He would stop in the middle of his writing, of his monotonous tramp from door to window, jot down a line of hieroglyphics, and turn again to his work. At lunch he kept his instruments on the table beside him, and a little notebook accompanied him on his evening walk about the Green. Sometimes he seemed to experience a certain difficulty in the act of writing, as if the heat of shame or even incredulous surprise held his hand, but one by one the fragments of paper fell into the drawer, and a full feast awaited him at the day's close.

As he lit his pipe at dusk he was standing by the window and looking out into the street. In the distance cablights flashed to and fro, up and down the hill, on the main road. Across the way he saw the long line of sober gray houses, cheerfully lit up for the most part, displaying against the night the dining-room and the evening meal. In one house, just opposite, there was brighter illumination, and the open window showed a modest dinner-party in progress, and here and there a drawing-room on the first floor glowed ruddy, as the tall, shaded lamp was lit. Everywhere Dale saw a quiet and comfortable respectability; if there were no gaiety there was no riot, and he thought himself fortunate to have got "rooms" in so sane and meritorious a street.

The pavement was almost deserted. Now and again a servant would dart out from a side door and skurry off in the direction of the shops, returning in a few minutes in equal haste. But foot-passengers were rare, and only at long intervals a stranger would drift from the highway and wander, with slow speculation, down Abingdon Road, as if he had passed its entrance a thousand times and had at last been piqued with curiosity and the desire of exploring the unknown. All the inhabitants of the quarter prided themselves on their quiet seclusion, and many of them did not so much as dream that if one went far enough the road degenerated and became abominable, the home of the hideous, the mouth of a black purlieu. Indeed, stories, ill and malodorous, were told of the streets parallel, to east and west, which perhaps communicated with the terrible sink beyond, but those who lived at the good end of Abingdon Road knew nothing of their neighbours.

Dale leant far out of his window. The pale London sky deepened to violet as the lamps were lit, and in the twilight the little gardens before the houses shone, seemed as if they grew more clear. The golden laburnum but reflected the last bright yellow veil that had fallen over the sky after sunset, the white hawthorn was a gleaming splendour, the red may a flameless fire in the dusk. From the open window Dale could note the increasing cheerfulness of the diners opposite, as the moderate cups were filled and emptied; blinds in the higher storeys brightened up and down the street when the nurses came up with the children. A gentle breeze, that smelt of grass and woods and flowers, fanned away the day's heat from the pavement stones, rustled through the blossoming boughs, and sank again, leaving the road to calm.

All the scene breathed the gentle domestic peace of the stories; there were regular lives, dull duties done, sober and common thoughts on every side. He felt that he needed not to listen at the windows, for he could divine all the talk, and guess the placid and usual channels in which the conversation flowed. Here there were no spasms, nor raptures, nor the red storms of romance, but a safe rest; marriage and birth and begetting were no more here than breakfast and lunch and afternoon tea.

And then he turned away from the placid transparency of the street, and sat down before his lamp and the papers he had so studiously noted. A friend of his, an "impossible" man named Jenyns, had been to see him the night before, and they had talked about the psychology of the novelists, discussing their insight, and the depth of their probe.

"It is all very well as far as it goes," said Jenyns. "Yes, it is perfectly accurate. Guardsmen do like chorus-girls, the doctor's daughter is fond of the curate, the grocer's assistant of the Baptist persuasion has sometimes religious difficulties, 'smart' poeple no doubt think a great deal about social events and complications, the Tragic Comedians felt and wrote all that stuff, I daresay. But do you think that is all? Do you call a description of the gilt tools on the morocco here an exhaustive essay on Shakespeare?"

"But what more is there?" said Dale. "Don't you think, then, that human nature has been fairly laid open? What more?"

"Songs of the frantic lupanar, delirium of the madhouse. Not extreme wickedness, but the insensate, the unintelligible, the lunatic passion and idea, the desire that must come from some other sphere that we cannot even faintly imagine. Look for yourself; it is easy."

Dale looked now at the ends and scraps of paper. On them he had carefully registered all the secret thoughts of the day, the crazy lusts, the senseless furies, the foul monsters that his heart had borne, the maniac phantasies that he had harboured. In every note he found a rampant madness, the equivalent in thought of mathematical absurdity, of two-sided triangles, of parallel straight lines which met.

"And we talk of absurd dreams," he said to himself. "And these are wilder than the wildest visions. And our sins; but these are the sins of nightmare.

"And every day," he went on, " we lead two lives, and the half of our soul is madness, and half heaven is lit by a black sun. I say I am a man, but who is the other that hides in me?"

THE HOLY THINGS

THE sky was blue above Holborn, and only one little cloud, half white, half golden, floated on the wind's way from west to east. The long aisle of the street was splendid in the full light of the summer, and away in the west, where the houses seemed to meet and join, it was as a rich tabernacle, mysterious, the carven house of holy things.

A man came into the great highway from a quiet court. He had been sitting under plane-tree shade for an hour or more, his mind racked with perplexities and doubts, with the sense that all was without meaning or purpose, a tangle of senseless joys and empty sorrows. He had stirred in it and fought and striven, and now disappointment and success were alike tasteless. To struggle was weariness, to attain was weariness, to do nothing was weariness. He had left a little while before that from the highest to the lowest things of life there was no choice, there was not one thing that was better than another, the savour of the cinders was no sweeter than the savour of the ashes. He had done work which some men liked and others disliked, and liking and disliking were equally tiresome to him. His poetry or his pictures or whatever it was that he worked at had utterly ceased to interest him, and he had tried to be idle, and found idleness as impossible as work. He had lost the faculty for making and he had lost the power of resting; he dozed in the daytime and started up and cried at night. Even that morning he had doubted and hesitated, wondering whether to stay indoors or to go out, sure that in either plan there was an infinite disgust.

When he at last went abroad he let the crowd push him into the quiet court, and at the same time cursed them in a low voice for doing so; he tried to persuade himself that he had meant to go somewhere else. When he sat down he desperately endeavoured to rouse himself, and as he knew that all the strong interests are egotistic, he made an effort to grow warm over the work he had done, to find a glow of satisfaction in the thought that he had accomplished something. It was nonsense; he had found out a clever trick and had made the most of it, and it was over. Besides, how would it interest him if afterwards he was praised when he was dead? And what was the use of trying to invent some new tricks? It was folly; and he ground his teeth as a new idea came into his mind and was rejected. To get drunk always made him so horribly ill, and other things were more foolish and tiresome than poesy or painting, whichever it was.

He could not even rest on the uncomfortable bench beneath the dank, stinking plane-tree. A young man and a girl came up and sat next to him, and the girl said: "Oh, isn't it beautiful today?" and then they began to jabber to one another—the blasted fools! He flung himself from the seat and went out into Holborn.

As far as one could see there were two processions of omnibuses, cabs, and vans that went east and west and west and east. Now the long line would move on briskly, now it stopped. The horses' feet rattled and pattered on the asphalt, the wheels ground and jarred, a bicyclist wavered in and out between the serried ranks, jangling his bell. The foot-passengers went to and fro on the pavement, with an endless change of unknown faces; there was an incessant hum and murmur of voices. In the safety of a blind passage an Italian whirled round the handle of his piano-organ; the sound of it swelled and sank as the traffic surged and paused, and now and then one heard the shrill voices of the children who danced and shrieked in time to the music. Close to the pavement a coster pushed his barrow, and proclaimed flowers in an odd intonation, reminding one of the Gregorian chant. The cyclist went by again with his jangling insistent bell, and a man who stood by the lamp-post set fire to his pastille ribbon, and let the faint blue smoke rise into the sun. Away in the west, where the houses seemed to meet, the play of sunlight on the haze made as it were golden mighty shapes that paused and advanced and paused again.

He had viewed the scene hundreds of times, and for a long while had found it a nuisance and a weariness. But now, as he walked stupidly, slowly along the northern side of Holborn, a change fell. He did not in the least know what it was, but there seemed to be a strange air, and a new charm that soothed his mind.

When the traffic was stopped, to his soul there was a solemn hush that summoned remnants of a far-off memory. The voices of the passengers sank away, the street was endued with a grave and reverent expectation. A shop that he passed had a row of electric lamps burning above the door, and the golden glow of them in the sunlight was, he felt, significant. The grind and jar of the wheels as the procession moved on again gave out a chord of music, the opening of some high service that was to be done, and now, in an ecstasy, he was sure that he heard the roll and swell and triumph of the organ, and shrill sweet choristers began to sing. So the music sank and swelled and echoed in the vast aisle—in Holborn.

What could these lamps mean, burning in the bright sunlight? The music was hushed in a grave close, and in the rattle of traffic he heard the last deep, sonorous notes shake against the choir walls—he had passed beyond the range of the Italian's instrument. But then a rich voice began alone, rising and falling in monotonous but awful modulations, singing a longing, triumphant song, bidding the faithful lift up their hearts, be joined in heart with the Angels and Archangels, with the Thrones and Dominations. He could see no longer, he could not see the man who passed close beside him, pushing his barrow and calling flowers.

Ah! He could not be mistaken, he was sure now. The air was blue with incense, he smelt the adorable fragrance. The time had almost come. And then the silvery, reiterated, instant summons of a bell; and again, and again.

The tears fell from his eyes, in his weeping the tears poured a rain upon his cheeks. But he saw in the distance, in the far distance, the carven tabernacle, golden mighty figures moving slowly, imploring arms stretched forth.

There was a noise of a great shout; the choir sang in the tongue of his boyhood that he had forgotten:

SANCT, SANCT, SANCT.

Then the silvery bell tingled anew; and again, and again. He looked and saw the Holy, White and Shining Mysteries exhibited—in Holborn.

THE GLORIOUS MYSTERY

SCROOGE: 1920
A NEW CHRISTMAS CAROL

SCROOGE was undoubtedly getting on in life, to begin with. There is no doubt whatever about that. Ten years had gone by since the spirit of old Jacob Marley had visited him, and the Ghosts of Christmas Past, Christmas Present, and Christmas Yet to Come had shown him the error of his mean, niggardly, churlish ways, and had made him the merriest old boy that ever walked on 'Change with a chuckle, and was called "Old Medlar" by the young dogs who never reverenced anybody or anything.

And, not a doubt of it, the young dogs were in the right. Ebenezer Scrooge *was* a meddler. He was always ferreting about into other peoples' business; so that he might find out what good he could do them. Many a hard man of affairs softened as he thought of Scrooge and of the old man creeping round to the counting house where the hard man sat in despair, and thought of the certain ruin before him.

"My dear Mr. Hardman," old Scrooge had said, "not another word. Take this draft for thirty thousand pounds, and use it as none knows better. Why, you'll double it for me before six months are out."

He would go out chuckling on that, and Charles the waiter, at the old City tavern where Scrooge dined, always said that Scrooge was a fortune for him and to the house. To say nothing of what Charles got by him; everybody ordered a fresh supply of hot brandy and water when his cheery, rosy old face entered the room.

It was Christmastide. Scrooge was sitting before his roaring fire, sipping at something warm and comfortable, and plotting happiness for all sorts of people.

"I won't bear Bob's obstinacy," he was saying to himself—the firm was Scrooge and Cratchit now—"he does all the work, and it's not fair for a useless old fellow like me to take more than a quarter share of the profits."

A dreadful sound echoed through the grave old house. The air grew chill and sour. The something warm and comfortable grew cold and tasteless as Scrooge sipped it nervously. The door flew open, and a vague but fearful form stood in the doorway.

"Follow me," it said.

Scrooge is not at all sure what happened then. He was in the streets. He recollected that he wanted to buy some sweetmeats for his little nephews and nieces, and he went into a shop.

"Past eight o'clock, sir," said the civil man. "I can't serve you."

He wandered on through the streets that seemed strangely altered. He was going westward, and he began to feel faint. He thought he would be the better for a little brandy and water, and he was just turning into a tavern when all the people came out and the iron gates were shut with a clang in his face.

"What's the matter?" he asked feebly of the man who was closing the doors.

"Gone ten," the fellow said shortly, and turned out all the lights.

Scrooge felt sure that the second mince-pie had given him indigestion, and that he was in a dreadful dream. He seemed to fall into a deep gulf of darkness, in which all was blotted out. When he came to himself again it was Christmas Day, and the people were walking about the streets.

Scrooge, somehow or other, found himself among them. They smiled and greeted one another cheerfully, but it was evident that they were not happy. Marks of care were on their faces, marks that told of past troubles and future anxieties. Scrooge heard a man sigh heavily just after he had wished a neighbour a Merry Christmas. There were tears on a woman's face as she came down the church steps, all in black.

"Poor John!" she was murmuring. "I am sure it was the wearing cark of money troubles that killed him. Still, he is in heaven now. But the clergyman said in his sermon that heaven was only a pretty fairy tale." She wept anew.

All this disturbed Scrooge dreadfully. Something seemed to be pressing on his heart.

"But," said he, "I shall forget all this when I sit down to dinner with Nephew Fred and my niece and their young rascals."

It was late in the afternoon; four o'clock and dark, but in capital time for dinner. Scrooge found his nephew's house. It was as dark as the sky; not a window was lighted up. Scrooge's heart grew cold.

He knocked and knocked again, and rang a bell that sounded as faint and far as if it had rung in a grave.

At last a miserable old woman opened the door for a few inches and looked out suspiciously.

"Mr. Fred?" said she. "Why, he and his missus have gone off to the Hotel Splendid, as they call it, and they won't be home till midnight. They got their table six weeks ago! The children are away at Eastbourne."

"Dining in a tavern on Christmas Day!" Scrooge murmured. "What terrible fate is this? Who is so miserable, so desolate, that he dines at a tavern on Christmas Day? And the children at Eastbourne!"

The air grew misty about him. He seemed to hear as though from a great distance the voice of Tiny Tim, saying, "God help us, every one!"

Again the Spirit stood before him. Scrooge fell upon his knees.

"Terrible Phantom!" he exclaimed. "Who and what art thou? Speak, I entreat thee."

"Ebenezer Scrooge," replied the spirit in awful tones.

THE GLORIOUS MYSTERY

"I am the Ghost of the Christmas of 1920. With me I bring the demand note of the Commissioners of Income Tax!"

Scrooge's hair bristled as he saw the figures. But it fell out when he saw that the Apparition had feet like those of a gigantic cat.

"My name is Pussyfoot. I am also called Ruin and Despair," said the Phantom, and vanished.

With that Scrooge awoke and drew back the curtains of his bed.

"Thank God!" he uttered from his heart. "It was but a dream!"

THE GLORIOUS MYSTERY

CONJURING TIME

CONJURING time, I suppose, is getting near. Elegant and slender gentlemen, with pale faces and distinguished black moustaches—I do not know why all good wizards are like this, but they are—are already being engaged to help our Christmas merriment. Some of them are thinking out and practicing in advance new and amazing tricks; I should not wonder if some of them had decided that rabbits were *demodes,* and that beavers must be produced from hats this Christmastide. But, anyhow, the magicians are making ready for those astonishing contradictions of the natural order of things which we call conjuring. And the good time that draws near will see their deeds. Old Robinson, old grandfather Robinson, pink with port and good nature at the children's party, is wholly certain that there is not a single guinea-pig in the pockets of his dress-coat. But the pale, dark man, with his sleeves ostentatiously drawn back, will walk across the room, bow with exquisite politeness, and saying: "Excuse me, sir, but I rather think they are homesick," will draw two engaging cavies from the very pockets in question. So Jones will discover with dubious emotions that his presentation gold watch has become a dormouse, and Smith minimus—aged nine—will bend his mighty intellect to the task of discovering by what power streams of varicoloured fire shoot suddenly from the magician's fingers.

And, in fact and in short, the usual conjuring tricks will be performed to the delight and entertainment of the usual Christmas parties; and good luck and good will both to the bewilderer and the bewildered. But what I am wondering is this: has anybody yet perceived the profoundly philosophical character of this Christmas game? I doubt it. It is just like pantomime.

I once went to a Lyceum pantomime and met Aristotle at the back of the dress circle—though nobody would believe me. He showed me, in eloquent Greek, that pantomime is the most philosophical kind of drama. "For," said he, "in this drama under consideration one dressed as a woman of middle age, whom we may rather suspect to be a man, declares that she has a friend who drinks soup with a sponge, adding that this feigned friend of hers is not a rich lady. Now when this is heard for the first time there is a little laughter, and at the second speaking of it the laughter grows greater, at the third saying the whole theater rocks, and when this gnomic utterance issues for the fourth time those present are possessed as it were with a Bacchic ecstasy of mirth, having entered into that state which I would almost call divine, where essences are eternal and the laughter of the gods is undying." I reported all this faithfully, but nobody seems to have believed it, and I had never a word of thanks from the Brothers Melville.

Yet so it is, and so it is with conjuring! The conjurer has been demonstrating for long years the truth which the old alchemists declared in their manner, which modern science is just beginning to apprehend. Read Robertus de Fluctibus—otherwise Robert Flood—read Bohme, read Law. You will be convinced that the universe was originally *fluid,* or one might rather say, plastic. At men's desire it would assume any shape; the mountains would become lakes, the seas, deserts; the diamond would dissolve into immortal wine. All this happy state ended on a certain dreadful event of which the theologians tell us: the world hardened, became rigid, obstinate; a rock remained a rock whatever you said to it; and if it hit you, it hurt.

It was only the conjurers—and a few other less entertaining people—who kept the old tradition alive. Now, of these very late days, science is beginning to get a faint gleam of the truth; that all things are one; that there is no particular reason why lead should not be turned into gold; that the atom, the smallest conceivable bit of material substance, is really a sort of stellar system on a minute scale, with a central sun and revolving worlds about it. When I was a lad I spent a good many months in groping amongst very odd books in a very old, mouldy garret in Catherine Street. In one of

them, a parchment quarto of the sixteenth or early seventeenth century, I found the sentence: "In every grain of
wheat there lies hidden the soul of a star." There you have
it; there is only one substance, and there is no reason why
anything should not turn into something else at a moment's
notice: if only you have the transmuting word, that is, if you
are a conjurer.

The conjurer has been telling us all this, if we had only
paid attention, for a very long time. Christmas after Christmas he has been demonstrating that it is the easiest thing in
the world for a pocket handkerchief to turn into a rabbit, and
that a cigarette case can become three white mice, and a gold
watch a very pretty little dormouse. That old, pink, portwiny
Robinson, of whom we were speaking, found, as we have
seen, that he was inaccurate when he thought that his pockets
were empty; emptiness, the conjurer showed him, was merely
a term for guinea-pigs, and it may be Peruvian guinea-pigs.
Of course, there have been people like the tiresome old lady
in "Cranford," who try to explain how it is done out of the
Encyclopedia; but we all know that this is nonsense.

And, just by the way, there is a capital trick, very
simple, that quite a number of people can perform without
any previous instruction. And it always gets roars of laughter—and, oddly enough, floods of happy tears. You remember old Jack, with whom you were "up" at Oxford in '80.
He has got on tremendously; he is a rector, he had a "living"
of £180 a year, a wife, and nine children. Well, you take a
Yorkshire ham, and a pork-pie as big as a tea-tray, and a box
of rare cigars, and a dozen of old port, and so forth, and you
put them all into a common hamper and direct it to old
Jack; and send a cheque for a hundred pounds by post, with
a word or two about the old days and screwing up the Dean
in his rooms at three o'clock one bright morning. Roars of
laughter! The joke is on old Jack, as the Americans say.
For he doesn't get a single one of these things. They all turn
on the way into old remembrance and loving kindness.

This is one of the best of simple parlour tricks.

LA DIVE BOUTEILLE

MR. TILLEY, who is a fellow and lecturer of King's College, Cambridge, and has undertaken the writing of this monograph on the great prophet of encyclopædic learning,* should know, amongst other things, that Geomany does not mean "divination of earthquakes." Let him read on this point the story of Aladdin; and then a whole library of books which will teach him how the Points are cast, the Twelve Figures obtained and placed in the Twelve Houses, and how the Judgment is formed.

And the book as a whole? Well: it is rather difficult to be quite fair. Let it be said at once, and with all frankness, that it is the very work to be consulted by anyone who wants to be well instructed in the Known Facts concerning Rabelais. The mythology of Rabelais has so long held the field; the man—one of the greatest men that ever lived—has so long been represented as a kind of learned buffoon, as the utterer of apocryphal wills, of preposterous death-bed phrases; by the malevolent Catholic as an Enemy of the Faith, by the malevolent Protestant as a monster of shameless indecency, that it is a relief to have the cold facts and the true public character of the Grand Pantagruel coolly and correctly exposed. Mr. Tilley has searched his authorities, sifted his evidence with an admirable impartiality; he shows us an excellent if rather dull personality, which is no doubt a very faithful representation of the external Rabelais as he seemed to his friends and contemporaries. He who reads Mr. Tilley's monograph will no longer harbour in his soul the Rabelais of phantasmagoria; the picture of the dissolute, runaway, drunken friar, who prostituted great talents to the service of lechery and wine-bibbing, who wrote the most "indecent" book that has ever been written. The grave humanist that

---

* *Francois Rabelais.* By Arthur Tilley, M.A.

was known to princes, doctors, cardinals, scholars of the sixteenth century is revived in those pages. Holywell Street is
no more; but Holywell Street is scattered abroad, not with
any advantage to the common decency. If Mr. Tilley's book
should have the effect of banishing the "Works of Rabelais"
from the modern, scattered, principality of Holywell; if we
are to be wearied no longer by the appearance of the Gargantua and Pantagruel beside "Maria Monk," "Gay Life in
Paris," and "Aristotle's Works," then Mr. Tilley will have
deserved well of the literary commonwealth. For, of course,
the right faith is that there is more true theology in Rabelais
than in all the works of all the elaborate idiots who have
written "Plants of the Bible," "Birds of the Jordan," "Lessons from the Kings," "Talks on the Judges," for the last
hundred years; there is more theology in Rabelais than in all
the reams of twopenny morality that have so foully and
foolishly embroidered and defiled the great texts of mystery.
It is doubtful whether the great Coleridge really understood
the true ethos of Pantagruelism; but he understood enough of
it to know that if Rome and Geneva could really comprehend
the message, then Rome and Geneva would be alike dumb-
founded.

Such being the work, it is well to have the facts of the
writer's life, his character so far as it appears in his external
history, coolly and accurately displayed for us; and Mr.
Tilley has certainly done this mechanical part very well.
More facts may be discovered, but it is unlikely that this
history of Rabelais will ever become out of date. The circumstances of his father's life are duly discussed; it is shown
that he was neither a taverner nor an apothecary, but an
advocate; the probabilities as to the exact place of the writer's
birth are learnedly weighed; it is shown that the scenes
which he must have known in boyhood appear, exalted and
glorified, in the great books. Then we have the question as
to the place of his novitiate in the Franciscan Order, his
transference to the Benedictines, the matriculation at Mont-
pellier, medical practice, literary work, wanderings in France,

journeyings abroad; in fine, all the history of Francois Rabelais, so far as it has been discovered and rediscovered, is told in Mr. Tilley's book, plainly, dully, distinctly. One trusts that he will have rid the English mind for ever of its mad conception of an East End hooligan in a monk's robe, that he has dissociated finally Francois Rabelais from the Drink Curse: that even booksellers will cease to catalogue the Gargantua and Pantagruel under the heading *Facetiae*. One is a little disappointed that an authority of Mr. Tilley's evident industry and accuracy shuld have not investigated a little more closely the traditional Gargantua of French folklore; it would be interesting, for example, to know whether anyone has attempted a Celtic etymology of the name; the two first syllables certainly suggest a Cymric origin. But perhaps this task had best be omitted; for if the word were shown to be pure Celtic we should have young Wales proving that the works of Rabelais are to be reckoned among the many great masterpieces of Welsh literature. Mr. Tilley says, by the way, that stories relating to Gargantua are "comparatively rare" in Touraine. The writer of this article remembers being shown in Touraine a field over which huge rocks were scattered; he was told that Gargantua had once passed that way, and being annoyed by some tiny pebbles in his shoes, had shaken them out on the land in question. The writer's informant was certainly not a man of letters; but, of course, the tradition may have been of literary and not pre-Rabelaisian origin. However, these are trifles.

It is when we cease to consider facts and dates and such matters that Mr. Tilley becomes tiresome and quite ineffectual. His account of Rabelais' work, of his philosophy, of his art, has about as much to do with the real things as an analysis of Paley has to do with the eternal mysteries of the Catholic Faith. *Sic probatur.* Mr. Tilley is dealing with the Fourth Book, the book which treats of the setting out of the Pantagrueline Company on the great Voyage and Quest of the Oracle of the Dive Bouteille. To illustrate this book our commentator has given us a careful analysis of the state of geographical knowledge in Europe from 1492 to 1550. In 1492, he says, Columbus practically discovered the American continent. In 1497 Vasco da Gama completed the work which Bartolomeo Diaz had begun, reaching India by the Cape of Good Hope. In 1513 Vasco Nunez de Balboa saw the Pacific Ocean stretched at his feet. In 1521 Ferdinand de Magellan had sailed through the straits which bear his name. There are thirteen pages of this; and the dissertation ends as follows:

> We may, then, with tolerable confidence, accept the identification and regard the Fourth Book as being, amongst other things, a noble monument to one of the most adventurous Frenchmen of his age, who died fighting against his country's foes.

Quite so: and the Pickwick may be regarded as being, amongst other things, a curious museum of legal practice in the 'thirties of the nineteenth century. Let us investigate the nature of the instrument known as a *cognovit* (an ill-bird that came home to roost at The Spaniards) ; let us enquire as to the method of keeping that book from which were read the words "Capias Martha Bardell"; above all, let us identify Mr. Justice Stareleigh.

Nor is Mr. Tilley more satisfactory when he proceeds to direct exegesis. In the first place he commits the capital error of looking at Rabelais through the glass of a literal morality; he considers Pantagruel, Panurge, and Brother John as if they were "characters" in a modern novel. He begs pardon for his author's grossness; it is inexcusable, he says, it is a blot on his work, it has brought on the book the penalty of comparative neglect; no great work is read so little. And again: Mr. Tilley explains the philosophy of the final chapters of the last book, of the great symbol of the Holy Bottle:

> Drinking, not laughing, is declared to be the special property of man, and by drinking the priestess primarily means acting.

Now, there is no space in the columns of a weekly paper to

expound all the heights and depths of the great Pantagrueline Philosophy, which has been so abundantly and completely veiled from the eyes of the lecturer at King's. But one or two points may be stated with some distinctness; and firstly we may declare, firmly and clearly, that Pantagruel, Panurge, and Brother John are *not* characters in a novel. All the analysis of their virtues and their failings, their shrewdnesses and stupidities in which Mr. Tilley indulges is nothing more or less than sheer nonsense. If we once begin on this false track we are lost, and worse than lost, we come inevitably to utter destruction—in a Rabelaisian sense. For, let us consider: accepting Pantagruel as the ideal of a Wise and Virtuous Prince, how are we to bear his taking into his employ and special favour one of the most cowardly, mean, spiteful, treacherous, murderous, filthy and profligate scoundrels that ever breathed? That is Panurge, regarded from the "serious" standpoint; and it is to be noted, by the way, that Brother John, another associate of the ideal prince, applauds with much heartiness one of Panurge's cruellest tricks. But it is clear that a really virtuous prince would not have such miscreants for friends and counsellors; and it follows that we must quite put on one side this view of the personages of the Rabelaisian Epic as "characters." They are in reality something much more subtle; they are symbols. We have said that it is doubtful whether S. T. C. had really grasped the full significance of the mythos; but he certainly saw many things which are dark to Mr. Tilley. He described Panurge as "the pollarded man," the man who was all Understanding and no Reason; and, with reserves, this interpretation may be accepted; though Coleridge's explanation of Rabelais' reasons for adopting such a symbolism—that it would not have been safe to tell the truth as to the Reason and Understanding in any other way—is, doubtless, nonsense. The full truth, however, is, probably, somewhat as follows. Pantagruel, Panurge, and Brother John are not three men: they represent an analysis of man, of humanity. It is necessary, of course, to remember that Rabelais was not a consistent artist or a consistent philosopher. It is doubtful whether he was wholly conscious of the message that he was delivering; and so while there are parts of his work which are little more than selections from the commonplace book of a sixteenth century humanist, there are others which follow closely enough the lines of the heroic romances which he imitated and parodied. But taking the scheme of the Pantagrueline Chronicles as a whole, it may well be that the three chief "characters" are the report of a vision of man. Pantagruel is the "overman," the being of pure spirit whose head is in the clouds while his feet touch the earth; he is the image of the eternal things that are in men; he is exalted and yet obscure, not very far removed from Divinity itself. And of this high personage it may be said truly enough that he harbours strange companions and wastrel counsellors: Panurage the intellect, and Brother John the hearty animal nature; it is on voyages and quests with these dubious fellows that the High Prince goes forth; and while Pantagruel meditates the serene vision of the mysteries his attendant rascals break in with their blackguardly and disreputable adventures of mind and body; it is so, and it always has been so since the soul of man lapsed from its estate of Paradise. Mr. Tilley, as a Master of Arts and a Fellow and Lecturer of King's is (doubtless) aware that the Serpent did not ascend beyond Daath in the Tree of Life; hence the position of Pantagruel will be clear to him. *Nov. 16, 1907.*

SANCHO PANZA AT GENEVA

THERE is a true story of a curate. He served a church in Northampton, and was talking to a smart young boot-maker, who was also a Wesleyan. The bootmaker allowed that Peter and Paul were gifted men, but he would not admit that they were, in any respect, to be classed with the great Wesley. "Look at our numbers," he said, "Peter and Paul between them didn't make so many converts, I know." Then in answer to some questions of the curate's: "Oh, the Ordinance, you mean? Yes, I don't trouble much about that. I daresay it was all very well for a lot of ignorant fishermen: I'm a foreman in a boot factory myself."

It should be mentioned that "the Ordinance" in Dissent-ing phraseology signifies the Holy Eucharist, commonly called the Mass; and this being understood it is interesting to read an eighteenth-century hymn on the Eucharist, from which the following verses may be quoted:

> Victim Divine, thy grace we claim
> While thus thy precious Death we show;
> Once offered up, a spotless Lamb,
> In thy great temple here below,
> Thou didst for all mankind atone,
> And standest now before the throne.
>
> We need not now go up to heaven
> To bring the long-sought Saviour down;
> Thou art to all already given,
> Thou dost e'en now thy banquet crown;
> To every faithful soul appear,
> And show thy real Presence here.

The hymn was written by Charles Wesley, and reflects, faith-fully enough, the Eucharistic teaching of John Wesley, the founder of the Methodist Society. In the same connection it is curious to note the prophecy of John Wesley that when the

Methodists left the Church of England, God would leave them.

On the face of it, then, it seems odd that the late Thomas Champness, who was evidently a most amiable and excellent man according to his dim lights, should have called himself a "Methodist" and a "Wesleyan." It would be quite singular if "Dr." Clifford and Mr. Campbell were to describe themselves as "Laudian Divines" or "Cavalier Clergy"; but the gulf between the teaching of Laud and "Dr." Clifford is certainly no greater than the gulf between the teaching of the Wesleys and the teaching of modern "Wesleyans." However, this is a point of more or less domestic interest; and if it pleases a sect of nebulous pietists to label themselves with the name of a High Churchman of the eighteenth century, perhaps no great harm is done, it being clearly understood that the "Methodist" of today has long departed from the method of the Wesleys. One is informed by one's lady friends that nobody is taken in by such terms as "sateen" and "flannelette."

There is little to be said about this "Life-Story" ("The Life Story of Thomas Champness," Charles H. Kelly). Thomas Champness, as has been noted, was a good man according to his lights; he was "converted," became a local preacher, was a missionary in Africa, returned, went on circuit, founded a mission called Joyful News, went to prison as a Passive Resister, died and was buried in the congenial soil of Lutterworth, under the shadow of the Wycliffe Memorial. Here are the notes of an early sermon by him:

> I. Joash, a promising young man, 2 Chron. xxiv.
>   (1) His attention to the advice of his servants.
>   (2) His zeal for the house of God.
>
> II. His fall.
>   (1) Began to keep bad company, 17.
>   (2) Neglected the house of God, 18.
>   (3) Hardened himself against reproof, 19.
>   (4) Became ungrateful, 20-22.
>   (5) Punishment, 24.

THE GLORIOUS MYSTERY

III. **Lessons to be learned from him.**
    (1) That early promise is often blighted (guilt and innocence).
    (2) That we should pay attention to the advice of those who
        are older than we.
    (3) Shun bad company.
    (4) Never neglect the house of God.

      To accomplish this get our hearts changed.

It is all about as inspiring a message as the advice of Polonius
to Laertes, and has about as much to do with real Christianity. It does not *quite* say, "If you would be respectable
and successful in life, it is absolutely necessary to be religious,"
but it comes very near to proclaiming that great evangel. One
remembers the old-fashioned geography -books which pointed
out that any traveller could distinguish between a Protestant
country and a Papist country, because Protestant lands were
always rich and comfortable. Protestants live on roast beef,
plenty of it; Papists on potatoes, frogs, and macaroni.
Protestants are always warmly housed, whereas Papists are
often almost as badly off as the foxes and the birds of the air,
which have only holes and nests. It is all very quaint, but its
chief curiosity lies in the fact that this squalid worship of
prosperity, comfort, and worldly success, is taught by people
who dare to claim the sanction of the New Testament for
their system; who have, indeed, the grotesque and sublime
impertinence to declare themselves "Scriptural" Christians
par excellence. The falsity and the impudence of this claim
are not matters for elaborate argument; we know the company that Christ loved to keep, the wastrels, the Bohemians,
tavern-haunters, harlots, of the Jewish Society—everybody
and anybody who might be free from the deadly taint of
respectability. We know, too, the precepts as to considering
the lilies and taking no thought for the morrow, the absolute
prohibition of all that savoured of worldly prudence, the all
but hopeless condemnation of the well-to-do and successful.
A humorist once told the tale of an old gentleman called
Primrose, whose name became an obsession to him, till at last
he fancied he resembled the flower in question and took to

sitting about the hedgerows (as he fancied) "in clumps."
This is a comic picture enough; but it is not so comic as the
idea of a dissenting shopkeeper taking the lilies as his guide
through life.   But how extraordinary the position of these
people is.   Suppose that after the end of a great career Sancho
Panza had suddenly proclaimed that *he* was in reality Don
Quixote; and that the true principles of knight errantry con-
sisted in keeping a whole skin and bones unbroken, in sleeping
under snug shelter, in eating two enormous meals a day, in
having a very comfortable sum put by in a capacious wallet,
and above all, in cherishing an utter disbelief in and contempt
for all enchantments, magic balsams, faery barks, thaumaturgic sages, and the whole universe of mystery and wonder.
It is an extravagant notion, but it is no bad analogy of what
has happened in the field of religion.   Of course we should
not have been in the least astonished if Sancho had stoutly
maintained that his master was mad and that knight-errantry
was nonsense; but it is a little too much when *he* pretends to
be the original adorer of Dulcinea.   And yet for three centuries Sancho has been bellowing that he, and he alone, is the
true mirror of chivalry, that he alone is the faithful and exact
follower and disciple of Amadis and King Arthur.   And
many people believe him, though his fat belly and greasy
chops are only too manifest; but then many people believe that
the Puritans of the sixteenth century, who made the recita-
tion of the Book of Common Prayer a penal offence, with
slavery as its sanction, were apostles of tolerance, and many
people believe that Oliver Cromwell, who abolished the
House of Commons and governed England by martial law,
was the founder of our popular liberties.   The upholders of
the old factory system (child slavery in the most ghastly
form) were all "Liberals"; and one thinks of an ancient
prophet who foresaw a day when the Churl should no longer
be called Liberal.   *Jam noli tardare,* we cry, looking for the
coming of that day; for then, no doubt, King Arthur will
come forth from Avalon and the Good Knight will ride in

his train, and Sancho's horrible masquerade will be ended for ever.

For, of course, the real truth is that Protestantism is a revolt against Christianity. This proposition, which is self-evident, would once have seemed highly absurd to the "many people" whose sapience and perspicacity we have just considered; but within the last few years, especially within the last year, even the typical blockhead called "the man in the street," has begun to see that there is "something in it." Of course the signs have never been wanting to those who cared to look; it was Luther who, finding that St. James the Apostle was decidedly not a Lutheran, pronounced his Epistle to be "of straw." Servetus and Socinus, too, were early products of the Protestant Reformation, and there were tendencies among the "Reformed" in France which were not exactly evangelical. Later, one notes that the Presbyterian congregations planted in England in the seventeenth century lapsed wholesale into Unitarianism, while in New England Calvinism went the same way, till it deliquesced into the vague spirit of Emerson. It has long been notorious that the Protestantism of the Continent of Europe generally is either negligible, or else "Liberal," which is a polite way of saying Non-Christian. The signs were many; but it is only within the last few months that Ichabod has been inscribed on the portal of the City Temple, while an acute journalist has discovered that the "New Theology" is the Reformation come home to roost. It will soon become absolutely clear that Protestantism is the negation of the vital principles, of the whole character of Christianity—that is to say, the negation of beauty, wonder, mystery, imagination, the negation of all that raises man above the level of the brutes, the abjuration of high heaven itself. It is not a recurrence of Paganism, but to something infinitely worse than Paganism in its lowest form—for Paganism had mysteries—it is a recurrence to the Pre-Adamite world, to the state of the beast-man before it had received the quickening.

June 8, 1907.

THE GLORIOUS MYSTERY

THE MORNING LIGHT

A FEW weeks ago a well-known daily paper had two
remarkable paragraphs, the one following immediately
on the other in such a fashion that total lack of humour on
the part of the assistant-editor may reasonably and safely be
inferred. The first paragraph sounded a well-known note—
the backward condition of Spain. Those poor benighted
Spaniards! With "mineral resources" expressly designed by
the Almighty to be exploited on the Stock Exchange; with
metal teeming in the earth, awaiting the touch of the company promoter to bless the world; with such bright examples
as Johannesburg in Africa and the Black Country in England
before them; these wretched Spaniards will do nothing. As a
consequence, of course, a great and good nation like the
United States takes their colonies away, business men, practical, hard-headed men refuse to love them, and they have to
eat common bread and drink common wine instead of revel-
ling on Chicago canned goods and "substitutes."

The paragraph in question did not deal with the symp-
toms; it went straight to the cause. The Spaniards are
wretched, it seems, because elementary education is so shock-
ingly neglected; the statistics given are terrible, they sound
like a nightmare which might beset a permanent official at
the Board of Education after he had eaten pork chops for
supper, from which he would awake with a groan of horror
and a sigh of relief, as he realised that after all it was only
an ugly dream. Good; we know why Spain is unhappy and
backward — there are no Council Schools. One is not
surprised: how can a people be fit for anything if the children
are not taught French, Physiology, Euclid—and the Violin?

And then, when one is feeling all right, and comfortable,
and proud of one's country, and glad one is Progressive, and
enlightened, and Liberal, and all that sort of thing—then on

the very tail of paragraph No. 1 comes paragraph No. 2, and paragraph No. 2 is a wail of despair over London hooliganism, over the badly behaved, loutish, vicious, ignorant, criminal young yahoos whom London turns out by the thousand. They are a hopeless race, it seems; there is no doing anything with them; they are a pest, and an ugly pest too.

Poor London marries young. A, let us say, was the child of an uneducated costermonger who knew nothing about the duodenum, and, if he played the fiddle, did so in a thoroughly amateurish, uninstructed manner after a course of wholly irregular lessons from an alcoholic person of Irish extraction. This ancestral costermonger could not have parsed the simplest sentence in the tongue of our vivacious neighbour, the Gaul. But A, his child, born in 1860, is destined to a happier state of things. He is caught by a kind inspector, and goes to the Board School. He is a father in 1878, and little B, his offspring, starts bravely as an Infant and attains to the heights of knowledge of the mystic seventh standard. B, too, leads his blushing bride to the altar at an early age, and C is "the consekens o' the manoover." C was born in 1898; he is now an elementary scholar and—it seems from paragraph No. 2—an elementary hooligan. And he is the third in descent to profit by the nostrum which would be the salvation of Spain, by the system, which having been practised for thirty-seven years, has succeeded in turning out a race of brutish savages! One of those two paragraphs should certainly have been "held over" for a day or two.

The fact is that it is quite time to recognise a great truth. This is, that you cannot make expert surgeons by the free distribution of cases of operating-instruments, accompanied, perhaps, by little books—"The Bistoury and how to Use It," "Half Hours with Great Operators," etc., etc. The amputating knife is a capital thing in skilled hands; but if the hands be unskilled and unfit it is a useless, even a dangerous toy. And, in like manner, instruction *qua* instruction, without certain qualifications, is no doubt useless, and perhaps poisonous. Everybody who had any sense knew this long ago, but the advanced, the progressive, the scientific went gaily into the educational adventure, with the result that they have spent a great deal of money, bothered a great many children, and effected nothing or worse than nothing— according to the showing of paragraph No. 2. After all, there were dons and schoolmasters in plenty before 1870; there were not lacking examples of the truth that a man may be highly, even elaborately instructed and remain a senseless ill-mannered, unintelligent boor, profiting as much by his knowledge of two great literatures as a wandering hog profits by the beauty of the landscape through which he strays. And this being so, it should have been evident to the Board School projectors that if Oxford and Cambridge, Harrow and Eton gave such results, it was not very likely that the Board Schools, presided over by Mr. M'Choakumchild and Bradley Headstone would do much better. However, they insisted that with compulsory education the Golden Age would come with a rush, and we have seen that there are still people who discourse this kind of folly; even when at the next moment they set down the evidence that it is folly, and folly of the most offensive sort.

And in spite of this evidence we have the authoress of "Labour and Childhood" writing such a sentence as this:

But the morning light is even now tearing aside the shadows of ecclesiastical authority and in the ear of Demos a fresh cry rings, fresh and new as from the lips of Morning: "What is Man? And what can you make of him?"

We have seen what education, in the authoress's sense, can make of him; it can make him something considerably lower than a badly behaved ape. We know, too, what the person called Demos does if he is left to his own devices. Aristophanes tells us a good deal about this unhappy individual; and there are some rather valuable notes on his little ways in *Henry VI, Part 2, Julius Caesar and Coriolanus*. His great achievement, however, is the United States of America. There are no shadows of ecclesiastical authority there. The morning light has torn aside the shadows to some purpose in that peaceful, happy land. One hopes that Demos likes it; but one gathers from his Socialist friends that he is not altogether enjoying himself.

Mr. Bray knows much better. "The Town Child" is not only a most intelligent book; it is highly entertaining, and written with a pretty and vivacious spirit that is not often found in works that deal with education. Take, for example, his instance of morality carried to the heroic pitch: the child, he says, may be told to go and speak kindly to his maiden aunt! There is not a dull page in a book which might so easily have been very dull indeed; and nobody who desires to talk sense on the education question—burning now, and likely to be white hot before very long—can afford to neglect this most admirable treatise. For Mr. Bray has cleared his mind of cant; he has nothing to say about Demos or "the lips of morning." He has studied the facts of his case, and has studied them in the light of first principles.

Mr. Bray is quite clear on the main point: he sees that the imparting of information on various subjects is, by itself, and in itself, a useless, absurd, and dangerous practice. What is wanted is not instruction but the production of an atmosphere, and our author is absolutely sound on the way to produce this atmosphere. "Take the children to High Mass as often as possible," he says, practically, "and whatever you do, see that they believe in fairies." It would be quite impossible to better this advice; and Mr. Bray very properly points out that the child who believes in fairies is infinitely nearer to the truth of things than the child who has been brought up on "scientific" principles. All this of course is obvious; but what a joy to find that anybody who is concerned with education recognises the obvious.

For, if we are Anglicans we must not be too proud. The English Church had control of the schools for many years, and rightly, since the English Church paid for the land, paid for the bricks and mortar, paid for the master and mistress. But what use was made of this great opportunity?

THE GLORIOUS MYSTERY

One fears a very bad one. To appeal to the excellent author of "The Town Child" once more; the Bible was read *ad nauseam,* read from the dullest, dreariest, stupidest point of view; sometimes as a forbidding code of negative morals, sometimes for the sake of the dates of the Kings of Israel and Judah, sometimes as a collection of queer stories. The Church built the school, paid the mistress—and taught her children that it was naughty to steal, the dimensions of King Solomon's Temple, and the tales of Jonah in the Bulrushes and Moses in the Lion's Den. The children's teeth are still on edge: through false priests and wicked bishops who pretended that this farce was the faith of the Holy Catholic and Apostolic Church. One must beg pardon: the children learned more: they learned how to shriek all the most maudlin Hymns in "Hymns Ancient and Modern" married to "music" that would disgrace a penny gaff. No! the only attitude that befits the English Church is one of profound penitence for a shamefully misused opportunity, and of a humble resolve to do better for the future, leaving all cant of "Bible Teaching" to "Dr." Clifford, and to the gang of imbeciles who follow his lead.

Mr. Bray is right in almost everything that he says, and his testimony is the more valuable in that he speaks from a quite independent standpoint. It is not the business of the reviewer to go behind the title-page, to know more than is written. Mr. Bray pleads for High Mass for children not as a Catholic but as an observant human being; as one might suggest, speaking without prejudice as to any medical theory, that if you are thirsty, it is not a bad plan to drink. And who that has eyes to see, and something bearing some faint resemblance to a brain behind those eyes, can fail to note the deadly, all-consuming thirst that now burns and racks the race of men and children too. There are the wonderful ones, the superhuman race—Miss (or Mrs.) McMillan is of these—who see the thirst, who have seen the poor perishing ones given salt and water in repeated doses for the last thirty-seven years, who still dare to cry that more salt and water is all that is needed, only the salt must be of the very best quality.

And their answer comes from all quarters. It comes from the poor yahoos, from these ill-used wretches who have passed all the standards, who have learnt about the pancreas, who can construe the selected passages in French, and demonstrate the Bridge of Asses which they have been made to cross; from these wretched and horrible lads and girls who should be tasting of the rare wine of the world and know nothing better than a drench of four ale; from those poor lost children who are a horror by day and a terror by night, who year by year grow less human and more bestial as the "morning light" tears aside more shadows of authority, human and divine. The answer comes from the French Republic, as one waits for news of a fresh religious order despoiled, of a fresh swindle in the highest official circles. It comes from America, home of every fraud, of every poisonous adulteration, of every monstrous crime, of every crazy and drivelling superstition; it comes from the "lips of morning," from the lips of Mrs. Baker Eddy, from the lips of a thousand quacks and charlatans.

One hopes against hope for England; one hopes that this book of Mr. Bray's may have its due effect with the people who are besotted merely, not malignant. One can only say:

Exurgat Deus et dissipentur inimici ejus: et fugiant qui oderunt eum a facie ejus.
July 13, 1907.

THE WORLD TO COME

"THE AFTER LIFE," a pious, credulous, and amiable book, is interesting as serving to illustrate the existence of a persistent and widespread error. Mr. Buckle, the author, has, with all reverence and industry, gathered together the places in the old and new Testaments which bear on "the future life," and on the foundation of his texts he builds up a theory of eternal existence. It is well enough done, his essay, as far as it goes; and one cannot help feeling that he, and many other pious Christians, who think in the same mode as he, entirely miss the real point, the essence of the question in which they are so interested. It may sound odd enough: but the truth is that the saints, the adepts, are very little interested in "The After Life." One must not press the analogy too far—all analogies must be tenderly and judiciously treated—but if a man were enjoying an excellent luncheon at 2, he would think it just a little out of place, a little untimely, if some one began to expatiate on the amazing dinner they would all sit down to at 8:30. "Certainly," he might say, "I know. But why not wait till dinner-time?" No; the saint is not over-interested in the future; perhaps because he lives in the everlasting now. The imbeciles, the pack of gibbering ignoramuses who call themselves "Freethinkers," the people who have taken out letters of marque to discuss every subject of which they know nothing, who are ready to dash in with their free and easy solutions of questions which have perplexed all philosophy and all religion in every age, are constant, among many other follies, in representing the Catholic Faith as chiefly concerned with a vague hereafter, as wickedly indifferent to the goods and ills of the present earthly state. They talk of the saints, these impudent blockheads, as persons who view with indifference the sorrows of earth, while they look forward to a future of harp-playing. One forgives them the jokes about the harp—one does not expect an appreciation of the sublime symbolism of Music from the hooligans and larrikins of thought—but they might at least get their facts right. But perhaps it is beneath the dignity of "Free thought" to trouble itself with the mere technical detail of facts; your Freethinker cannot be bothered with the wretched dry-as-dust business of knowing anything accurately on any subject whatsoever. "Blether" is so much more "simple" and "big-hearted" and the rest of it. Of course there are many good Christians who think of this matter of eternity with Mr. Buckle: but one judges an art—and a religion—by the great masters, the supreme artists. And the great artists of sanctity are not over curious about "heaven"—because they are in it.

But here is another oddity. Let it be enunciated as a maxim that in certain matters it is unsafe to go beyond the curate at the Sunday School. One must confess that this sounds the extreme of hardy paradox; and yet it is undoubtedly true, and there is an illustration of this truth in the works of that profound and mystic Saint-Martin, the *Philosophe inconnu*. Saint-Martin is discoursing of the future life, and on the "title of our admission into the future regions," and he speaks as follows (I quote from the admirable "Life of Louis Claude de Saint-Martin," by Mr. A. E. Waite):

We cannot obtain a seat in our theatres unless we have taken the precaution to secure a ticket which admits us. This ticket is issued only under the seal of the manager; furthermore, unless we book our seats in advance, we risk being crushed in the crowd which is gathered at the doors waiting for tickets to be issued; there is even the chance that we may not get a seat at all. This emblem, altogether temporal and terrestrial, instructs us that we are here below for the purpose of purchasing a ticket of admission to the divine festivals; that if we neglect the precaution of securing this title we shall assuredly not enter into that gathering of delight and rejoicing; that we must not put off till the last moment this needful piece of prudence, having regard to the inconvenience to which such delay may expose us; that this precaution is the more easy to take because places for the sale of tickets may be found everywhere; that we are, hence, inexcusable if we do not provide ourselves accordingly, etc, etc.

[134]

THE GLORIOUS MYSTERY

It is a charming piece of fantasy, but after all what more is there in it than the curate's maxim: be good and you will go to heaven? The phraseology of Saint-Martin is more attractive than the curate's certainly, but the pith of the matter is the same in the one as in the other; and it is worth noting by the way that all splendour usually dwells in all simplicity. Bobby Brown of St. Juniper's Sunday School can have no better advice; nor can the most exalted of sages.

Of course there is a very large race, which has existed in all ages and in all countries, which knows a great deal more than the curate, which mocks at the lesson given to Bobby Brown. It is a race worth considering.

One comes sometimes in out-of-the-way country places on a certain horrid and deadly spot. Sometimes it is a barn-door on the verge of the wild land; sometimes it is in the heart of the dark wood. In some such place one sees victims of vengeance, set there to be a terror to ill-doers, ill being, for the moment, calculated according to the standard of the game-keeper. Here, crucified against the door or to the tree trunks, are the wretched criminals of the wood and the waste—the poaching cat, the owl, the adder, a dreadful and shocking spectacle. So in the history of the mind one sees the ghastly and unseemly bodies of those who have known better than the curate; a warning to us to do otherwise. And this sort of vermin is called Occultist. They are of all times and all ages; they performed of old their wretched Mumbo Jumbo Rites in all the dark holes of the earth as they perform them now. One may read with reverence and awe and religion the divine *Phaedo* of Plato; one bows the knee before the great assurance and high faith of Socrates as he drinks the hemlock most devoutly, resigning himself with joy to the everlasting compassions. *Anima naturaliter Christiana,* we may say, and perhaps an *ora pro nobis* were not so much amiss, and no very deadly error. But while Socrates was a-dying, Mumbo Jumbo was "initiating" at Samothrace, and filling simple Grecian skulls with sham science and sham religion, with an apparatus of nonsense which—so far as it tends anywhere—tends to make true religion an impossibility. It is the same everywhere; perhaps the state of "savagery" might be best defined as a state in which Mumbo Jumbo —or "Occultism'——has finally got the upper hand, in which a heap of observances, sometimes devilish, sometimes silly, often both, has overwhelmed the pure and shining light of the soul. In certain African tribes, it is said, there still lingers a vague rumor of the Most High, but the really Established Church is fetish, and preaches salvation by the sacrament of eating your deceased great-uncle's brains and entrails, compounded according to art.

So it was in the early days of Christendom. The great and high mystics St. John and St. Paul, the authors of such *dicta* as "Love one another" and "It is raised in power" were opposed by the grotesque rabble of the Gnostics, of the "knowing ones," by the church of insane delirium, which proclaimed the highest morality and prac- tised the most revolting vices. One has only to read the *Pistis Sophia* to see how deeply the gulf yawns between Christian Mysticism and Occultism, between High Wis- dom and barbarous gibberish, and perhaps there is no better way of demonstrating the ultimate identity of evil and nonsense that a study of the Gnostic sects, with their amu- lets, and Abraxas gems, and Abracadabras, and Æons, with the most extensive and peculiar information about heaven, and the most complete piggery on earth. Later on the Albigenses were the milk-and-water descendants of these malign lunatics, and the Albigenses have their descendants to-day, whom I will not mention, because their vote is a thing to reckon with. In a more direct line of descent from Gnosticism is the horrible, squalid and noisome im- posture known as Theosophy, which for the last twenty years or more has infested foolish drawing-rooms and (occasionally) foolish newspapers; accumulating a record of sham miracles, sham deities, sham gospels and of other things still more unsavoury, that is probably unequalled in the history of the folly and wickedness of the world. For Madame Blavatsky one had a certain tenderness, in spite of her flagrant impostures and the really devilish nature of much of her teachings. Her learning was humbug, her books were humbug, her signs and wonders were most impudent and arrant humbug—but, she was undoubtedly on the grand scale: she is not altogether unworthy of being mentioned in the Great Calendar of Quacks beside Joseph Balsamo, called Cagliostro. But for the later prophets of this Neo-Gnosticism, whether fugitives from justice or not, whether believers in the "Bacon Theory" or in some other nonsensical doctrine, whether found out in childish tricks or still undiscovered—for these, the "Low Tobies" of the canting crew, one can have nothing but undisguised contempt and dislike, not unmingled with the qualms of nausea. When directors of such companies as the "Hansard Union" come forward as the apostles of the "Ancient Wisdom Religion," it is time to cry "enough:" when women who have been associated for many years with the propaganda of the crudiest and silliest atheism deliver the Mahatmas' messages—then human speech fails and dies away. Memory is short enough, no doubt, but there are those still left who remember the "Fruits of Philosophy" Trial.

And it all comes of not minding the curate! Dr. Pusey was a learned curate—a learned, devout, orthodox, unilluminated man—and one has read the account of the wretched Mrs. Besant's conference with him. She began to vomit forth her blasphemies, and the Doctor replied: "Woman, remember that you are speaking of your Saviour and your Judge"—or some such words. "How illiberal, how narrow," says the precious man in the street, "how devoid of human sympathy, of Christ-like comprehension." And one knows the result of that disregarded warning; the years passed in the service of Old-street, of an idiotic but poisonous atheism: and then the new career

which must not be too precisely defined. She found a slip
of paper in her blotting-pad with something like: "Judge's
plan is right—follow him and stick," scrawled over it and
she assured the world on the faith of *that* that she had
received communications from the supernatural sphere. An
admirable journalist has told the whole story in "Isis very
much Unveiled"; it would be impossible to add anything
to that detestable and ridiculous tale, with its catastrophe
of detected cheats and quacks who just avoided the dock.
No: there are decidedly certain points on which it is not
safe to know more than the curate. We may improve his
manner, perhaps, but it is not wise to meddle with his
matter.

And the great artists of sanctity are, as I have said,
not over anxious about this question of the *vita venturi
saeculi*. It has been held by high mystics that there are
certain of the saints now on earth who enjoy a greater
bliss than certain of the saints who have passed beyond;
and it is most probable that this conjecture is well founded.
We have to deal with an experimental science, of extraordinary exactitude, the last experiments of which science
are made by very few indeed—the masters are always few
in every science and in every art. We are, of course,
liable to be vexed in our discussion of these matters by
the interruptions of those who "don't believe" in the saints
and think sanctity a pack of nonsense; and these interruptions again have their perfect analogy in the arts. A writer
in the *Daily Mail,* a week or two ago, spoke of Mr. Caine,
Miss Corelli and Mr. Crockett as "this fine galaxy"; and
we imagine that this person would be highly amused by
real literature if he ever saw it. The interruptions of the
ignorant are of very little consequence.

It is probable then that there are those still living who
have made the Great Experiment and have entered into
the possession of the eternal beauty, who see through the
material shapes of the world as through a thin veil, who
hear through our ugly and discordant voices the everlast-

ing song, the unending *pneuma,* who suffer no more from cold or heat or hunger or any sorrow. The old chronicler says of King Arthur that in this world he "changed his life," and it may be that a few who have not known fear have entered into Avalon in our days, have attained to the Holy Isle beyond the glassy floods.

July 27, 1907.

GOOD LITTLE BOOKS*

IT IS rather unfair, perhaps, to include the Bishop of
London's mission sermons under a title which is not
meant to indicate approval, for, within their limits, these
addresses contain plenty of good, practical advice, delivered
with a certain rather attractive earnestness. One notes, by
the way, however, that while gambling is denounced as a
great cause of evil, there is not the same insistence on the
radical evil of the whole commercial spirit. No doubt
gambling does bring a number of people to terrible grief;
but, compared with the horrible results of the factory system, it is the merest pin-prick on the body politic. The
foolish gambler is ruined; perhaps his family is ruined too;
it is very sad and a great pity. But what is such an affair
as this, what are dozens or hundreds of such affairs when
weighed in the scale against the existence of those blots
on humanity, Manchester and Sheffield, with ever-widen-
ing circles of ugliness, ruin, degradation, misery, and shame?
A boil may be tiresome enough; but, really, a patient in
the last stages of carcinoma would not be seriously affected
by such a trifle. "Principal Rainy" is a note on the life
of a very amiable man who rose to great distinction in
a very unimportant Scotch sect; if one is interested in
the points of variance between the "United Frees" and the
"Wee Frees" it must make capital reading. If one is not
so interested one is inevitably reminded of Dr. Johnson's

---

* *The Call of the Father.* By the Right Rev. Arthur F. Win-
nington Ingram, D.D., Lord Bishop of London. *Principal Rainy.* By
Robert Mackintosh, D.D. *The Silver Lining.* By J. H. Jowett, M.A.
Christus Redivivus. By S. Henry, B.A. *Old Testament Miracles in
the Light of the Gospel.* By A. Allen Brockington, M.A. *What
About the New Theology?* By W. L. Walker.

dictum as to the comparative merits of Derrick and Smart. "The Silver Lining" contains this passage:

What is the second promise of the evangel? "I will give him a white stone." This phrase was running through my brain when I was away for my holiday recently, and in passing along a pebble-strewn beach I picked up a white pebble. I looked at it very intently and inquisitively—and spiritually, in the hope that it would communicate something to me of the significance of the Apostle's figure. It was wonderfully pure; it was intensely hard; it was exceedingly smooth. My Lord will give me a "white stone." What is the significance of it? My interpretation was this: "I will endow thee with a character pure as a white stone that lies upon the beach, hard and tenacious as that stone, beautifully refined, with all obtrusive and painful angularities smoothed away. . . . Perfectly pure I will make thee—and hard!" Oh, not the hardness of insensitiveness, but the hardness of strength. Said one of my young fellows, speaking of another man, "His muscles are as hard as nails." That is the hardness we want in the spirit.

One has heard so much of the superiority of Protestant over Catholic oratory, that the passage quoted becomes quite interesting. "Christus Redivivus" is an oddly written book in praise of Christian optimism as opposed to Buddhist pessimism. On one page there are seventeen exclamation marks in twenty lines. "Old Testament Miracles," meaning to be persuasive, does not attempt to give any philosophical rationale of the events which we commonly call miraculous. A "miracle" may be defined as an extraordinary event or act, of very rare occurrence, the causes of which we do not understand. We do not in the least understand how it is that the human will can annul for the moment the law of gravitation, in the act of lifting the arm; but this event is of such common occurrence that we do not call it miraculous. But of course all the talk about "interfering" with the "laws of nature" is beside the mark; the "miracle" is simply the lower law giving way to the higher, and taken by themselves miracles are of little evidential value. It is credibly stated that certain Hindu fakirs can actually perform feats which are strictly miraculous—a rope is thrown into the air and remains rigidly suspended in space, a boy climbs up the rope, rope and boy vanish, and in a few moments the boy is seen running towards the spectators from a little distance off. Now, this is a miraculous event—it is miraculous if it be an effect of the process very loosely called hypnotism—but it proves nothing as to the truth or falsehood of the fakir's religious belief, whatever it may be. Such actions as these may very well be of the world of the *psyche,* not of the *pneuma;* they show, of course, that the old-fashioned materialism of the seventies was nonsense, but they may not show much more. "What about the New Theology?" asks Mr. Walker. The proper answer is "nothing whatever." A serious literary critic does not sit down to demonstrate the fact that Mr. Caine and Miss Corelli are not good writers; a student of painting does not indite a book to show that the photographs in the *Daily Views* are unworthy of a place beside the masterpieces of Velasquez, and a theologian, conscious of strange and unruly appetites, of a desire to read a little heresy by way of a change, does not go to the very ugly and barbarous building on or near the Holborn Viaduct. The Gnostics were as foolish and heretical as the "Templars," but there is a sort of picturesqueness about them—most of it due to the "delusion of antiquity" no doubt. Still, we cannot help feeling an interest in the sanitary appliances of prehistoric Crete, which we are unable even to simulate in the corresponding objects of modern Lambeth.

And all of these six volumes (with one doubtful exception) are "good little books," a title which one hopes has been taken in the sense intended, as implying more or less of contempt. For they are all *mesquins,* petty, mean; dealing with little things, little people, little thoughts or (worse still) with great things in a little way. And moreover (it is really the same truth put in a rather different fashion), in none of these books is there any sign that the writer understands in the smallest degree the real object of the religion which he so fervently champions. The nearest approach, oddly enough, is in the book which comes so close to absurdity, the book of the exclamation marks; but "Christus Redivivus" approximates to the right stand-point as melodrama approximates to romance. For the rest, we must frankly say that they are nought. They are not worse than such books usually are, they are better perhaps than hundreds of sermons which were preached last Sunday and will be preached next Sunday; and we merely single them out as a text on which to denounce and reprobate the great genus to which they belong. It is time that this sort of thing should be put a stop to; that the *Ars Artium,* the Art of the Great Experiment, should be no longer de-graded and made ridiculous in the eyes of all intelligent men by Mr. Feeble Goodygoodyman, with his passion for the obvious, the moralising moral, the everlasting common-place. A tenth-rate drawing-master in a fifth-rate provincial town does not venture to discuss the first principles of the art which he fails to adorn; or if he does venture he only gets laughed at. But there seems a vague sort of notion abroad that anybody who writes about religion is entitled to some kind of respect, as if the Great Matter which he is rendering absurd threw an aegis of protection over him. If AB scribbles rubbish about football he will probably hear of it pretty soon, and be sharply corrected by people who know better; but the Reverend AB can ladle out twaddle about the Epistles or the Penitential Psalms amid reverential silence, if not applause. Again we say it must be put a stop to; the final mysteries of the universe are of much greater consequence than football, and require the very best treatment that the highest minds can afford. Actors have a phrase about X who "can't act for nuts, but is very good to his dog!" Well, assuming this to be the case, X is not very likely to get an important engagement at a leading London theatre; and *simili modo* the Reverend X must be restrained from *his* very absurd and incompe-tent performances in a far higher part. Let him go on being "good" by all means; but goodness does not necessarily imply the *charisma* of prophecy.

For one class of book it is to feared that there is no remedy. Over England, Scotland, the United States, there are scattered at the present moment an enormous number of modern sects, some actively noxious, some silly, some harmless—more or less. Each has its own marks, though these may elude the casual observer; each oak-leaf on the tree, it is said, is to be distinguished from any and every other oak-leaf. So with the sects; there are doubtless distinctions, if one cares to observe them, between a Seventh Day Adventist and a Christadelphian; while a Plymouth Brother is again quite different from either. But there is one point common to all these varying sects, and that is that not one single one of the whole catalogue has, from any intellectual or spiritual standpoint, any existence at all. If two theologians were discussing some theological question and a third person said: "Oh, but the Baptists (or Independents, or Wesleyans, or Mormons, or Extotheenthians) think so and so on that point"—well, the theologians would lift their eyebrows and continue their discussion, being perfectly well aware that what the Baptist says is not evidence—so far as theology is concerned. Sandemanianism doesn't count, doesn't exist in the field of religion, though an admirable analytical chemist may be a Sandemanian. But the worst of it is that in the nature of things the Sandemanian cannot be expected to recognise the nullity of his formulas, his theological non-existence, and so we have a book about Principal Rainy and the United Free Church of Scotland, which is really no more than saying "nought times one are nought, nought times two are nought, nought times a hundred and forty-four thousand are nought," and so on to infinity. And the result is the same when the Non-ens is refuted in place of being applauded; the book about the "New Theology" is merely "nought from nought leaves nought." It might be possible to get something funny out of these nullities—a sort of "Alice in Wonderland" book might, perhaps, be made out of those City Temple phantoms—but the worst of it is these books never are funny. And yet they will continue; there shall never fail apparently, a "Memoir of the Reverend Alexander McCaw of Dunblather and Stillcracksie." It must, of course, be admitted that if Mr. McCaw, apart from his theological non-entity, had been a strong force in the political movements of his district, he might well be entitled to commemoration.

Then there is another and a deeper point. What does the popular (and unadmirable) hymn say? "He died to make us good," or some such phrase. This is the great and deadly error which is not far from pervading all western Christendom, which certainly pervades Anglo-Saxondom more or less completely. It is an absolutely false statement; the end of Christianity is not morality, nor anything remotely resembling morality. The error in question has always pervaded the quarrel called the Education question. The dissenting people have shown, or have tried to show, that boys who have not been taught the Apostles' Creed steal no more apples than the boys who are perfect in the Church Catechism: while the Church people have demonstrated , or think they have demonstrated, that where dogmatic theology is neglected men beat their wives madly and live and die for beer. Now this is *a* point, and an arguable one: but it is not *the* point, or at all events it should not be. We are not Christians in order that we may be good; we try to be good in order that we may be Christians: morality is one of the means by which we hope to attain the end; and the end is that perfect bliss which comes to the man who enters into the joyful law of conformity. Any man, be he Catholic bishop or be he schismatic preacher, who announces any other gospel but this and calls it Christianity, lies and knows he lies. Morality is no more the aim of Christianity than a knowledge of perspective and anatomy is the aim of painting, or a knowledge of grammar and spelling the aim of literature, or a knowledge of metre the end of poesy. He did *not* die to make us good; He died that He might restore a banished and wretched race to the pleasures and delights and beauties of the Lost Paradise: let him who preaches aught else be anathema. Hear the Divine Liturgy of St. James:

> Thou who didst make man from the earth after thine image and likeness: and didst give him the delight of Paradise . . . and lastly didst send forth into the world Thine Only-begotten Son, our Lord Jesus Christ, that He might come and renew and restore in us Thine image, *et cetera.*

Those who know these things know why the Law is spoken of in the New Testament as "beggarly elements:" the Law is what the alchemists call the gross work, the purging process by which the matter of the operation, that is the human spirit, is freed from its impurities and excesses of all sorts, that the final transmutation may be duly effected. The gold is for the chalice, made to be the splendid vessel of the Blessed Mysteries; who could be so foolish as to maintain that the final end of gold is the crushing machine and the furnace?

Yet, how widely is this extraordinary imbecility of mistaking the means for the end believed in. You may find it in the skulls of archdeacons and in the brains of poets. When Mr. Swinburne speaks of the pagan who swears that the Galilean shall not take away the laurel, the doves, and the pæan, or the breasts of the nymphs in the brake, he is manifestly labouring under this grave confusion, trusting in the Right Reverend Bishop Stiggins as an exponent of Christianity. The truth is that the veritable joys which are figured imperfectly by these symbols are to be attained in the Catholic Church and nowhere else; and the only object of the *askesis* is the attainment of the state of Paradise. One would think this no very difficult proposition; it does not seem very hard to understand that a man who wishes to relish the finer growths of the Medoc

[147]

must abandon the practice of habitually getting drunk on Plymouth gin—in some cases, if his palate be naturally delicate and sensitive he may have to abstain from Plymouth gin for good and all. The truth is obscured, one supposes, by the preaching which teaches satiation by not-drinking-gin; which seems to have forgotten the very existence of the rare wine of the kingdom. *Calix meus inebrians quam praeclarus est*; says the Psalmist—and our false prophets exhibit to us a ginger-beer bottle, and assure us that it is the true Sangraal. And Mr. Jowett says that the mystic white stone of the Apocalypse symbolises—a good character, hard as nails.

A sort of amiable penitentiary is the end of things according to this wretched school; but the deacon in the Rite of Malabar sings:

Open to me the gates of righteousness, O Thou Merciful One, whose door is open to penitents, who dost invite sinners to draw near to Thee; open to us, my Lord, the Gate of Thy Loves, that we may enter in and sing praises to Thee day and night. *Aug. 10, 1907.*

THE GLORIOUS MYSTERY

FAITH AND CONDUCT

[After publication of the foregoing review, the following reply was made by an anonymous critic.]

IT IS rather a shock to find that the Bishop of London does not "understand in the smallest degree the real object of the religion which he so fervently champions." Of another of the writers reprobated a reviewer recently said: "He has all Browning's sublime optimism and spaciousness in dealing with great and simple facts and beliefs." Can the Ethiopian so soon change his skin, or the leopard his spots? Then may he also turn into a Mr. Feeble Goodygoodyman "with a passion for the obvious, the moralising moral, the everlasting commonplace," who was accustomed to exhibit "rare humour and breadth of mind." But I wish to say a word about "another and a deeper point." Your reviewer considers that "He died to make us good" is the "great and deadly error which is not far from prevading all western Christendom." May not the error find its origin in the words of Christ and be perpetuated in one of the Catholic Creeds: "Who for us men, and for our salvation came down from heaven . . . and was crucified also for us under Pontius Pilate"? If "for our salvation" does not mean "to make us good," what does it mean? How can we "enter into the joyful law of conformity" except by becoming good? And surely it is a Catholic belief that we were made "members of Christ" before we consciously began to try to "follow the example of our Saviour." "Faith and conduct" is the Catholic order, not "conduct and faith," and we were made Christians in order that we might become Christian.

I am wondering also whether your reviewer considers his trite remarks about "miracle" and the Hindu fakir's juggling trick a "philosophical rationale of the events which we commonly call miraculous."

ONE OF THE GOODYGOODIES.

[To which Mr. Machen replied]

I am very much obliged to my correspondent for calling my attention to a certain *lapsus* of mine. My only defence is that, owing to various circumstances, the article on "Good Little Books" was written rather hurriedly—hence the slip in question. My mistake, of course, was to allude, very badly and crudely, I admit, to the bare possibility of a Bishop not understanding everything. This possibility, though it may no doubt be maintained in the schools as an abstract, daring, and speculative opinion, is, I am quite aware, not to be shouted from the housetops; as there are persons in existence capable of declaring, on encouragement, that a Dean may be a booby and an Archdeacon an ass. As it is, there are to be found individuals who whisper that there are Canons who are not in possession of the highest genius. May I correct my error and make amends by professing my belief in the infallibility of all Anglican Bishops, more especially in the Bench that drove Newman out of the English Church, most especially in the present Bishop of Bristol, who discovered the other day that the Venerable Bede and King Henry VIII, were rather like one another.

I am not quite clear about the other point. "If 'for our salvation' does not mean 'to make us good' what does it mean? How can we enter into the joyful law of conformity except by becoming good?" Let us take a fair analogy. X, let us say, died in laying the line that enables us to reach Y; the whole object of X was to bring people in safety to Y. It seems to me, under submission, that people take a ticket to Hampstead, in order that they may get to Hampstead. The "Tube" journey may or may not be delicious; it is surely not the end, but rather the means to the end. Many people are horribly sick and uncomfortable between Dover and Calais, and the Nord is (or used to be) a rather jolting line; still one must get to Paris. I have passed by the very interesting example of an old fallacy that occurs in the first sentence. I forget my Logic Books, I am sorry to say, but the essence of the fallacy in question is the avoidance of the point at issue. I think it is called *ignoratio elenchi*. My correspondent and I are agreed that salvation is the end—or rather your correspondent pretends to agree with me in this sentence; but I am afraid that is all his artfulness and skill in logic fence—where we differ is in our definition of the word salvation.

I say that salvation means the state of unity with Deity; my correspondent thinks that salvation means being good. But, though his learning has led him to the discovery of the Apostles' Creed, he must not assume as proved that which has to be proved. "How can we 'enter into the joyful law of conformity' except by becoming good?" How can we get to the first floor except by the stairs? Therefore, I suppose, the stairs *are* the first floor? My correspondent may call his state of mind, as evinced by this method of ratiocination "goodygoodyness": I know of places—large, cheerful establishments with high walls all about them—where his mental condition would be called by quite another name. "We were made 'members of Christ' before we consciously began to try to 'follow the example of our Saviour.' " A seed has a certain potency (else it is not a seed), but its end is the flower. The seed does not exist that it may die in the earth, but that it may be quickened and raised to the glory of a perfect blossom. " 'Faith and conduct' is the Catholic order, not 'conduct and faith.' " Is this unreservedly true? Surely there is a text in the New Testament to the effect that if a man will do the Works of the Christ, he shall know the Doctrines of the Christ? Finally, I see that your correspondent is "wondering." I am content to leave him wondering.

THE GLORIOUS MYSTERY

THE APOSTOLIC IDEAL

ONE must always recognise the tremendous potentialities that are latent in human nature. This is the defect of science, and of scientific reasoning, falsely so called; it assumes a logical sequence of antecedents and consequents, it postulates a scheme of natural order which is never broken, thereby showing the entire absurdity and impossibility of such an event as the Incarnation—or, in a minor degree, of the genius of Shakespeare. We love Science; we spell it with a large S; we want to believe that it rules everything and keeps the world warm as with a blanket. We do our very best in the cause of Science; when one man gives up his life for the life of his enemy, we murmur: *Darwin, Tyndall, Spencer, Clifford, Huxley: intercede for us. We believe and confess: A died for B owing to some evolved peculiarity in the monkey; and the art of Lincoln Cathedral is entirely explicable as the outcome of a primitive desire to shelter Ancestral Ghosts from rain.* I say we do our very best; for we see all the Blessings that Science has given us. We can reach Hell (otherwise Manchester) six times as swiftly as our ancestors; we can stand in Tartarus (or Sheffield) in so brief a time that the superstitious and besotted old schoolmen would have cried out Black Magic if they had been told of such a feat; we can walk in the Ways of Death (the manufacturing districts generally) in time for lunch after having breakfasted in London. Many other, indeed innumerable, are the benefits and mercies of this blessed Science, which disdains nothing that concerns man, however lowly it may be. The privileged artisan, who in the Middle Ages would have been a miserable, downtrodden serf, groaning under the exactions of his feudal superior, of an immoral and corrupt priesthood, now has the happiness of being an iron-worker, enjoying all the priceless benefits which Mrs. Bell has lately described for us. We may live in the Bottomless Pit, certainly; but at all events the sanitation is irreproachable.

And yet, as we have noted, there remains this one defect: there is always the unforeseen appearance which defies all scientific laws. A wholly undistinguished family of burghers produces Shakespeare, from baronets comes Shelley, from a livery stable Keats, from the parsonage Tennyson, from Corsican notaries Napoleon Bonaparte, from the market-garden Burns. Of course Science still has her consolations; though, in her modesty, she will hardly dare to be positive, still she hints that Shakespeare behaved oddly enough in his youth and died in middle age, that Shelley was considered queer, that Keats had consumption, that Tennyson suffered from whooping cough, Napoleon from cancer in the stomach, and Burns from whisky—in short, that no one of these personages conformed absolutely to the type of the Perfect Grocer, which is written in the scientific heavens, and consequently that no one of these examples is of any consequence. Yet, some secret instinct prevails, an evolved reverence no doubt for the Miraculous Flea Catching and Tree Climbing Monkey, and we continue to believe in the Remarkable Man, the man who is really the God from the Machine.

It is fortunate for the Church of England that in her hour of great peril she does not lack for such a champion, such a defender. We know that the situation is desperate; again and again a voice rings in our ears bidding us note the tremendous fact that the House of Commons does not wholly approve of the Church of England, that the County Councils are indifferent, that the Trades Union Congress is lukewarm, that Lady Wimborne has seen a man riding on a donkey on Palm Sunday, that Mr. Spender thinks something must be done, and that the Tooting Congregationalists are in open revolt. Let us listen to no uncertain testimony; it is not that of a foe, but of an English Bishop, a Successor of the Apostles, a Bishop of the Holy, Catholic, and Apostolic Church, a Bishop, as he himself prefers to call it, "of our grand, historic, English Church";

Forty years ago the House of Commons was practically a Church Senate. What was it now? With each successive widening of the franchise—and here was a spectacle calculated to make all true Churchmen seriously reflect—Parliament had become less of a Church Senate and more of a Nonconformist Assembly. This vast digression of the Church and upheaval of Nonconformity was no mere question of party politics. It cut far deeper than the surface shiftings of Parliamentary tactics and majorities. It reached down to the very root of the national life. "At bottom it will, I am convinced, be the beginning in England of a great war between clericalism and Christianity. The noise of the coming battle may be heard on every shore and in every province of Christendom. But confining our attention to our own land, how strange it is that so few Churchmen seem capable of reading the signs of the times! We have had a superabundance of warnings. The passing of the Cowper-Temple clause under a Liberal Government was one, the passing of the Kenyon-Slaney clause under a Unionist Government was another. The majority of the members of the present Parliament are by no means irreligious men, yet they are not by any means friendly to the Church of England as at present administered.'

"What a moral, what a warning!" as an old lady in one of Mrs. Ewings' beautiful stories once ejaculated. Conservatives no longer like the Church, Liberals do not like the Church; abroad the French Government is displayin its heartfelt, burning zeal for pure, simple Bible Christianity after the exemplar of that worthy Protestant Bill Sikes; and as the holy, orthodox Bishop shows further on in his speech, 1,200,000 members of the Trades Union Congress voted for secular education, against 120,000 on the other side. Nay; if the Trades Union Congress, with its peculiar knowledge and specific training in the Things of Eternity is against us, what need of any further witness. If the majority say guilty, what more do we want? The majority cried, "Crucify Him, Crucify Him." It was done.
I am away from home, I am sorry to say, and so I

cannot consult my books. So I ask the pardon of the dear Bishop, and of all other theologians, if I have to give a certain anecdote loosely, from memory, instead of accurately, from book. St. Polycarp, the disciple of St. John the Divine, was brought before the representative of the Roman State, and also, incidentally, before a raging mob—I mean, before the House of Commons and the Trades Union Congress of the day. The saint answered the representative of the Emperor civilly enough, though, as it happened, he did not seem to be aware that in opposing the will of the State he was guilty of sectarianism; he refused to abjure his faith. But when the official suggested that Polycarp should explain his position to the democracy, the saint replied to the effect that he did not deem the democracy worthy of the slightest notice! "A strange clergyman!" as Sir Daniel Ridgeley observes in "His House in Order." And then the State and the democracy burned Polycarp alive.

Possibly these things were written for an example to us, to warn us what will be our fate if we fail to defer in all things to the popular will. *Vox populi, vox Dei;* I have not even a Bible with me, I am sorry to say, so I cannot give chapter and verse for this solemn warning of the Good Book.

But this by the way. We have seen by the Bishop's words how very far we have strayed from righteousness, how near we are to deserving the Gospel imprecation: "Woe unto you when all men speak ill of you"; how remote we are from the promise that in this world we shall be extremely comfortable. And yet the Bishop, who is clearly the Man of the Hour, the almost miraculous product of a time of desperate danger, does not leave us in absolute despair. No; Dr. Diggle, Bishop of Carlisle, has words of comfort for our erring Church. He says that even if Disestablishment and Disendowment came, "he would by no means be overwhelmed with despair for the future of the historic Church." Thank Heaven for this trumpet note of encouragement and consolation! Think of it; think of the courage, the splendid optimism of this grand Bishop. Translate the message into plain English; let it run: "Even if the few thousand pounds *per annum* which the English Church receives from Catholic hands for preaching Protestantism were withdrawn, even if bishops had no longer seats in the House of Lords—even then I should by no means be overwhelmed with despair." Still, the dear Bishop seems to say—I would prefer the lightest hint of the House of Commons to all the words of Holy Writ, of the Apostles, of the Canons, of the Councils, of the Primitive Doctors, which are especially commended in the Book of Common Prayer. Still in my diocese (if the House of Commons and the Trades Union Congress permit the existence of such things) shall the majority of churches be fast shut from Sunday to Sunday, still shall Festival and Fast be neglected with my approval, still will I neglect to honour Our Lady by the title bestowed upon her in the Book of Common Prayer, still will I despise everything that is sacred, holy, and of ancient order. When, by some rare chance, anything in the Prayer Book pleases me, I will make much boast of our glorious Reformation; in other cases I will jeer at "the rubrics of the Tudor Kings."

Clearly the Bishop of Carlisle is born for the healing of the English Church. Imagine it; he will not give way to absolute despair *even* if Disestablishment and Disendowment come upon us for our sins against popular opinion. *Even.* Every word is worth considering; even if a popular assemblage, which may be composed of Jews, Turks, infidels, heretics, and atheists, have no longer so much as a pretense for interference with the affairs of the Catholic Church in England, even if the precious balms of Royal Commissions and fraudulent Privy Council judgments be denied her, even if retired Divorce Court Judges, wholly void of ecclesiastical learning, are no longer set to decide the most delicate and intimate points of ecclesiastical discipline, even if the most Holy Sacrament of the Altar is no more liable to be abstracted and exhibited in court by the greasy assistants of Messrs. Dodson and Fogg, even if priests who have given their wealth, their comfort, their earthly happiness, all the joys of life for God's poor folk are no longer apt to be tormented to death and madness by slow legal process, with the blessing and approbation of the dear, good Bishops, inheritors of all Evangelical blessings pronounced upon the poor, upon them that have despised all judgments of this world, preferring to abide by the voice of eternal doom. Even if the Church of England be Disestablished and Disendowed, still Dr. Diggle, Bishop of Carlisle, will not give way utterly to despair.

Irony will always have its uses; it is natural vent of that *saeva indignatio* which burned and tore the heart of Dean Swift—foreseeing, it may be imagined, all the monstrous pageant of wickedness and lies and blasphemy and imposture that was logically bound to follow in the Hanoverian train. But there are things so holy that irony, though it were of the weight of "Gulliver's Travels," does not suffice for their defence; and it is time now to have done with jesting with Dr. Diggle. One may, in a grim and fantastic mood, construct fantasies on the tales of the world's vileness and devilry and wickedness; Bill Sikes may appear in a *Punch* cartoon; Armour may provide a text for certain pleasantries, as when the devil, in the American paper, having rashly peeped into Packingtown, is wheeled in a bath chair by the shores of the Infernal Lake, and exclaims, as the fire and brimstone fumes mount to his nostrils, "This does me good." But there is a point beyond which irony becomes ill-placed, indeed irreverent; and I am tired of Dr. Diggle, *pour rire.*

Why do we suffer the accuser to sit in the chair of the saints, in the chair of those doctors who have rightly divided the Word of Truth, who have counted the voice of all the whole world, of Kings and of People, as less than a speck of dust when weighed against the Faith delivered to the Saints? This man dares to talk of Disestablishment and Disendowment as a misfortune. Was the Church, then, Established and Endowed in the days of the Christ, in the days of the Apostles, in the days of the Martyrs? The true misfortune of our poor Church is this—that false prophets occupy the places of the Apostles amongst us. All the blood and all the torments of all the blessed and holy saints from the beginning of the world cry out for vengeance against them and their fellows. All the memories of all holy and orthodox priests of the Church of England in especial clamour against them. The Carthusians, whom the tyrant Henry slew with rope, with slow torment, with starvation; Laud, murdered without a show of justice by the State, by the "People of England"; all the faithful Caroline clergy, who gave up their goods rather than obey this filthy idol called "the People"; all the good priests of later days, especially denounced, be it said, by Dr. Diggle —all these utter their voices in condemnation of them. One does not know the stories of all these martyrs; perhaps one never will; one does know the general outline—the life given up wholly for the poor, the wretched, the unhappy, the oppressed, the life spent amongst the hideous slums, amongst hideous people; the True Faith taught, the Sacrifice offered for Quick and for Dead—Religion, not babble, hypocrisy, wealth-worship, weak pietism, and other shams and devilries, once more exhibited to the world. And the end of such stories is always the same—"the Bishop was regretfully forced to let the law take its course." And then the long years of persecution, of popular infamy, of legal process, of slow, deliberate, malignant torture. The Bishops! Tait, Jackson, and the like—I know not what black calendar would have to be ransacked to find worthy companions to such names as those. Whose blood was it that choked Robespierre? How is it that such bishops can find voice, while the Life and Death of the Priest of St. Alban's by Holborn is still within memory? Yet this man stands up. Hear him:—

THE GLORIOUS MYSTERY

At the same time (the Bishop continued) I am full of hope for the Church of England if only she can get rid of seminarism, mediævalism, the idolatry of tradition, and the schismatic tendencies of ecclesiasticism; and can become catholic, national, reasonable, spiritual, resolved to inspire the nation with the grand ideals of brotherhood and catholicism taught by Our Lord and His Apostles.

What does he mean? Seminarism, one supposes, implies the teaching to priests the matters which concern priesthood—a horrible thing truly that theologians should be instructed in theology, just as engineers are taught engineering. Mediævalism; that is fine indeed! Let the Church abjure the spirit of the great and glorious cathedrals, the wonders of all time, let the Church abjure the spirit of the Morte d'Arthur, of the Dante ,of St. Thomas a Kempis, of St. Thomas Aquinas, of Everyman. Let the Church receive instead the high doctrine of Marie Corelli, of the Red-Nosed Man, of Mr. Chadband, of "Dr." Clifford; let it learn to enjoy the exquisite art of the buildings in which the "Free Churches" perform their strange and uncouth travesties of Divine Worship. The "idolatry of tradition"; again one wonders what the man means. Is he so free from "seminarism," is he, in other words, so densely and grossly ignorant that he is unaware of the high authority assigned to tradition in the Prayer Book of that which he calls "our grand, historic, English Church"? How can anything be historic without tradition; nay, how can anything exist at all without tradition? Does this bishop imagine that a man can trim a hedge without tradition, does he think that a partridge can be roasted without tradition? And what are the "schismatic tendencies of ecclesiasticism"? Is a Freemason guilty of "schismatic tendencies" when he refuses to admit me, an unqualified person, into the lodge? And are all the schismatic sects "ecclesiastical"? There are three hundred of them, I believe, in England at the present day; I was not aware that there was much "ecclesiasticism" in many of these bodies. What does the Bishop mean by "Catholic"? Does he conceive, can he even pre-

THE GLORIOUS MYSTERY

tend to conceive, that the term Catholic implies a body of doctrine and ritual which will please the House of Commons, the Trades Union Congress, and the populace generally—and, it seems, more especially the rabid Atheists at present in power in France? Let us waive aside all theological pre-possessions of whatever kind, let us investigate *in vacuo,* as it were; we cannot, in the face of the New Testament, in the face of history, maintain that the Christian Church was founded with the object of pleasing everybody—Christians apparently excepted.

There are many other gems in this address, delivered "under the shadow of the stately cathedral," as the reporter puts it. Here is one:

> Time was when the vision of a glorious Catholic Church—a Church universal and loving—seemed to be dawning on the world: a Church whose unit was the family, whose multiple was the city or province, whose total was to be all mankind.

The unit of the Church in the Apostolic Age was the Bishop.

Again Dr. Diggle says:

> Where the spirit of exclusive sectarianism was, there the Christ was not; and wherever the Christ reigned, the exclusive spirit of sectarianism was exorcised. One of the greatest foes of the Christ was sectarianism. "It was so," Dr. Diggle proceeded, "in the beginning from the days of Paul, and Apollos, and Cephas."

Did the Christ show this spirit when He called a respectable religious denomination hypocrites and vipers? Did St. John the Divine display a sectarian spirit when he hurried out of the bath ,on being informed that the dissenter Cerinthus was present? Did the martyr, holy Polycarp, show the sectarian spirit when he addressed another dissenter, Marcion, as "the first-born of Satan?"

And, then, this personage censures the Roman Church for promulgating "heresies and novelties absolutely unknown to the Primitive Church." The Primitive Church! This

[161]

personage, who repudiates ecclesiasticism, appeals to the Primitive Church, which "did nothing" without the bishop. This personage who abhors tradition, appeals to the Primitive Church, which had a devout reverence for the tradition of the Apostles and the Fathers. This man, who sneers at certain English canons because they are three centuries old, appeals to the first ages of Christianity. The period of the "Tudor King" is, then, musty in its antiquity, compared with "the more widely illumined national conscience of the present day"; but the first five centuries of Christendom are, it seems, too long ago to count! And he appeals to the Primitive Church; to the age of strict dogmatic definition, of miracle-working saints, of the great Liturgies of the East, of the unfailing teaching of the Great Eucharistic Sacrifice—of all the things of which Bishop Diggle profoundly disapproves.

Finally, the Bishop brings the worst charge of all. It seems that so inveterate has the sectarian spirit become in "the Tractarian Movement," that some of its disciples are venturing to echo the denunciations against rich men and riches uttered in the New Testament by the Christ, to echo also the benedictions pronounced by Christ Himself upon the poor. A horrible outcome of the "sectarian spirit," indeed. The Tractarians will be saying soon that man was not sent into the world to "do business."
Oct. 5, 1907.

THE GLORIOUS MYSTERY

ECCLESIA ANGLICANA.—I

IT WOULD be very inconvenient, and indeed tiresome, if every fresh crime that occurred had to be discussed, not on its particular demerits or on its excuses and palliatives, but on broad, general principles. For example, suppose Mr. Sikes to be still in the enjoyment of his faculties and talents; suppose Nancy to be again murdered with every circumstance of horrible brutality; how very odd we should think it if our half-penny Press proceeded to treat the case on broad and charitable grounds; to argue on the natural rights of man, with reference to Mr. Hobbes's theory of the State of War; to show from the *Leviathan* that Nancy had suffered no injustice whatever; to demonstrate from Saxon examples the purely civil nature of Bill's offence. We should find it odd, and tedious, too; since we have finally settled that premeditated murder is a capital crime. We should not wish to argue about abstract theorems and historical precedents; we should simply desire that sentence of execution should immediately be issued against Bill.

And yet in another and much more important field we seem still to be quoting the *Leviathan* and the Anglo-Saxon precedents—*mutatis mutandis*. Week after week I see notes in the journals in which bishops, deans, chancellors, editors have to be laboriously brought to book by the application of arguments which should be axioms, by the force of facts which have been notorious for two thousand years. For instance, only the other day some Diocesan Chancellor, writing under the bilious protection of the *Westminster Gazette,* uttered the awful threat that if something or other wasn't done pretty quickly the clergy would be free to hear confessions. It should have been sufficient to quote this singular piece of imbecility—the gamekeeper is not obliged to demonstrate the noxious character of stoats and vipers before he nails their bodies to the barn-door—but *The Academy,* no doubt justly, felt bound to remind the preposterous Chancellor and his preposterous editor that the practice of Auricular Confession is fully provided for by the Prayer Book and the Canons of the English Church. Again, there was the Bishop of Newcastle, who thinks, or pretends to think, that the "judgments" of the Privy Council are binding on the consciences of the priesthood; here, again a hammer and a couple of nails should have been the only requisites; but *The Academy* was once more obliged to restate the general principle that vipers are undesirable and offensive reptiles before proceeding to execution. In other words, it seemed necessary to affirm—for the ten thousandth time—that the dioceses of the Ecclesia Anglicana owe obedience to the whole Church Catholic, and not one whit of any kind of service to the blunderings of a body of corrupt ignoramuses, even though the said body be called the Judicial Committee of the Privy Council.

Possibly it may be necessary to continue to demonstrate the already demonstrated, to prove to each several reptile his reptilious and venomous character before one breaks his back and nails him to the door; but it certainly seems time to state general principles generally without the confusion which must be introduced by particular culprits and especial crimes. For it is manifest that the state of the Church of England is not far from desperate; that if it is to exist in any real sense much longer, the truth must be told with no uncertain words. I am speaking for those who do *not* conceive of the Church as an amiable organization for the promotion of general good nature and the civic virtues; with those who hold the contrary opinion we have no communion, less bond than we have with a fetish-worshipper or a Red Indian sorcerer; since the latter are at least firmly convinced of the super-natural order and of a certain world of transcendence.

And here is the root of the matter. We waste our

THE GLORIOUS MYSTERY

time about trivial and ridiculous details; even we, who are good Catholics, allow ourselves to be drawn into tiresome and profitless discussion as to the precise date of the first Prayer Book of Edward VI., we enquire patiently as to the true meaning of a "plain" alb, we waste the hours in proving that the "Royal Supremacy" of the sixteenth and seventeenth centuries did not mean what it has come to mean now, we show to admiration that such a man as Laud did not wish the Church to be ruled by an assemblage of Jews, Turks, Infidels and Hereticks, that Henry VIII. would have burnt most of the members of the present House of Commons, that Queen Elizabeth would certainly have hanged a good portion of those who now claim authority and judgment in the most holy and awful mysteries. And then we show that Bishop A in 1690 certainly wore a cope, that Bishop B in 1720 prayed for the dead, that Bishop C in 1800 had a mitre. And so forth, and so forth, at infinite length, and for the last seventy years. Interesting? Certainly; a good deal of this research is extremely interesting to antiquaries, and Church lawyers, and ecclesiologists. But it is not by these means that the Church of England can be saved from extinction. It is of very little use to know about the Ritual of Bishop Cosin's chaped in the seventeenth century if, now in the twentieth, we are ruled, and suffer ourselves to be ruled, by bishops who in any other portion of the Catholic Church would be doing lifelong penance in the cell of some remote monastery. Personally, I take the warmest interest in ecclesiological matters; but it seems to me that what the Church and the time need is not so much priests who are unerring guides as to the uses of the Rood Screen in the Middle Ages as priests who will set up the Rood *episcopo volente seu nolente,* without thought or care for the judgment of the Chancellor, who, if we may judge by the *Westminster* sample should be rather at the whipping-block of the ignorant dunce than in the chair of the Ecclesiastical Judge. No; the moment is not for luxuries of ecclesiological knowledge, for pleasant odds and ends of ritual learning, it demands men who are Catholics to the core, who are of unflinching, immovable principle, for whom nothing but the Church exists, to whom the decisions of the House of Commons and the Privy Council are of considerably less import than the Laws of Howell Dda.

I remember how, many years ago, I went with my father to a meeting of the English Church Union. There were not many members, and most of them were poor parsons; the coat of one of them, I recollect, had turned a light green with age. The mass was sung in the little church of Tintern Parva, on the height overlooking the great and glorious abbey. Here alone, indeed, was carven in fair stones and manifested in broken arches and ruinous walls all the matter of our work, all that we loved and hated. There, in the wonderful and enchanted valley, had once risen the miracle, the restoration of lost Paradise, a perfect and transcendent work of art, a shrine for the Graal of Heaven, for the Life-giving and Quickening Bread of the soul. The dull and heavy and shapeless stones had once more received life and beauty; then had stood in its glories the Holy House of the Mass, a priceless sacrament, a marvellous testimony to supernatural truth, to the Great Fact —the only fact of any consequence—that the world is not wholly Devildom, that the aim of men is not altogether to "do business." And there, too, was the sign of that which we hated; the holy place was roofless and the wall decayed; the altar was thrown down, and the carven work in ruins; the Sacrifice was not offered any more, and the Tabernacle of God was no longer with men. I cursed the "Protestant Reformation" then with heart and soul; and still do I curse it, and hate it ,and detest it, with all its works and in all its abominable operations, internal and external; I loathe it and abhor it as the most hideous blasphemy, the greatest woe, the most monstrous horror that has fallen upon the hapless race of mortals from the foundation of the world. And now, in these late days I look into the leading "High Church" paper and see mild censure of Lord Halifax for "letting the cat out of the bag," for uttering his most righteous abomination of that Masterpiece of Hell and Death which is called The Reformation.

The little meeting of the English Church Union, which was held in the mid-seventies, was not of the mind of the "High Church" paper. Some nonsense, called The Public Worship Regulation Act, had just been made law; and "Ritualism," it was said, was to be put down. Protestant England, Puritan England had spoken, and spoken firmly; in other words, Bishops and "Statesmen" and Leading Articles, and the "man in the street" had combined once more in that great concert of malignant balderdash, that inexpressive song of ignorance and wickedness and cant that would be an additional horror in Malebolge itself. Everybody felt that the "Ritualists" were done for—everybody, that is, save the "Ritualists" themselves. I shall never forget the manner in which the preacher—I think he was a priest named Ives—spoke of the utter contempt in which he and his Catholic brothers held the court established by the Public Worship Regulation Act, of their firm resolution to treat all its procedure and decisions as null and void and non-existent, of their firm confidence in the triumph of the Catholic Cause. The priest Ives— if he was Ives—was not at all afraid of "letting the cat out of the bag"—and one knows the sequel. In a few years Lord Penzance's court was practically annihilated by the people whom it was going to put down. It went astray at every step, it committed every possible error, its decisions were upset again and again on technical grounds; it was continually in such hot water that Lord Penzance must have often sighed for the putrid, peaceful atmosphere of the Divorce Court—the legal sphere which he had previously adorned. The cat was very much out of the bag; and it was a cat with long teeth and sharp claws, and Lord Penzance was the mouse. Even Tait, that most malignant of persecutors, had to give way, had to acknowledge that one could not "put down Ritualism," even with Acts of Parliament, Privy Council "Judgments," and a brand new court making a funny though rather shabby pretence of being a very old one.

And it is these Churchmen and Catholics of the seventies that we need now. I daresay that the Rite of Tintern Parva was in many respects ecclesiologically incorrect; still Lord Penzance and the House of Commons and the House of Lords, and the Judicial Committee of the Privy Council had to bite the dust, and the Catholics were victorious. And then came the time of peace, and then the days of Kensit the Notorious, and ecclesiological arguments before ar.\bishops—and, I am afraid one must add, cowardice and collapse. One wonders whether it is too late to recover those early ardours, whether it is too late to restate once for all the fact that a man is either a Catholic Priest, or else no priest at all, and that in the great cause which we are fighting what the Venetian Ambassador saw in the sixteenth century is not evidence, and what Cosin did in the seventeenth century is (comparatively) of no consequence. For take this one single point of incense at Mass; the point is this: Has incense been recognised as a proper accompaniment to the Offering throughout the whole Church from the fourth century onward? If the reply be in the afirmative, then there is no more to be said, and any priest who omits this ceremony at the bidding of Councils or Commons or Lords or Bishops, or of all combined, is nothing more than an apostate.

A small thing, a grain of incense? Certainly; but no smaller now than it was in the days of Nero. Men were once ready to die in hideous torment for the sake of this little grain. We have not the splendid opportunities of the blessed and holy martyrs; no priest will be burned alive or sawn asunder in these days; but shall we not make the best use we can of what we possess? We can still gain the contempt of the world, of those in power and high place, by adhering to our principles. We can win the scorn of the *Westminster Gazette*, and of its unctuous "Liberalism"; we can have the pleasure of being denounced in unnumbered leading articles, the futility and absurdity and dishonesty of our position can be pointed out to us by the "Popular Press" in general—by that wonderful Press which can hardly make three statements on any matter whatsoever without committing four gross blunders. We can draw down on our heads the wrath of the "plain man," of the "practical man," of "the man in the street," and the faithful among the clergy can attract the neglect and quiet persecution of their biships—the neglect and quiet persecution changing to open and virulent malice and "legal proceedings" if it seem likely that such would prove at any time the more popular plan. The men of the 'Seventies were not afraid to go to gaol for their "millinery," as that sapient and instructed Popular Press then called it; they were not afraid to stay in gaol, and the term "self-made martyrs" had no terrors for them. Surely these are not chances to be despised. One may say that the denunciations of popular journalism are too contemptible to be esteemed; and no doubt this is so far as the instructed are concerned; but one must remember that the mass of men are uninstructed—else there were no Popular Press. The greater number still believe that the newspapers know all about art, letters and theology; and so we may have the satisfaction of having the hiss of the world against us.

That is: if we are sure of our first principles; if we are quite certain that the Reformation and the Privy Council and the House of Commons have nothing whatever to do with Holy Church, its dogma, or its rites and ceremonies. In every family history there are deplorable events which are mercifully suffered to fall into oblivion; for the future let it be understood by the Bishops and their friends that any references to the deplorable events in the Christian Church in England will be treated by Catholics with silent contempt; that obedience will alone be given when the

THE GLORIOUS MYSTERY

Bishops speak with the voice of the whole Church Catholic, founding their utterances upon the Apostles, the Saints, the Martyrs, the Doctors, the Canons, the Councils. To take a concrete instance: let us hear no more the uncouth, *male sonans* phrase—Solemn Celebration of the Holy Communion. What we wish to hear is High Mass and nothing but High Mass; for the word which was good enough for St. Ambrose is good enough for us—we will have none of these "comfortable," safe Anglican phrases, these cowardly, wretched opportunisms, these inventions of men who fear the Bishops and the newspapers more than they fear Almighty God and the Holy Catholic Church. It is "disloyal" they say, these miserable time-servers, to speak of the Mass: nay, but it is most deeply, most damnably disloyal not to speak of the Mass; and the priest who affirms daily his belief in the Catholic Church, and refuses to call the High Sacrament of the Altar by that name is no true Catholic, but rather a disloyal apostate, a rotten branch on the living tree.

I am amused as I think how trifling all this must seem to some of the readers of this paper—to some, perhaps, who are fully aware of the marvels and miracles that are wrought in the arts by things that seem small enough, by trifling juxtapositions of words, of tones, of colours. They will say that I am violent over matters of no moment; and yet I believe that they would hesitate to affirm that Wordsworth's great Ode on the Intimations of Immortality would be "just as good" turned into prose, if only the sense were carefully preserved.
Dec. 7, 1907.

THE GLORIOUS MYSTERY

ECCLESIA ANGLICANA—II

IT IS sometimes necessary to be violent. There are occasions and cases in which soft phrases, roundabout hints, elegant circumlocutions, and "opportune" remarks are quite definitely useless, and the present condition of the Church of England seems to me to justify a complete lack of ambiguity. Hooker was a great man; he wrote what most people have thought a great defence of the Anglican position—and the end of it was ruin and desolation of the seventeenth century; foals baptised in cathedrals and sanctuaries hideously profaned. One cannot make war with rosewater; it seems obvious enough. The odd thing is that the defenders of the Ecclesia Anglicana do not seem to have found out yet the obviousness of another maxim—that one cannot defend the English Church by saying nice things about Protestantism. In time, one trusts, the truth of this doctrine may be recognised as axiomatic, and the genius may even now be born who will convince Bishops that the Catholic Faith is not buttressed when they shake hands with Dissenting preachers, nor is our holy religion sustained and fostered when our Fathers in God introduce notorious heretics at Court. I tried to advance these paradoxes (as they now seem) as clearly as possible in the preceding paper; I tried to make it plain that the prerogative question was not what the Privy Council said, not even what pattern of surplice Cosin wore, but rather the question of Catholicity or non-Catholicity. If a clerk in holy orders of the English Communion is not a Catholic priest he is one of the most melancholy humbugs and imposters that the world has produced. If he is a Catholic priest let him accept the consequences of the situation—most of them very uncomfortable—anl let him cease writing letters to the *Guardian,* showing that the decisions of the Judicial

Committee of the Privy Council are part of the Deposit of Faith.

And then comes the subsidiary point on which I touched at the end of the article—the infinite importance of little things, of a grain of incense, of a queer set of clothes that a priest puts on when he is to say Mass; there are many such trifles, as they seem to most people. It is so painfully easy to show on rational grounds that these "trifles" don't matter, and can't matter, that all anxiety about them is a peculiarly puerile and imbecile fuss; that one quite understands the frequency with which this demonstration is made. A journalist with a few inches to fill could hardly find a simpler topic, the words flow from the pen; it is like putting one two under another, drawing a line, and writing four beneath. Of course, it is so evident as to be past argument, and yet how would the journalist like it if I strolled into his wife's drawing room with my hat on and my coat off? But, surely, the fact of a man's head being covered or uncovered is the veriest trifle; surely a waistcoat and shirt sleeves are as decent as a coat, and (in hot weather) more sensible. Yet I should be kicked out of the house, and the doom would be a just one. Then there is another point; admitting that incense and candles and queer clothes called vestments do seem, on the face of it, little things, should there not have been some sort of arrest of judgment when the character and acts of the men who were attached to these little things came into consideration? Sir Walter Besant was not a "churchy" man by any means, but he confessed that he did not know what would have happened to the East End of London if it had not been for the "Ritualistic parson." Now, if a man born and bred in the "comfortable"—sometimes in the luxurious—classes has confessedly and openly given up all comfort, and all ease, and all pleasantness, has exiled himself to the darkest pit of the City of Dreadful Night, has devoted himself, body and soul, to the physical, mental, and spiritual salvation of the wretched, starving and degraded victims of our infamous commercial system, has made himself the bedmate of vermin, the companion of every horror for the poor's sake, would it not have been as well to hesitate, to wonder whether the "trifles" this man loved were such trifles after all? Of course, it is splendid to cherish noble and philanthropic sentiments; it is splendid to get a seat in Parliament by making speeches about the people; it is most splendid of all to write leading articles showing that Sir Arthur Campbell-Balfour's heart is bleeding for the distresses of the poor—but, after all, the man who actually feeds starving bellies and puts clothes on shuddering flesh is entitled to some consideration. No; it certainly seems as if there had been a little haste when Mackonochie of St. Alban's and Lowder of St. Peter's, London Docks, were set down as lovers of trifles. The conclusion is improbable.

And, then, of course, there is the argument from the Arts. "Tunes impressed on the brain through the medium of the auditory apparatus are delightful; but still more agreeable are those which are received without the assistance of the sensory channels." This statement is made in a clear, more scientific, terminology than:

Heard melodies are sweet, but those unheard
Are sweeter.

And yet something seems lacking in the prose form; one is inclined, surely, to regret some, at least, of the changes that have been made; one would like to restore the measuring of the syllables, and, if the paraphrase were continued, some of us might say that we missed the rhymes. It is, surely, not necessary to work out the analogy; it will be quite sufficient if we accept the general principle, and agree that the logical understanding is not the supreme judge, not the one and only and final Court of High Appeal. Dr. Johnson knew no better, and so he said that Lycidas was rubbish. Let us not be found to be echoing this judgment by saying that incense and candles and vestments are childish trifles.

And, then, comes the grand question of all. It is conceivable that one might be forced in certain quarters to abandon the defence of the method of, say, Poesy, and turn one's attention to the defence of the thing itself, of its very existence. I daresay that many a "sturdy" Englishman does not see much use in poetry of any sort; there must be "plain" men in vast quantities who are quite sure that Keats was a singularly foolish fellow, who wasted time over writing verses, instead of inventing steam-engines and looms and blast furnaces, and so forth. I think we may fairly rule this interesting school of thought out of court; the existence of a literary journal rather assumes that literature is a worthy and excellent art, and in a review of the Arts it is not necessary to be continually defining and re-defining the first principles on which Arts are based. But it is otherwise with the great Ars Artium—the source and origin from which all art proceeds, whence arose Architecture, Painting, Music, Imaginative Literature; that Primal Ecstasy which makes man to be man, which—and not "reason"—distinguishes him from the brutes. Let it be said, then, that we define Religion in such terms as these, and that we utterly abjure and detest the common belief that it is a respectable agency for promoting good manners, good morals, and good nature generally. In other words, the Christian Church is not a philanthropic institution in its essence, though it may be such accidentally; its object is to bring heaven down to earth, and to raise men up to heaven, to restore him to that Paradise from which he has lapsed.

Who can blame those who have not understood this? Who can blame them, I say, here in England, where for three hundred years they have been taught by precept and example, quite otherwise; where the essence of the priesthood has been understood to lie in the giving of coals, blankets, and port wine, and in the possession of a comfortable vicarage; where the high office of the preacher is taken to consist in exhortations to good behaviour, respectability, and success? By the blast-furnace of The Reformation the fair face of the

Church has been seared and made hideous, and religion, the summit of all arts, has become a sort of sanctified Man in Blue, a transcendental policeman, promising, on the one hand, success in business and the esteem of one's neighbours, and on the other hand threatening the frown of the well-to-do in the present and everlasting torment in the future. And this farrago of lies and blasphemies is called the "sober religion" of the Englishman. The "sober" religion! *Calix meus inebrians quam praeclarus est*—this "temperance" beverage of mine how "sober" it makes me feel. The Apostles on the Day of Pentecost did not behave like people who have been drinking weak tea.

Nay, let us away with it; let us, good Catholics, co-operate with anybody, with anything, if we can but crush this infamy of a "religion" which boasts of its sobriety, which finds the imagery of the "Song of Songs" alien to English modes of thought, which explains the miracle of Cana in Galilee as suitable, no doubt, to Syrian habits. We want to turn out the snug parson from his snug parsonage; we want to expel the large Bishop from his large palace; we want to put an end, once for all, to the thaumaturgists who are perpetually changing the great and glorious vessels of strong wine into vessels of gingerbeer. The Catholic Church in England shall not be ruled for ever by the Athenæum Club, by the organ of Mr. Hooper, and by the Judicial Committee of the Privy Council.

For this ruling, this guidance, are quite inconsistent with the aim for which the Church exists. Neither "eminent" personages nor Printing House Square journalists, nor dishonest and blundering lawyers are masters of the mysteries; and the Church of God is wholly concerned with the mysteries, and with nothing else. The object of the Ecclesia is to operate the Great Redemption, to be a voice ever crying in the wilderness of materialism that the lesser joys, the true delights are above, and that the lesser joys and delights, so far as they exist, only exist as faint and dim copies of the everlasting realities. It is the office of the Church to mutter the perpetual incantation, to sing the song of magic neumes, which is efficacious against all the horrors and blasphemies and follies and piggeries which we know now was civilization," which are, in reality, the brutish and devilish instincts of man codified into a system.   The world, said Coventry Patmore, is a dungheap, and has always been a dungheap; the world has "done business" from the beginning; it has worshipped success; it has adored the pleasant humbug; it has poured wealth into the hands of the adulterator; it has crowned and laurelled every kind of fraud and abomination; it stoned the prophets; it starved the poets; it crucified the Christ.   In every time and in every place one might see enthroned the abomination of desolation sitting in the place where it should not. We, who add to all vices the supreme vice of cant, pretend to ourselves that all this sort of thing went out with Heathendom, or, at all events, with Popery; and we pretended to believe that ours was an age of progress, of the dawn of the millennium.   Still we persisted in this belief as we slowly destroyed every goodly and kindly custom, every excellent rite that had survived to our days; as we planted factory after factory in the pleasant lands; as we turned the hillside into a heap of abominations; as we changed the old English speech into a vile Cockney jargon; as we fouled the clear rushing stream with filth indescribable; as the cottage walls fell down, and the labour barracks and the slum quarters, and the millionaire's hideous mansion rose up over all the length and breadth of the land. And then, having enslaved the people in our industrial system, having substituted cogs and wheels for their souls, and given them poison for their drink, and pollution for their meat, we erected some fountains for puppies, ordered a hundred-and-fifty thousand copies of—well of some popular work of fiction—and decided that we were an enlightened and humanitarian people, with a taste for literature.   Above all we were thankful that we did not live in the dark ages.   And then the awakening: the proclamation, coming from the lips of advanced Socialism, that humanity was fallen into a pit of misery and ugliness

THE GLORIOUS MYSTERY

and degradation infinitely deeper than any dungeon it had dug for itself in the past.

One gives all honour to Socialism, because it has had the honesty to recognise the truth, to dwell no more in the lying tents of "Liberalism" and "Conservatism." One gives no honour at all to its safecure of £365 a year for everybody—a new version of "the hair of the dog that bit you." It is time now for Holy Church to enter the scene, to proclaim once again that man does not live by bread alone—or by an income of £365 per annum—but by heavenly mysteries. Holy Writ long ago instructed us that our conversation was in heaven; and perhaps without undue violence or paradox it may be asserted that heaven is not a synonym of the house of business or of the House of Commons. Let the dead bury their dead; arise and follow me. This was said long ago; let us interpret it. Let all the whole tribe of fussy and charlatanic and maniacal philanthropists, all the crowd of humbugs and fools who are for ever holding meetings and passing resolutions, and seeking for better bread than wheaten, and teaching the violin to starving children, and exhibiting masterpieces of art to hungry savages, and closing public-houses, shutting up skittle alleys, adulterating beer, promoting Pleasant Sunday Afternoons, agitating for the reformation of the Solar System, for the instruction of Berkshire pigs in the Binomial Theorem, and the substitution of "Grape Guts" for roast beef—let all this hopeless race, sunk in their dead (and chiefly lunatic) works, still persist in their follies and malignancies; but let us, who have seen the light, arise and endeavour to ascend to it. With contempt for all worldly consequences, with more than contempt for the opinion of the respectable, let us decline misery and aspire to happiness, to the true life of man, which, again and again, be it repeated, lies not in so many farthings or in so many thousands of pounds a year, but in certain hidden regions of mystery, the gates to which are the sacraments of the Church—of the true Church, not of the Erastians' "Establishment," which is merely a ministrant of blankets and behaviour, not of the living and quickening

[177]

bread which cometh down from heaven, not of that celestial drink which inebriates, from whose raptures arise all delight, all the wonder that is called Art.

Away with the Church of the Blankets, the Behaviour, and the Invalid Port. Let it sink down to everlasting Styx, and minister to the souls of Henry VIII. and Queen Elizabeth and "safe" Bishops, and the deceased members of the Judicial Committee of the Privy Council. Here on earth we want none of it; its more than dubious vintages, its (probably) adulterated cottage loaves are of no service to them that are hungry for Everlasting Bread, for the juice of the Eternal Vine. Let smug Anglicanism disappear and cease to be; let Morning Prayer, sung to Barnby in F, no longer offend the ears of the angels; let not the image of the Slain and Risen lurk any longer behind the vestry door; let not our cathedrals be odorous only of escaped gas and the heating apparatus; let not the sermons of our teachers be compact of feeble and obvious pietisms, or else of pleas for the Girls' Friendly Society. Let the Holy Water Stoup stand once more in the porch, so that those who enter may comply with the Scriptural precept; let the Great Rood shine on high, imaging the Veil through which we are bold to enter into the Holy Place; let the tapers which symbolize the interior light glow about the altar and in the mystic dance of the procession; let the green boughs and flowers and garlands once more witness to the redemption of the earth; let the smoke of the incense lead us by the subtlest of all senses into the inner region; let the incantation of the Church's ancient awful song echo once more from the dim roof that we may fitly make and celebrate the Sacrifice of the Lamb, slain from the foundation of the world.

Dec. 14, 1907.

" MODERNISM "

THERE are many paths, many ways; and it is usually an ungracious and a foolish person who does nothing but proclaim in strident accents the fatality and futility of every track save that which he himself is following. But, when every allowance of charity and reason has been made, it remains that one road is always to be disallowed, and that is the way on which those stand who proclaim that the goal does not exist—that there is not, indeed, in any real and efficient sense, any way at all. There have always been people of this sect; it is conceivable that in the wilderness there were scientific and rational Jews, broad, liberal-minded men, who perceived that the journey of the tribes was a vivid Oriental allegory; that, while the desert was real and true enough, the talk about the land flowing with milk and honey was a mere flourish, a pious fraud, justified, perhaps, by the literalism and simplicity of the days of bondage, but without any true fulfilment in the nature of things. "Here," these enlightened ones might have said, "is the only Promised Land which we or any one else will ever see. In the natural order we shall never get out of the wilderness, for the very good reason that there is nothing but wilderness in the universe; the Land of Canaan is a poetic dream. Still, if we journey faithfully, if we are constant in the performance of humanitarian and philanthropic work, if we help our fallen brother, if we carry the burden of the weary, if we cherish kindly sentiments about everybody—then the desert shall blossom like the rose, and we shall achieve not the mythical splendours and delights of an imaginary Promised Land, but the very real reward that always attends unselfishness." And, in the same way, there may be many allowable and indeed admirable divergencies in the region of the arts; a man may love Homer with such a fervent and consuming devotion that he has no corner left in his heart or soul or mind for the cultus of Sophocles; or, again, one may be so rapt into the mystery world of Malory that "Pickwick" may seem vile, unclean, profane, a vulgar tale of mean streets and mean people, in which the Holy Vessel has become a brandy-bottle. Very allowable are both these loves and these hatreds—one would never be angry with a man who said that he loved the "Arabian Nights" too well to tolerate the naturalism of "Tom Jones"—but here, again, there is a path that is condemned, which is marked with a "No Thoroughfare," which bristles with man-traps and spring-guns; and this is the path which denies the very existence of art of any kind; which looks on all literature, painting, music, architecture, as an odd remnant from the pre-scientific days, from the time when primitive man, beset by all kinds of illusory terrors, illusory loves, groundless desires and apprehensions, devoted himself to performing a vast conjuring trick, of the which trick we call some portions Religion and others Art. So, according to this school, Aphrodite is hocus-pocus, the Parthenon is hocus-pocus, Chartres Cathedral is hocus-pocus; Homer, the New Testament, and the Queste of the Sangraal are all hocus-pocus. This is called the scientific standpoint, and it owes its name, no doubt, to its utter lack of all *scientia,* properly so called. One is sorry to have to say that "What we Want," an open letter to Pius X. from a group of priests, translated by the Rev. A. Leslie Lilley, belongs very distinctly to the "scientific" school, to the way which is No Thoroughfare, which means waste of time, waste of temper, weary feet, heated brains, and a wood of thorns at the end of the journey. To take an example. These Italian priests—who, I suppose, would call themselves Modernists — speak as follows:

When we have . . . . to explain the relations between God the Father, Jesus, and humanity, while we recognise all the beauty of the doctrine built up by Scholasticism, and agree in its religious content, we yet cannot have recourse to the ontological terms, "person," "essence," "nature," "hypostases," "processions." As the modern habit of mind does not attach to these any meaning which corresponds with reality, it is returning to exactly the same moral and intellectual conditions as those of the first Christians, or of the humble and simple-minded Christians of our country districts, who know nothing of these rational categories. . . . . So, again, to explain the Eucharistic Mystery, we cannot, for similar reasons, adopt the theory of Transubstantiation unless no one is to understand.

Now, at first sight, and on reading the first words of the passage that I have quoted, it might be imagined that these Modernists were the most faithful Catholics in the world, devout believers in the Christian faith as it is expounded in Holy Writ, by the Fathers, and in the scholastic philosophy. Their sole anxiety would seem to be as to the terms they are to use in teaching the faith; their only protest is against the compulsory employment of the technical language of a highly systematised theology in their discourses to simple and unlettered folk. One can confess with all one's heart that if this be the basis of Modernism, then Modernism is the most reasonable thing in the world, and one would be sorry to understand that the Roman Catholic clergy were forbidden to use any modern equivalent word or words for such terms as "hypostasis" and "circumincession." But is this all the content of Modernism? What about the passage on the Eucharist? Here it is no longer a case of preferring a clear word before an obscure; the priests simply say: "We cannot adopt the theory of Transubstantiation," and in place of this "theory" they give an explanation of the great Mystery of Faith which, one imagines, would have pleased Zwingli, which would scarcely have satisfied Calvin, which Luther would most certainly have anathematised. This is surely not agreeing with the religious content of Christianity, unless the faith was hidden from the faithful till the arrival of the Swiss "Reformer"; and when on another page we find these Modernist priests expressing their sympathy for Mr. Tyrrell, we are forced to conclude that their assent to the propositions of Scholastic Christianity is a mere passing politeness, not meant to be understood literally. For, to take the question of the Eucharist, Mr. Tyrrell's doctrine is as follows:

[181]

THE GLORIOUS MYSTERY

Dogma apart, and taken at its lowest, the Eucharist remains for you the sacrament of communion and incorporation with that mystical "Christ crucified" [*i.e.,* the Christ regarded as the "central and supereminent figure round whose Cross are gathered the Christs of all ages, races, religions, and degrees"], an act by which you offer yourself to be received into that Divine company or spiritual organism, to be made a sharer of its faith, its hope, and its love, to give your own body and blood "for many for the remission of sins."

Now this doctrine may be amiable and charming and liberal and broad-minded; but it is not Christianity in any common sense of the word; and so, it seems to me, we are enlightened as to what these Italian priests really do want. They want that which "Dr." Clifford, Canon Hensley Henson, and "Dr." Campbell want—that is, a Christianity which is robbed of all its essential character; a system which is no longer a magical and mystical religion, but a scheme of universal philanthropy seen against a background of vague Deism. I do not think I am unfair; there is, of course, a certain sense in which a eunuch is a man. I need not say that I recognise that the Italian priests would require a very different "set" from that in favour with our English heretics. "Dr." Clifford would deny the faith in the midst of a "Liberal" demonstration (regarded as the supreme act of worship); Canon Hensley Henson would make the Resurrection of Christ contingent on a vote of the House of Commons; "Dr." Campbell would declare the Holy Eucharist to be an intelligent anticipation of a vegetarian and non-alcoholic Communist breakfast *chez* Mr. Eustace Miles; the Italians, doubtless, would still sing Mass in honour of nothing in particular and of noble sentiments in general; but the result in each case is the same. I am not at all surprised to find that Modernism has been defined as "the heresy which contains all the heresies and errors of the past"; indeed, one could find no better definition than this; no better phrase to summarise that impulse in men which continually surges up, declaring in very various idioms that there is no world of vision and wonder, that there is but earth and humanity, and that we have got to make the best of both. This is, indeed, the heresy of all heresies, masquerading sometimes under the most curious disguises, putting on now and again the vestments of the "occult" sciences, but always constant to the one idea, that man is the master and measure of all things. "Ye shall be as gods, knowing good and evil"; as in the Garden, so in the modern world, in the world of Modernism. I speak with apology; for I, an Anglican, have no right to intervene in the internal matters of the Holy Roman Catholic and Apostolic Church; still, there are points which truly concern "common" Christianity, in which the old-fashioned Wesleyans, if such there be any longer, are deeply interested; and, whether the Roman Church be pleased or displeased, it seems to me fitting that one voice at least should be raised against this Atheism in a chasuble, against this shabby and squalid attempt to show that the Faith of the Saints is a synonym for the doctrine of the "man in the street." Ah! we desire to live in charity, to believe the best of all men; but how can we reconcile these things? Our Modernists profess the warmest attachment to the Gospel; they say that they, and they alone, are the successors of the first Christians; and yet they stumble against this or that dogma because it cannot be understood. Have they read the texts:

> The Jews then murmured at Him, because He said, I am the bread which came down from heaven. And they said, Is not this Jesus, the son of Joseph, whose father and mother we know? how is it then that He saith, I came down from heaven?

> The Jews therefore strove amongst themselves, saying, how can this Man give us His flesh to eat?

> Many, therefore, of His disciples when they heard this, said, This is a hard saying; who can bear it?

> From that time many of His disciples went back, and walked no more with Him.

And so, say the Modernist priests, we cannot adopt the theory of Transubstantiation "unless no one is to understand." And so, I am sorry to confess, say hundreds, perhaps thousands, of

THE GLORIOUS MYSTERY

Anglican priests, who confess the truth in their hearts, who deny it in their acts, who prophesy smooth things in Zion, who talk of the Catholic Faith as if it were a musical comedy—something which must be presented in popular style if it is to catch on. There is the cleric who shudders from the herse at *Tenebrae:* his Bishop tells him it is not a lawful ornament of the Book of Common Prayer; and the same cleric has "lantern services," with sacred songs by Ira D. Sankey: a magic lantern and a white sheet, and the doggerel of an American heretic being, doubtless, lawful according to the Book of Common Prayer. Let us not be bold to exult over our Roman brothers; with us, as with them, there is a school which declares that everything is lawful which outrages the Catholic Faith. The school is a strong one, it seems, in both Churches, but, at least, it should appear under its own colours. Let it appeal, if it will, to the judgment of the profane vulgar; but, in face of those words of St. John the Divine, let these philanthropists no longer pretend to be Christians of any shape or fashion. Their part is with the disciples who went back and walked no longer with Him, not with the faithful who believed in order that they might understand.

Nay; let it be understood once for all, the Catholic Faith is not a Christy Minstrel or music-hall performance which has to commend itself to the suffrages of the majority. It may be quite true that they who live to please must please to live, but a Catholic priest is not by any means to be reckoned in this company. The Catholic religion is, or should be, the everlasting witness of heaven above on earth below; the continual reminder of the futility, and vanity, and absurdity of most of our mortal aims. It is the stalest of old tales this; it is the oldest of old texts, and yet it must be re-enunciated again and again, for it is very evident that it is not yet of common knowledge. There are, I suppose, many definitions of Christianity, but I believe that the definition which really prevails, which is of authority in the very best circles of the Anglican Church, is this—How to belong to the

Athenæum Club, decently, respectably, splendidly. No doubt there are many divisions and sub-divisions in a treatise which has not yet been issued. For example, there must be a heading—Worldly Prosperity. On the one hand, it is shown that betting, unless on the largest scale, with persons of acknowledged social position, is highly disreputable, irreligious, and a national scourge; while operations on the Stock Exchange, prudently conducted, on the best information, with fortunate results, are the backbone of English commercial life, and a credit to our common Christianity. Though at the same time failure in this path may be very disgraceful. Example: The Dean and Chapter of St. Paul's Cathedral accepted Eucharistic plate from Mr. Hooley when he was successful, and returned it when he became the object of popular denunciation. And so forth, and so forth; and I am reminded of an advertisement that I once saw in Shepherd's Bush: "Funerals conducted with Decency, Solemnity, and Respectability." And, again, there is another curious instance: A pious woman has opened in Western London a chapel of rest and meditation, which she has caused to be adorned with paintings, illustrating the passage from things temporal to things eternal. To this place enter the Bishop of London, who immediately observes that it would be a capital spot for meetings. For meetings! Cannot one see it all? Here, in this quiet place of rest, where men may stay and think for a moment how vain is all their work, how vain is vanity, and all in vain; how behind the ugly fog of business, and Imperialism, and Liberalism, and Conservatism, and Churchwardenism, there are still the everlasting splendours; that even in modern "civilised" London the Quest of the Sangraal is not impossible; that behind the songs of the "Merry Duchess of Guttenberg" resounds the inexpressive chant of the angels. Here, says the Pastor of the People of London, is the place for public meetings. Here, beneath the glowing walls, let us discuss the Mission to Borrioboola Gha; let us consider how we shall insist on trousers and chemises, and the decisions of the Judicial Committee of the Privy Council as part of the faith once delivered to the saints, while we decide that we must not press the petitions:

> By the mystery of Thy holy Incarnation; by Thy holy Nativity and Circumcision; by Thy Baptism, Fasting, and Temptation; by Thine Agony and Bloody Sweat; by Thy Cross and Passion; by Thy precious Death and Burial; by Thy glorious Resurrection and Ascension; and by the coming of the Holy Ghost.

Lest, of course, the simple natives do not understand. Here, beneath the symbols of the eternal, let "Mr. Chairman" take his stand; let the Bishop of Blank Negation rise to "a point of order"; let the blessed words "Hear, hear," "No, no," resound; let there be re-enacted under decent, Church-like disguises, the meeting of the United Metropolitan Improved Hot Muffin and Crumpet Baking and Punctual Delivery Company, with a capital of five millions in five hundred thousand shares of ten pounds each. Here let the mystery of iniquity of brewing beer be denounced, here be demonstrated the saving truth that the wine of Cana was non-alcoholic, here be advanced the claims of the great-grand-nephews of the clergy, here be finally proclaimed to the world the Great Gospel of Anglo-Saxondom—that the prosperous shall inherit the earth. Where is the prophecy of Isaiah:—And in those days, saith the Lord, there shall be a Chair upon the earth, and a Vice-Chair amongst the nations. And they of the uppermost parts of the earth shall say "Hear, hear," and many Resolutions shall be passed in My Name, saith the Lord of Hosts. Where is the passage from Isaiah showing that the City of London and the House of Commons shall be as it were as fountains of water, and as the shadow of a great rock in a dry and thirsty land? When the Lord turned again the captivity of the Stock Exchange: then were we like unto them that dream.

It should be enough for good Catholics to demonstrate the utter wickedness of all this "modern spirit"; it should be enough for thinkers of mediocre intelligence to demonstrate the silliness of it all—as though one should say, argon has been discovered; the Peckham Protestants Protest against the Literal Resurrection, so we must give up the Mass; but it is perhaps necessary to show that this modern scheme, besides foolish and false, is also futile. It really does not pay; and against that sentence Modernism surely cannot appeal. Three hundred years ago or more the Blessed Reformers discovered that Englishmen were dolefully ignorant of the Christian Faith, because the services were in Latin; the said services were accordingly translated into English. See the result; of all creatures on earth the Englishman Churchman is most ignorant of his religion; the Common Prayer-book is a puzzle to him; auricular confession is to him a Popish innovation, fasting on Fridays a superstition; the disciples of the medicine-man can give a more intelligent account of the mysteries than he. So this squalid, and stupid, and ungodly scheme has failed in the one aim which it attempted, and the result of "popularising" the Catholic Faith has been to drive half the population outside the pale of the Church. And from the point of view of literature—Has any one pondered the Prayers on Special Occasions, composed and issued by the late Archbishop Tait? And our music? Is it necessary to argue the question as to the superiority of plain song over the efforts of Smart and Goss? And our hymns? Here is the one side:

> Ecce panis Angelorum,
> Factus cibus viatorum:
> Vere panis filiorum,
>   Non mittendus canibus.
> In figuris præsignatur,
> Cum Isaac immolatur:
> Agnus Paschæ deputatur:
>   Datur Manna patribus.
> Bone Pastor, panis vere,
> Jesu nostri miserere:
> Tu nos pasce, nos tuere:
> Tu nos bona fac videre
>   In terra viventium.
> Tu, qui cuncta scis et vales:

THE GLORIOUS MYSTERY

Qui nos pasci hic mortales:
Tuos ibi commensales,
Cohæredes et sodales
Fac sanctorum civium. Amen. Alleluia.

And the other:

Jesu, gentlest Saviour,
Thou art in us now;
Fill us full of goodness
Till our hearts o'erflow.
Multiply our graces,
Chiefly love and fear,
And, dear Lord, the chiefest,
Grace to persevere.

And now our Fathers in God are attempting the cure. Having discovered that half England is Anabaptist, or Independent, or Wesleyan, they are going to draw the strayed sheep back into the fold by showing that the English Church is more Anabaptist than the Anabaptists, more Independent than the Independents, more Wesleyan than the Wesleyans; it being also provided that "our beloved Church" affords more snug lying for "reverent Agnostics" than any other community. In a word, we proffer all the comforts of home, and everything as nice as mother makes it; so daily do we blaspheme and deny the Holy Catholic Church, the Cloud of Witnesses, the Assembly of the Firstborn, and the Lord that bought us. The tactics of the quack medicine vendor, the intelligence of Earlswood, the religion of the Prince of this World (who has another name)—to these ends has come Britain, once the abode of the saints. Our Bishops may not be passionately certain as to the Resurrection; but, at all events, they forbid us to sing the hymns of the fourth century—pending, no doubt an enabling Act of Parliament and the latest results of scientific investigation.

I am sorry that space does not allow me to deal with "The Spiritual Return of Christ Within the Church," by Richard de Bary, or with "The Golden Sayings of Brother Giles" both of which books may be earnestly recommended as antidotes to the fooleries that we have been considering.
April 18, 1908.

THE GLORIOUS MYSTERY

DISSENTING LOGIC

" I COULD never bring myself to any admiration of the schoolman's famous formula, *Credo quia impossible.*" These are the first words of Dr. Horton's Preface to his book, "My Belief: Answers to Certain Religious Difficulties." It would be very interesting to know the name of the schoolman in whose works the cited phrase occurs; but it would have been as well, perhaps, if Dr. Horton had given the true source of the paradox. Qu. Sept. Flor. Tertullianus, who lived about a thousand years before the great period of the Scholastic Philosophy, writes as follows:

> Natus est dei filius; non pudet quia pudendum est: et mortuus est dei filius; prorsus credibile est, quia ineptum est: et sepultus resurrexit; certum est, quia impossibile. *De Carne Christi. V.*

However, a trifling point such as this does not obscure Dr. Horton's meaning. "For my own part," he goes on, "I believe only what appears to me certain," and he assures us that he is only to be convinced by strong and irrefragable arguments. This being the author's position, it may be interesting to examine one or two of the arguments on which, as he says, Christian Belief may most certainly be founded.

Personally I was very much struck by an argument to prove the authority of the Bible. Dr. Horton, it may be said at once, dismisses all authority of Church or Chapel; the Bible, he says, will not fail to prove itself if you read it without any theories whatever.

Here is one instance from thousands which can be quoted: A man was in Durham gaol, doing a term of penal servitude for attempted murder. A Roman Catholic, he had registered himself as a Protestant for certain supposed advantages in the prison life. He therefore found a Bible in the cell, and read it to pass away the time. One day, as he read the New Testament, it occurred to him: "If this book is true, the priest is not. I can pray to God myself." He knelt and asked forgiveness; he vowed that he would go back to the village where he had committed the crime, to show that he was changed. . . . . He began to speak as a local preacher; his work was blessed, and now he is a missionary in India.

"A book that works in that way," says Dr. Horton, "carries its own authority with it." It may be so; but it seems to me that the corollary to the story and the deduction is that a mind which works in Dr. Horton's way carries very little authority with it. The prisoner in question was a murderous ruffian, he was a lying ruffian, he was also a hypocritical ruffian, and, above all, he was an excessively ignorant ruffian. "I can pray to God myself!" Will Dr. Horton be so kind as to cite the rule of the Roman Catholic Church forbidding any layman to pray to God by himself? As for the conversion, it may have been honest; but I believe that the life of a Protestant missionary in India is often a comparatively comfortable one. In another place the author shows that the "historical trustworthiness" of the New Testament is established "beyond the reach of critics"—by the reports of the British and Foreign Bible Society. These are the "reasons" which convince our sturdy follower of argument, our stout Protestant, who will not believe unless under the strictest logical compulsion. But they are interesting, as they serve to illustrate the very important distinction between paradox and nonsense. The *credo quia impossible* is paradoxical in expression; its meaning no doubt is: I believe in certain religious mysteries, amongst other reasons, because they are mysteries, because they transcend all the facts of every-day and commonplace experience; because religion, by its definition, implies transcendence; because a religion which propounded nothing beyond average human konwledge would not be a religion at all, though it might be a capital moral code. This is the "schoolman's" paradox which our cautious, hardheaded Doctor cannot away with. It is seen in analysis to be reasonable in the highest degree; while Dr. Horton's "reasons" are clearly no reasons at all, but rather the effervescences of a somewhat weak sentimentality. That Durham prisoner who was so evidently determined to be as comfortable as possible, those famous missionary reports—in cold logic they amount to something less than nothing. Even if these instances had been advanced to prove the proposition: Many men have been affected by reading the Bible; they would be weak enough; but, cited as they are to show the authenticity of the New Testament, they are almost incredibly impertinent. The truth of the Koran, of the Book of Mormon, and of Madame Blavatsky's "Secret Doctrine" could easily be proved by such "arguments" as these.

Let us take another instance of Dr. Horton's logical abilities. He argues that, since a man without religion would not be a man at all, therefore there is no such thing as a man without religion. Technically, the enthymeme seems fallacious, and there is the confusion between potency and actuality; every man, no doubt, is born with the one, but there are very many men who never attain to the other. It is true that the author would call a man who was afraid of spilling salt or going under a ladder, or believed in carrying a *mascotte* to the roulette-table religious; but this is to give a word which is generally, if vaguely, understood a new meaning and a confusing meaning. And it is, moreover, certain that there are many people quite devoid of religion who do not even believe in "luck" or fate. It seems, then, on a comparison of the Preface in Praise of Argument with one or two casual instances of the arguments actually employed by the author, that he would be wiser to rely on his intuitive rather than on his ratiocinative faculties. He is no doubt right in his conclusion that the New Testament is trustworthy, but this conclusion is not legitimately drawn from the premises of the converted gaolbird and the Bible Society. The Serpent, Dr. Horton will remember, rose up to Daath in the Tree of Life, while the higher faculties remained uncorrupted.

THE GLORIOUS MYSTERY

I am afraid that a further examination does not do much to shake my conclusion as to Dr. Horton's weakness in the mere logical process. I hasten to say that there are some excellent things in the book, though it must be noted that the author refrains himself with sedulous care from the paradoxes that he derides in that old "schoolman" of the Preface. Perhaps Protestantism discourages brilliance; perhaps our amiable Doctor agrees with Cartwright, who wrote, "Being the Canon bars me wit and wine," for there is nothing that can be called striking either in matter or manner from one end of the volume to the other. But though in one place the author cites material prosperity as evidence in favour of Protestantism, he recants this most unbiblical, most unchristian, and most wicked position in another chapter, and says, very sensibly, that the motor-race will not more promote true happiness than did the *meta fervidis evitata rotis*. It is melancholy that any one calling himself a Christian should dare, in the face of the express words of the Christ, to say that material riches and their results are an evidence of the Divine favour, and a testimony to the truth of Protestant dogma or no-dogma; but it is well, at all events, that the author throws over the motor-car, even if his logical consistency is again in question. It is charitable to suppose that there was no good deal of truth in the accusation uttered the other day at the Baptist Conference. The ignorance of the Bible, it was said, was scandalous, even in candidates for the ministry. Still, this is more or less of a domestic matter; and, though the Catholic Church has always urged the extreme importance of Biblical studies, the tolerance of the present day would not suffer us to compel Dissenting preachers to read their Bibles.

But, to proceed with our examination of "My Belief": Dr. Horton desires to prove that God is not unknowable, since we can surely know Him by His Works. As, the writer says, I know the mind of Holman Hunt by his pictures, so I know the Mind of God by the evidence of created things— of the Universe. This granted or (in Dr. Horton's mind) proven, he proceeds to deduce from the consideration of the aforesaid Universe a God of Wisdom, Beauty, and Benevolence. For example:

> If a wound is made in the body, immediately a process is set up which can only be compared with a gang of workmen sent posthaste to a wrecked train. . . . . It is an Intelligence other than my own which restores the balance, invigorates the weak part, heals the wound.

And, again, all things, animate and inanimate, are said to be "steeped in the magic of beauty." And, further: history shows that there is a continuous progress, a perpetual ascent of man. "The ape and tiger within us gradually but surely die. Man is in the course of appearing." And this progress is highly moral; witness the fact that Henry V. was smitten down with disease within a few weeks of Agincourt, that the Crown of England lost its possessions in France for ever. Furthermore, we may infer the nature of God from human nature, with all its faculties and powers. I believe, by the way, that there is an error of fact in one of Dr. Horton's instances from Nature. He says that bees are mere automata, that they "have not the sense to overcome the slightest unaccustomed obstacle." The threatened lack of a queen is surely an unaccustomed crisis in the hive, and we know that the bees in such a case will administer "royal food" to a common grub, which thereby becomes in due season a queen. An even stronger instance is that of the experimenter who tilted the bees' house to one side, endangering the equilibrium. A sufficient number of bees immediately mounted to the other side to maintain the balance, while another gang tried to make the hive secure in its new position.

However, these instances do not affect the main argument, to which we now return. Take the case of the wound. The *vis medicatrix naturae* proves, according to the author, a God of Wisdom and Benevolence. What does suppuration prove, then? What do inflammation, mortification, and death of the patient prove? That gang of healing workmen declares the goodness of God? Whose glory, then, is declared by the other workmen whose operations are Plague, Tetanus,

THE GLORIOUS MYSTERY

Typhoid, Diphtheria, Smallpox, and the rest? What sweet influences are manifested by the fair sisters Sarcoma, Epithelioma, Carcinoma? All things, too, are steeped in the magic of beauty? The Pterodactyl, the Hippopotamus, the Rattlesnake, the Cobra, the Devil Fish, for example? And is it so absolutely clear that there is a continual ascent of man, a continual progress to better and holier things? Is it, for example, certain that Chicago is infinitely superior in all things to Athens in the days of Sophocles? Are its morals better? Is its Wisdom more exalted? Is its Art immeasurably more beautiful? Is its literature as noonday to twilight compared with the literature of Athens? Can it produce a drama which would drive Æschylus, Sophocles, Euripides to despair and suicide? Is it socially more pleasant to inhabit? Is it politically more pure? Do its public buildings cause the Parthenon to appear a mean hovel? Would its police-courts abash the Judges celebrated in the Eumenides? Or—with a change of scene and time—would Plato have sat humbly at the feet of Dr. Aked, that fervid social reformer, and chaplain to Mr. Rockfeller? And the Tiger and the Ape? I read the newspapers now and then, and I seem to have detected, not infrequently, the tracks of these beasts. It will be noticed that I have chosen Athens, which was pagan, I regret to say; I think the case might have been more strongly presented by the instance of a mediæval city, but I am aware that Dr. Horton does not hold with Popery. And as to the moral purpose of history, this is shown, it seems, by the illness of Henry V. and the loss of the English possessions in France; the moral being, of course, that theft does not prosper. How then was it with the case of the Saxons who stole Britain from the Britons, with the Normans who stole England from the English, with the colonists who stole the country of the Massachusetts? I would instance the Turk, who is still at Constantinople, but I must not do so, because the inhabitants of Byzantium were not Protestants. Dr. Horton has visited Cairo, and, the Coptic Christians not being Protestants, he confesses frankly enough that the intelligent onlooker might hesitate between the claims of the Christian Church and the "splendid mosque on the citadel." And then there is the argument from the nature and powers of man. How do we know that Casanova, Tiberius, and Charles Peace were not the really typical men, the examples that we ought to follow, the indices pointing to our true source and origin? Nay, how do we know that savagery is not our proper state, that history is not the record of our lapse from happiness, while that which we call "civilisation" is the cause of all our miseries? Shakespeare was a man? Certainly; and the dunce, the fool, the monomaniac are men too.

Now it must be said that in a later chapter Dr. Horton admits a great deal of all this; he does not perceive, it would appear, that the earlier argument is thereby nullified. He is content to say that on a shipwrecked vessel the useful man is he who gets out the boats and points to the shore. Most certainly; but the handy man in question would not shout through the swelling storm that it was getting calmer every minute; he would not assure his fellows that the boiling waves were firm land; he would not point to the savage rocks and say, "Look at the pier"; he would not say that the dozen or so of unhappy wretches just swept overboard were safe ashore; he would not deduce from the general circumstances and surroundings of the moment the safety and, indeed, luxury of going to sea. The other passengers might possibly regard such an one as a dangerous lunatic and as the crowning misery of their misadventure. Again, I must say that it is a pity that Dr. Horton does not study the Scriptures more carefully and thoroughly; if he were to do so he would discover that the Bible does not depict the world of Nature or the world of Humanity as a kind of Cokayne, or pleasant Lubberland, where the ripe fruit drops into the open mouth, where the gaping wound is invariably and automatically healed, where the fiercest animal is a tabby kitten, where vice is perpetually being punished and virtue is always finally rewarded. This sort of conception has become obsolete even in that most conventional of all spheres, the stage; it is odd, indeed, that a Dissenting teacher should compose a scenario of the Universe which makes one think that he has confused the Creator of all things with Messrs. Sims and Pettitt. Let him search the Scriptures; he will not find that the world is at all like an old-fashioned Adelphi melodrama. We often hear sectarians speaking with awe and respect of "the spirit of the age." In the Bible, too, we are told somewhat concerning the Prince of this World; but the Personage in question and his dominion are not precisely held up for our admiration.

I have noticed several statements in "My Belief" which seem to me questionable, or more than questionable:

> If God is the one Power . . . . He can and will make Himself plain.

Well, if God has made Himself plain to the Holy Catholic Church, then He has not made Himself plain to Dr. Horton. Dr. Horton says it is better to be a Buddhist, a Mahometan, an antique pagan, or an atheist of the Continental type than to be a Catholic Christian, Catholic Christianity being a pest and a scourge. This sentiment is expressed in various passages throughout the book; it is tersely and distinctly enunciated on p. 80:

> If Catholicism is Christianity, the world must deliver itself from Christianity . . . . if Catholicism as it is known to us in history if the best that Christianity has to offer, the world which is bent on liberty, light, and truth must consent to let the dream of Christianity die.

It seems that the world has changed in the course of the centuries. There is no need now for the consolatory declaration, "I have overcome the world," since the world (of Latin Atheism) is bent on liberty, light, and truth. I have always been under the impression that the world in question was chiefly bent on Loot, or, as they call it in France, Liquidation. Still, however that may be, the problem remains. Dr. Horton says that God has not made Himself known in Catholicism, nor yet in Calvinism or early Protestantism—only, it would seem, to Dr. Horton and his Hampstead congregation. *Patiens quia Æternus* indeed; and one is a little reminded of the Welsh preacher's sermon. He was enumerating the Redeemed, according to their denominations, somewhat in this manner:

Baptists—a few. Wesleyans—a few. Independents—a few. Presbyterians—a few. Churchmen—a few. (With sudden vehemence) Welsh Calvinistic Methodists ! !—*a great multitude!*

Then there is a place which contrasts "simple Christian teaching, which finds its ready entrance into every unprejudiced human heart, the teaching of the New Testament itself," with the "corrupt historical systems"—*i.e.,* of course, with the Catholic Church of Christ, as before. Now, one would like to ask Dr. Horton, the Logician, the Friend of Reason, whether there is an *a priori* probability that Religion, a scheme of things which professes to give an everlasting, heavenly clue to the whole Universe, would be "simple." Is the human heart "simple"? Is Psychology "simple"? Are the Sciences "simple"? We know that none of these is simple; we know that in the speck of dust in the sunlight there lie latent all the mysteries, all the tremendous problems which have awed and perplexed the hearts of the greatest sages from the foundation of the world. Is it then reasonable to suppose that a system which professes to be the clue to the awful labyrinth of all things could possibly be a simple system? Then, passing from probability to certainty, was the religion of Christ, of His Apostles, of the New Testament, in fact a simple religion, winning its way to every heart which was not foritfied against it by violent prejudice? If this be a true description of Scriptural Christianity, why did the disciples murmur and say, "This is a hard saying; who can bear it?" Why did many of these disciples go back and walk no more with Him? Why was Christ crucified? Why was St. Stephen stoned? Why were the saints hewn asunder, thrown to wild beasts, hideously tormented, burned with fire?

THE GLORIOUS MYSTERY

Why was the Gospel a stumbling-block to the Jews, foolishness to the Greeks, and felony to the Romans? Why were the companions of the Lord, the Holy Apostles themselves, in darkness more or less complete till the very Day of Pentecost? Why was it said that no man could know the Lord save by the miracle of the Holy Ghost? Nay; but the disciples and the Apostles surely had no prejudice against the truth; the Jews were a devout people, the Greeks were the most eager enquirers after Truth that the world has ever known, the Roman law was amazing in its broad-minded toleration; every cult was welcomed by it—except that one cult, which, according to the Sage of Hampstead, is so "simple" so entirely self-evident. But it will be said, perhaps, that Dr. Horton believes that the ancient world was stubborn, prejudiced, "invincibly ignorant"—to borrow a phrase from the enemy— while since the coming of the Christ the universal human heart has been transmuted and changed. But this is not so; for Dr. Horton is explicit as to the doctrine that all religions of all ages and all climes are revelations from God. Judaism was a revelation:

> But so also was the religion of Bel-Merodach in Babylon, the worship of Athene and Apollo in Greece, the jejune cultus of ancient Rome.

It is impossible, then, to regard the ancient world as fortified against this "simple" faith of Christ by obstinate and demoniacal prejudice, since the ancient world was in possession of "the revelation of God according to its capacity and willinghood." In fine, then, though Christianity is so "simple," so self-evident that all but the most inveterate are compelled to give it their assent, at the same time the very Apostles of the Lord failed to grasp its meaning, and Jewry, Greece, and Rome rejected it and its teachers with vehement disgust. And at the same time this self-evident religion, so simple as to be axiomatic, became hopelessly corrupted in a century or two from its foundation, the corruption being otherwise known as the Catholic Church; and this faith, which no one in his sober senses can escape crediting, is at present so far from being credible in modern England that

> The proletariat of an English city . . . . probably come nearer to being *without religion* than any other population in the world.

Also

> Thoughtful and intelligent Europe is now non-Christian;

and

> Christians are in a minority, derided by the intellectual, railed at by the workers, ignored by the fashionable.

It seems to me that Dr. Horton has been unjust to himself in his famous Preface. He says that he cannot receive the *Credo quia impossibile*. Surely he is mistaken; he can do much more than believe in a verbal paradox. He can believe at once that all A is B and that some A is not B—a feat so novel and so surprising that I do not remember to have seen any technical name for it—in the Logic Books.

To proceed. On p. 64 we learn that:

> Christianity was a Judaism which discounted the external and ceremonial side of religion, laying the whole stress on the inward life, the state of the heart.

This statement is, I must say without circumlocution, absolutely and entirely false—directly at variance with the plain and literal text of the New Testament, at variance with the express words of the Apostles and their actions, at variance with the express words of the immediate successors of the Apostles and their actions. I cannot weary the readers with the catena of texts that I have cited on other occasions again and again; I will not insult them by supposing that they are ignorant of the rites and ceremonies of Baptism, the Lord's Supper, Unction of the Sick, Bestowal of the Holy Ghost; I will not insist in detail on the plain and notorious fact that the Christ gave His solemn approval by word and deed to the whole system of the ceremonial law. I simply declare that Dr. Horton's statement as quoted above is not true, and I refer him, in the approved Protestant fashion, to Rev. xxii. 15.

My materials are by no means exhausted, but my space is limited. I have approached "My Belief" from the logical point of view, because Dr. Horton himself indicated that point of view in his Preface. "For my part," he says, "I believe only what seems to me certain"; and, again, declaring his belief in mysteries, he points out that the steps which lead up to these mysteries are "strong and irrefragable arguments." I have examined a few of these strong and irrefragable arguments; and now I should like to lighten the end of this review with a point which is more or less a matter of taste:

> I recall (Dr. Horton says) a feeling which came over me in Athens; after studying the noble remains of ancient art, the ruins of the Acropolis, the temple of Theseus, and the sculptured reliefs of the Ceramicus, I felt a strange and sickening revolt against the tawdry mummery of the Orthodox Church, which seemed not only lifeless, but deadening.

Now we will not be so uncharitable as to suppose that Dr. Horton formed his judgment as to the "commonness of this *ci-devant* Christianity" on the evidence of a casual, hurried visit to a ceremony which he did not understand. The American gentleman certainly did form his judgment on English justice in some such manner, but I will not condemn Dr. Horton as guilty of such folly as that. We will rather believe that he has made an exhaustive study of the Eastern Church—of that Church which has kept the faith through centuries of sword, impalement, torture, and cruel oppression, which offered up anew its martyrs a few years ago. We will credit the Hamstead Doctor with a careful examination of the Eastern Liturgies also; and we can only regret that he found nothing in the Orthodox Church of the East but commonness and tawdry mummery.

Here is a bit of mummery from the Divine Liturgy of St. James:

THE GLORIOUS MYSTERY

We render thanks to Thee, Lord our God, for that Thou hast given us boldness to the entrance in of Thy holy places, the new and living way which Thou hast consecrated for us through the veil of the Flesh of Thy Christ. We therefore, to whom it hath been vouchsafed to enter into the place of the tabernacle of Thy glory, and to be within the veil, and to behold the Holy of Holies, fall down before Thy goodness; Master, have mercy upon us; since we are full of fear and dread; when about to stand before Thy holy altar, and to offer this fearful and unbloody sacrifice, for our sins and for the ignorances of the people. Send forth, O God, Thy good grace, and hallow our souls and bodies and spirits, and change our hearts to holiness, that in a pure conscience we may present to Thee the mercy of peace, the sacrifice of praise.

And here is a vulgar, deadening prayer from the Divine Liturgy of St. John Chrysotom:

None is worthy among them that are bound with fleshly desires to approach Thee, nor to draw near, nor to sacrifice unto Thee, King of Glory; for to minister to Thee is great and faerful, even to the heavenly powers themselves. Yet through Thine ineffable and measureless love, Thou didst . . . . become man, and didst take the title of our High Priest, and didst give to us the Hierurgy of this offering of the unbloody sacrifice, as being Lord of all; for Thou only, O Lord our God, rulest over things in heaven and things on earth, who sittest upon the cherubic throne, Lord of Seraphim, and King of Israel, only holy, and resting in the holies.

This sort of thing must be very disgusting to a man accustomed to the stately ceremonial, the dignified ritual of the English Independents.
May 16, 1908.

FALSE PROPHETS

I HAVE often wondered how far one is justified in arguing as to a man's sagacity and common sense from the
particular to the universal. It is a tempting course to pur-
sue; human nature, having discovered that in one particular
instance Smith has been guilty of hopeless and undisputed
folly, is apt enough to conclude that Smith is always and
in all respects a fool. "What does he know about books (or
ships, or motor-cars, or Moorish art)?" one is inclined to
say; "look at the way he lost all the money his father left
him." It is tempting; but it is not quite reasonable. A man
may be downright Earlswood so far as money is concerned,
and yet his views on plainsong may be worthy of the highest
respect; and a Seventh-Day Baptist may be a skilled, daring,
and trustworthy pilot. It is clear that we must go warily; it
will not do to say without reserve that folly in A necessarily
etxends right down the alphabet even unto Z. Take the
pilot; he is a member of an absurd sect, not from any defect
in his reasonnig powers, but from circumstances, from accident—because his father before him kept holy the seventh
day, or because his wife was a member of the Connexion; his
theory of the Sabbath does not interfere in any respect with
his theory of rocks and shoals. A grocer may be a very good
grocer and a substantial citizen in spite of his belief that the
Reign of the Saints will commence on August 15th, 1926, at
nine o'clock in the morning precisely; but if he embarked in
an enterprise for planting tea and rice in the Thames Valley
we should be justified in a profound distrust of his reasoning
powers, more especially if this scheme of culture were backed
by quotations from the Book of Daniel and the Apocalypse.
For it would be clear in that case that the man's specific folly
had overflowed its "compartment"; that his whole being was
in process of being overwhelmed by a flood of nonsense; that

even his technical knowledge had been submerged by the tide of the Millennium. When a man is not merely mistaken, but obviously nonsensical, in his own business, there is every reason to suppose that he is universally foolish.

The worst of it is that this truth is not accepted in the region of theology. The theologian seems, indeed, to be the chartered libertine of thought, and the most important of all subjects is the one in which every man appears to have a license to make an ass of himself without reproach. The pious young curate and the well-meaning old Bishop can do no wrong. Listen to the sermon. In the first place half of it is inaudible, because the preacher has not had the common decency to master the very simple art of speaking in public— in spite of the fact that the art in question is to be an important part of his life's work. And, secondly, the preacher's voice rises and falls in a sort of monotonous sing-song, which, if it means anything, seems intended to convey to the hearers the fact that the speaker has no sort of interest or belief in one single word that he utters. And, thirdly, the matter of these ill-delivered remarks is sheer silliness or dreary commonplace. And then people tell you that Mr. A. is such a *good* man, which is a wholly impertinent statement, and moreover a false statement. For if Mr. A. were really a good man he would take the trouble to learn his business; true piety would dictate at the least a dozen lessons in voice-production, pronunciation, and elocution. One is reminded of the tale of the old Scotchwoman. She was "taking up the character" of a new cook, and the woman's late mistress dwelt at length on the servant's undoubted morality and respectability. "Damn her respectability," was the comment; "can she cook collops?" And, after all, the ability to cook must logically be considered as the cook's differentia, and so the ability to preach should be held as essential to the definition of a preacher.

But the clergy—I should explain that, out of deference to the liberal, broad-minded spirit of the age, I include Dissenting teachers under this term—the clergy have a still

wider license.   Not only may they preach without having
mastered the first elements of the art they profess, but they
have also liberty to utter nonsense wholesale, to preach and
to write in such sort that if they had lived in the days of the
Scholastic Philosophy they would all have received the title
of "Master of Contradictions."   And no farrago of obvious
fallacies, of absurdities, of false reasonings, seems to have the
slightest effect on the position that these persons may have
attained.   Take the case of Mr. R. J. Campbell, of the City
Temple.   He wrote a book, a book which proved to be a mass
of contradictions and mutually-destructive statements.   I am
not going to fall into the fallacy of concluding from this fact
that Mr. Campbell's cause is evidently a bad one.   The cause
may be a very good one; what is evident is that in Mr. Campbell it has found a most atrociously incompetent advocate;
this there is no gainsaying.   And yet, so far as I am aware,
the publication of this volume of absurdities has had no
appreciable effect on the preacher's position.   I don't suppose
that he is the poorer by a single pew-rent; one sees his name
still quoted with respect, his views on this or that are to be
read in the newspapers, his alliance is welcomed in various
quarters.   Why is this so?   I suppose because he is like the
curate; he is such a *good* man.   But I deny his goodness.
Having set himself to conduct a certain argument, he should
have considered it his duty to familiarise himself with the
fundamental laws of ratiocination.   A really good man would
never conclude in *Barbare* or *Celarant,* nor would such an
one place the propositions "all A is B" and "some A is not B"
side by side on the same page.   Mr. Campbell may be respectable in a sense, but he certainly cannot cook collops; and yet
he is famed in certain circles as a most accomplished *chef.*
Is the suppressed premiss—A man can talk the wildest rubbish about religion, and yet remain an excellent religious
teacher, so long as he utters kindly and humanitarian sentiments, so long as he is anxious that everybody should have
£200 a year?   This might be true in a sense if religion were
defined as a scheme for providing everybody with £4 a week;

but I believe that the universal consent of humanity has declared that religion is something much more than this. Socrates and the King of Borrioboola Gha, St. Paul and Buddha, Calvin and St. Ignatius Loyola are at least agreed on this point. And even if the £4 definition were true, the doctors and pastors of the Comfortable Faith would be all the better, one would think, for a modicum of reasoning power. Surely no cause, whatever its nature, can be advanced by the utterance of rank absurdity. And yet large masses of the English people continue to put their trust in these masters of contradiction and unreason; they still gaze in admiration and respect at the process which Dr. Johnson called "milking the bull." We have always professed our belief that reason is man's noblest attitude; it is very clear that a great many of us regard reason as the merest trifle—an amusing accident, like a movable scalp or double-jointed fingers. The sea-captain who first noted a rapid fall in the barometer, then observed a strange glare in the sky and the gathering of wild and stormy clouds, and, putting these facts together, concluded that the weather was going to be exceptionally fine, would, it seems probable, soon forfeit the confidence of his owners, even though he were a notoriously humane man, bursting wtih altruistic sentiment. And yet it is in such spiritual captains that hundreds of thousands of Englishmen put their trust; and one wonders what the end of our voyage will be.

I see a ray of hope in a recent issue of a daily paper. Possibly readers may remember the review of a certain book called "My Belief," the author of the book being Dr. Horton, a personage of the greatest distinction in Dissenting circles. "My Belief" was, like Mr. Campbell's book, a tissue of contradictions and absurdities; I exposed a very few of these in the review in question. I do not know whether the review was read by the Hampstead Independents; but I am quite certain that no exposure of their pastor's bad logic and false reasoning would diminish in the slightest degree their reverence and respect for his teaching. I do not know why this is so, unless it be on the theory which I have advanced before in these columns—that men have the power of casting away their best possessions. Still, I suppose one must do one's duty; one must continue to affirm that a lobster is not a red fish that walks backward, though one knows that the affirmation will persuade nobody. But Dr. Horton has ventured beyond the region of theology. He has recently declared that the best way to avoid the horrors of war is to be thoroughly unprepared for it; and I have great hopes, more especially as this egregious folly has been exposed by Mr. Arnold White in the *Daily Chronicle*. For this is not a questoin of theology, of Death and Judgment, Heaven and Hell, and such obsolete trifling. This is a matter of our skins and our purses, our front lawns and our back gardens, our very existence as a nation. And my hope is that people who would listen to Dr. Horton's theological nonsense with grave and bland respect may be led by this absurdity in a "practical" sphere to doubt their wisdom in submitting themselves to such a teacher *in divinis:*

> I wonder (says Mr. Arnold White) whether Dr. Horton has ever devoted a day of his life to the study of German preparations for war against England, and whether he thinks that the happiness and morality of family life have been increased by the successive attacks on Denmark, Austria, and France. . . . . In the triangle between Wilhelmshavn, Rheine, and Emden, screened by the Frisian Islands, is all the apparatus for sudden attack on England. . . . . I have satisfied myself by personal inspection that Dr. Horton possesses a front door with bolts and locks. On what principle can it be wrong for England to defend herself against international hooliganism if it is right for Dr. Horton to pay a police-rate and lock his front door against Hampstead thieves?

Mr. Arnold White goes on to warn the preacher that, if his advice is followed, the result will be the bloodiest war in history; and, I say again, I have hopes that those who have accepted gladly any and every delirium in theology will reconsider their position, and ask themselves whether teachers that preach red ruin, and blood, and woe, and destruction on earth are likely to be safe guides to heaven. Unfortunately, as I have said, vague sentiment appears able to cover every absurdity, monstrosity, and fallacy in the things of the soul. We listen and applaud, I know not why. But the simplest Englishman has the love of country in him; he has a pride in the ancient story of the realm; he knows that in time of peril he would give his life for the land, for his hearth and his home. He may be neither theologian nor logician; but he can at least understand the Gospel of Ruin preached in plain words; he may, perhaps, have talked to Frenchmen and Frenchwomen who remember the disgrace and misery and shame and desolation of 1870; and then he may ask himself whether he will put his trust in false teachers any more; he may ask himself whether, this one rivulet being so rankly putrid and envenomed, the fountain from which it springs is likely to be a well of water unto everlasting life.

There is, it seems to me, something of awful tragedy in the situation. From every quarter comes the same warning. Lord Cromer has uttered it in the House of Lords; Mr. Arnold White repeats it; Mr. Hyndman, the militant Socialist, declares that the danger is instant and tremendous. And Dr. Horton tells us that now is the time to lay down our arms and scrap our ironclads. And I repeat that if such a man as this is sitll regarded with respect as a teacher in things sacred or in things profane, then the doom of England, both in body and in spirit, must be near at hand.

Aug. 8, 1908.

THE GLORIOUS MYSTERY

INTOLERANCE

A FORTNIGHT ago a weekly journal commented on a singularly horrible case of "lynching." A negro was taken out of the custody of the law, dragged to the market-place of Grenville, U.S.A., and burned alive to the accompaniment of shrieks of joy from men, women and children. The editor deduced from this incident—and, no doubt, quite rightly—that the claims of America are somewhat extravagant, especially in matters of moral and humanitarian progress; there is every reason to suppose, indeed, that most Americans are—to quote Sancho Panza—as God made them, and some of them a great deal worse. But this legitimate conclusion apart, the fact of these lynching horrors may suggest to some of us that a certain very important question, supposed to be settled once and for all, and long ago, has not been really settled—is, in fact, still an open question. We are quite sure that the English Parliament, the Calvinistic authorities of Geneva and New England, and the Spanish Inquisition were intolerant when they made "heresy" a capital offense, and I suppose that the detail of hanging or burning is a mere detail; in Geneva and England and Spain they burned their heretics, whereas in New England they were satisfied with mere floggings, mutilation, and hanging. But the point is this: Are we in reality more tolerant than they were? "We" includes us all; not merely the citizens of Georgia and Florida who burn and hang negroes, but also the Englishmen who condemn the murderer to the death in the horrible shed, the common thief to the torture of hard labour in a gaol. Many years ago a person who displayed an unctuous piety in his shop-window and robbed the widow and orphan in the back-parlour received a heavy sentence amidst general delight and applause; and a certain paper published a brutal cartoon, showing this man stripped to the waist and receiving a severe flogging from a prison warder. It seems clear, then, that on this occasion we were intolerant of a mixture of cant and thieving; and I daresay the delinquent would have fared very badly indeed if he had been caught by a mob of his victims. Of course, Englishmen of the present day are not so cruel as the American lynchers— partly by reason of different social conditions, partly because the judicial system of America is notoriously ineffective; but the questions of cruelty and intolerance, though often confused, are quite distinct. If the Inquisition were established in England, and I, as Grand Inquisitor, gave orders for the secret and painless poisoning of Dr. Horton of Hampstead, I should be guilty of the greatest intolerance; but if I ordered Dr. Horton to be grilled at a slow fire in Trafalgar-Square the intolerance would not be increased; the element of cruelty would be super-added to it. There is, of course, a use of the word "intolerance" which is frankly absurd and nonsensical, resembling pretty well the American use of "carnival"—a big fire is a "carnival of fire," and a massacre is a "carnival of blood." So, when one sees the heading "Priestly Intolerance," and finds that the Rector of Stoke-on-the-Wold has declared that an unbaptised person is not a member of the Holy Catholic and Apostolic Church, one is aware that the word "intolerance" is simply used in this instance *nonsensicaliter;* we need not trouble ourselves with an amusing though idiotic perversion, which will probably stimulate a flow of illogical controversy in the pages of the *Stoke-on-the-Wold Mercury.* The tolerant man is, surely, the man who is willing to bear with and endure actions or opinions for which he has the profoundest dislike; it would be tolerance, for instance, if one gave a large sum of money for certain fishing rights, and then allowed the country folk to poach all the salmon. Or suppose a man to be extremely fond of flowers; he would be tolerant if, watching a party of happy children snapping off all his prize rose-blooms, he took no action. And if a father, walking in the fields, were to see his little girl brutally attacked by a tramp and were to abstain from all interference, this man would be tolerant in a very high degree. From these examples it would seem to follow that there are some cases in which tolerance is silly; some in which it is infamously wicked; but this is a consideration apart, which may or may not be dwelt on in the course of this article. But I hope that I have established the true meaning of the word. It is a bearing with something that one hates. A man cannot be said to "tolerate" his dearest friends; a gourmet does not tolerate an exquisite dish; I do not even "tolerate" people who are indifferent to me, since if there be no dislike, no hatred, there can be no burden to be borne. The Pope does not tolerate Roman Catholics, and the "Free Church" Council does not tolerate Dissenters.

Are, we, then, more tolerant than our ancestors? I suppose most people would answer in the affirmative, because, they would say, we no longer burn Unitarians after the mode of Calvin, disembowel Jesuits after the mode of Queen Elizabeth, or hang Quakers after the mode of the blessed Pilgrim Fathers. And it is certainly a long time since anybody has been bothered in England for sneering at Transubstantiation. But is there any true tolerance in all this? Take the case of Transubstantiation; we do not burn people for disbelieving in that dogma, not because we are more tolerant, but because we don't think it matters twopence whether anybody believes in it or not. And so the Calvinists of Geneva would leave the Servetus of these days alone, for the good reason that they don't care a rap what a man believes in, so long as he doesn't touch their pockets. Let us understand this quite clearly. You were punished in certain countries at a certain period for disbelieving in Transubstantiation (and for expressing your disbelief), not because the people of that country and that age were more tolerant than we are now, but because the people in question regarded the dogma of Transubstantiation as a matter of the most vital and tremendous importance—of infinitely greater consequence than ease of body and rest of reins, Free Trade, Imperial Supremacy, the properity of the mining industry of South

Africa, and a Universal Pension Scheme. Right or wrong, these people that we are talking about would have pronounced a race that had no industries or millionaires, but believed in Transubstantiation, to be a happy race; while they would have declared that a nation entirely composed of Rockefellers who disbelieved in Transubstantiation was a miserable race. You stole the purses of those people, and they hanged you without animus as a mere piece of social policy and convenience; but if you tried to steal their treasure—their faith—they executed you with unction, because you were attacking something for which they had an enormous value. It is for precisely the same reason that negroes are burned in the Southern States today; that the vengeance of the English after the Indian Mutiny was terrible and relentless. I remember the story of a native prisoner doomed to death. The men in charge of him were not content with the rope; they smeared him with the fat of unclean beasts, thus shutting the man out of Paradise, according to his own belief. This was intolerance in a very high degree, as great as anything in the acts of Torquemada, the only difference between the two intolerances lying in the subject-matter. The faith of the Church, the honour of Englishwomen: each was very dear to its intolerant defenders.

I do not know that there is any ground for restricting the word "toleration" to the sphere of religious or irreligious opinions. The word is no doubt often used with that connotation, but for no reason that I know of, unless it be that people like to boast of a quality which they do not possess. As I have pointed out, where there is no great love on the one hand and no great hatred on the other there can be no question of either tolerance or intolerance. The "man in the street" will hear that Smith is a Roman Catholic with the greatest indifference; he does not care two straws about Smith's religion. But let him be informed that his wife is staying at Brighton under Smith's protection, or that Smith is the promoter of the company that has robbed him of ten thousand pounds, or even that Smith wrote that savage attack on his last book, you will see the bright wells of toleration dry up in the shortest possible period. The "man in the street" will not burn Smith alive; that mode of resentment is impossible to him. He will not kill him even, because hanging is unpleasant; but he will, if he be a man of courage, very likely thrash Smith black and blue, or if he be more skilled in diplomacy than in the handling of riding-whips, he will do his best to ruin Smith for life. In a word, the "man in the street" is as intolerant as the man in the Inquisition—when you attack anything that he really treasures.

There are, of course, people who believe, or think they believe, that speech should always be tolerated, while action, in certain cases, should be punished. This would be an absurd and illogical belief if it were really held, since speech, if it be not entirely futile, is almost certain to result in action. First you have the inflammatory discourse, and then the stones are crashing through Mr. Asquith's window. But nobody really holds this belief. If a man tells you that in his opinion speech should always be tolerated, do not believe him; or, if you do believe him, just inform his employers that he has "done time" for embezzlement, tell his wife that you have seen him under circumstances not altogether compatible with marital fidelity, and let his club hear of that little card-sharping transaction of a few years ago: and then instruct your lawyer to defend the action. When a man says that speech should be free he really means to say: "I do not object to speech to which I have no objection." It is an obvious attitude enough, but it is not tolerance.

I have always felt that there must have been a slight confusion on this point in the mind of J. S. Mill—a man who, I am sure, endeavoured most earnestly to clear his mind of cant. Mill, so far as I remember, considered a prosecution for blasphemy as intolerant, but saw nothing amiss in a prosecution for indecent or unbecoming conduct in public. Surely the two cases are exactly similar—we prosecute for blasphemy because it is unpleasant to us; we prosecute for indecency for the same reason. So soon as the great majority of people cease to resent blasphemous utterances the prosecutions on that count will cease, and it is quite conceivable that society should allow a like liberty to words and acts which we should call "indecent," "filthy," "disgusting," and "obscene." Of course the matter of truth or falsehood does not enter into the question of blasphemy in the slightest degree. There are many true statements which would not at the present time be allowed public utterance. A man would not be permitted to demonstrate certain undoubted facts in physiology, with the aid of diagrams, to a Hyde Park audience; and if the great mass of English people become convinced atheists a man will not be permitted to demonstrate the existence of God in public places. A Republican would not be tolerated at a meeting of the Primrose League; a convinced Legitimist would not be allowed a hearing in the circles of French Republicanism; bank managers are for the rigid repression of burglary. In a word, we are all extremely tolerant of persons whom we do not dislike and of opinions and actions to which we have no objection.

Aug. 22, 1908.

THE DARK AGES

ONCE upon a time, it seems, the world was in a very bad way. According ot Mr. H. Jeffs, the author of "The Good New Times," there was no drainage in the fourteenth and fifteenth centuries, nor for long afterwards; "there was no pure water-supply, no care taken of the food of the people . . . . no sanitary conveniences of any kind." Moreover, the whole fabric of society was bad and corrupt:

> Each lord was a tyrant in his own domain, whose will was law. The people were serfs of the soil; neither their bodies nor their souls were their own. . . . . The labouring classes of the Middle Ages were as ignorant as the cattle which they tended. It is true that the nobility were little less ignorant as far as reading and writing and book-knowledge were concerned. The thought of educating the working classes, however, would have astonished the nobility beyond all measure. . . . . To educate the labourers would have been to teach them that they had minds of their own and souls of their own, and that would have suited the book neither of the owners of the land nor the priests, who were the paid upholders of things as they were, and who were so sunk in superstition—they regarded superstition indeed as identical with religion—that they dreaded . . . . any illumination to the minds of the people as a whole lest that illumination should lead them to doubt the superstitions which gave the priests the control over them.

And so forth at some length; and the conclusion is, according to Mr. Jens, that we owe all the blessings we enjoy today, including sanitation, education, and pure food—I forget, by the way, how many children are slaughtered yearly by putrid and tuberculous milk—to the Open Bible; or, in other words, to our old friend the Glorious Reformation.

It is wonderful doctrine! As it happened, soon after I had read "The Good New Times" I glanced at a review of a book on jewellery, with an illustration of the famous Tara Brooch:

[215]

The ring and expanded head of the pin are ornamented with examples of nearly every technical process, being enriched with enamel-work, niello, and inlaid stones. The metal is hammered, chased, engraved, and filigreed with extreme delicacy.

There are, of course, many examples of this wonderful Celtic work—in stone, in illumination, in metal; and at some of these works the modern experts can only express amazement, wondering with what eyes, with what hands of exquisite and delicate cunning such masterpieces were created. The microscope only proclaims more clearly the absolute and impeccable perfection of the work. These things were done, in all probability, by degraded and superstitious monks, sometimes for their convents, sometimes for a brutal and ignorant nobilty; but it must be remembered that it was the common labouring men, who were as ignorant as the cattle they tended, who built the churches and cathedrals; and the great Romances were in many cases written by lay-people, who had no pure water-supply. From the unfortunate labouring classes also proceeded the wealth of folk-lore, of song, and story, and proverb; to them, too, belongs the glory of Agincourt, Crecy, and Poitiers. They were very badly fed, says Mr. Jeffs, and one wonders if he has ever seen the *menu* of a Japanese soldier. Rather they lived hardly, somewhat in the style of a German peasant of today perhaps. They no doubt ate a good deal of the coarse bread, which is a main preserver of health in the writings of the doctors, and a chief part of the horrible doom of Protection in the speeches of the politicians.

Mr. Squeers spoke to Bolder slowly, "for he was considering, as the saying goes, where to have him." One has to approach Mr. Jeffs in a somewhat meditative and cautious manner, not because it is difficult to know where to have him, but because he offers so many vulnerable points. The matter is too large to be dealt with in the course of a review; it must suffice to say that a person who believes that the great Opus of the Middle Ages—its poetry, its romance, its architecture, its craftsmanship, its devotion, its social structure—was the work of ignorant and brutal lords, superstitious clerics, and brutish commons is . . . . not very wise.

And the worst of it is that Mr. Jeffs is not altogether consistent. In his opening essay he warns us not to look at the past through the glasses of poets and painters; and yet in another address he says, very truly, that it is the object of Religion to make every man a poet. Surely not that every man may become an expert and discursive liar? And then, after abusing the Middle Ages in the fashion that we have seen, he has an elaborate eulogy of the mediæval ideal and practice of chivalry. And when he has told his working-man friends how infinitely happier they are now than they ever have been he goes on to say:

> Somehow none of these [modern] labour-saving contrivances seem ["seems" were more in accordance with the genius of our language] to save the labourer. They rather keep him more and more upon the rush. One is inclined to wish sometimes that we could return to the calmer and more leisurely ways of the seventeenth and eighteenth centuries. Man is becoming the slave of his own machines. . . . . Can anything more brain-bedulling and heart-sickening be conceived than . . . . such soulless labour?

Let Bolder—otherwise Mr. Jeffs—step back unharmed to his place. He is clearly an intelligent and amiable man after all—if he would only get rid of a set of obsolete, absurd, and ignorant superstitions, which are infinitely more ridiculous and more nocent than any tale of dragons and laidly worms that ever amused a mediæval fireside. Indeed, there were once dragons and laidly worms upon the earth, but there never was a time when "the Open Bible" was anything but a pest and a danger; there never was a time when the whole social structure was as corrupt and abominable as it is now; there never was a time when the working-man's condition was so thoroughly deplorable.

But these "Brotherhood" addresses furnish incidentally an interesting text. Mr. Jeffs considers, in his superstitious moments, that poets, painters, and romancers are, in plain language, liars; they are people, he thinks, who see life falsely and make a false report of it to the bewilderment and confusion of the more sober lieges. This opinion is interesting because, I suppose,, it is a very general one; it is, in other words, the common opinion to which a man who should have known better has given currency. It is, of course, as false and wicked and foolish a lie as are most of the opinions and beliefs of "practical men." Great wit is not in the least allied to madness; it is at the opposite pole to madness, which, with few exceptions, is due to intense stupidity and to lack of the imaginative faculty. To these causes should be added Protestantism, which, after all is probably only a "shorthand" name for stupidity exercising its lack of intelligence on religion. Nevertheless the "practical" man has long opined that artistic genius of any kind is a form of lunacy, and that poets and painters spend their time in looking into a kaleidoscope and telling us what they have seen. This nonsense, this most poisonous lie, being, as I have observed, both widely spread and obstinate, it is perhaps worth while to give it the fullest and most emphatic contradiction; to assert once more that, so far from poets and painters seeing amiss, it is they, and they alone, who really see at all. The artist, the man of genius, is of necessity the man of clear and piercing and transcendent vision—the man whose eyes are purged from the mists and fogs and cataracts that afflict the most of us, that make us see an elephant where there is but a mouse, which make us chatter about "hallucination" and "indigestion" when, by the mercy of heaven, we are now and again permitted to behold the apparition of the angel. The "plain man," the "practical man," the "man in the street"—this monster of many names is, indeed, the inhabitant of a world of monstrous delusions and of a distracted phantasmagoria. To him Syon seems an insanitary village, and the seers, the saints, the poets, and the painters are but madmen in various disguises. It is not difficult to guess the reason; the plain man is aware that men of genius often die in poverty, and to him poverty is the last and bitterest Gehenna, the sin that shall not be forgiven, neither in this world nor in the world that is to come. Tell him that there are certain people who despise money and money-making, and he wonders whether such persons are lunatics or criminals, and, being charitable according to his lights, is good enough for the most part to give genius the benefit of the doubt—to vote for Broadmoor rather than for the gallows. A friend of mine once said very wisely that one great difference between the Middle Ages and the present time was this—that, though there were money-grubbers in those days as now, yet even the money-grubbers of old were aware that it was the saint, the solitary, the ascetic who were in reality the true "men of affairs," the men who had got hold of a business eternally profitable, and pursued that business without rest, without weariness, without distraction. And in a lesser degree the men of genius are the real "men of affairs," the men who are truly practical, since they have received the vision of things which are real and eternal and beautiful, which are worth seeking with heart and soul and mind and strength. That the other opinion is ever muttered outside the walls of a madhouse is an astonishing portent. That there are actually human beings who believe that the existence of powerful machinery capable of printing a magazine of rubbish, impertinence, triviality, and malignity at a terrific speed is a matter of the smallest importance to any creature that God has made: this is in truth a tale wilder than anything in the "Arabian Nights" or in the mediæval Mirabilaries. Unfortunately, however, it is a tale only too true; and those who prophesy against these crazy and fantastic delusions are likely, it seems, to meet with no better reception than did Cassandra, whose warnings (the popular journalist is respectfully reminded) all came true. There is, indeed, an evil savour of blood and woe, and madness and ruin, about the house; and unless the lords of it and they that serve in it repent speedily and repent deeply, its doom is certain. The rule of madmen is sure to be disastrous; the rule of cunning and dishonest madmen will most certainly lead to a peripeteia at once and final and awful beyond all expression.

July 11, 1908.

www.ingramcontent.com/pod-product-compliance
Lightning Source LLC
Chambersburg PA
CBHW020601030726
47497CB00007B/2036